FURY FRAYED

Of Fates and Furies
Book 1

MELISSA HAAG

ISBN 978-1-943051-82-3 (eBook Edition)
ISBN 978-1-943051-04-5 (CreateSpace Paperback Edition)
ISBN 978-1-943051-71-7 (Paperback Edition)

The characters and events in this book are fictitious. Any similar to real
persons, living or dead, is coincidental and not intended by the author.

Editing by Ulva Eldridge
Cover design by © 2019 Cover Art by Cora Graphics
© Depositphotos.com

To everyone willing to take a chance on a new book,
Thank you!

To everyone who wasn't willing,
My crazy, amazingly dedicated readers will eventually convert you.
You're welcome!

FURY FRAYED

I have no idea what I am, but I know I'm not human.

Megan's temper lands her in Girderon Academy, an exclusive school founded in a town of misfit supernatural creatures. It's the one place she should be able to fit in, but she can't. Instead, she itches to punch the smug sheriff in his face, pull the hair from a pack of territorial blondes, and kiss the smile off the shy boy's face. Unfortunately, she can't do any of that, either, because humans are dying and all clues point to her.

With Megan's temper flaring, time to find the real killer and clear her name is running out. As much as she wants to return to her own life, she needs to embrace who and what she is. It's the only way to find and punish the creature responsible.

CHAPTER ONE

THE RAPID THUMP OF MY FEET AGAINST THE CEMENT SENT students scattering from the sidewalk as I sprinted from school. I needed to get home before Mom did.

"It wasn't my fault this time," I said under my breath. I raced around the corner, navigating the route home at high speed. "She pushed me into the locker. What was I supposed to do?"

I knew what I was supposed to do. Not fight. Yet, my temper never listened. Why couldn't I just be like other people my age? Moody but not irrationally angry?

I shook my head while neatly jumping over a kid on a tricycle. His mother squawked from her place on their porch. The look she shot me sent my temper flaring again.

"He's fine!" I shouted. "Maybe you should get off your ass and stand by him if you don't want people jumping over him." However, I was already four houses away when I finished my rant, so I doubted she'd heard more than "he's fine."

Focusing once more on what I planned to tell my mother, I rejected my first approach.

"Come on, Megan. You can do better," I said to myself. "I was upholding the school's anti-bullying policy. I saw that girl shaking down people for their lunch money and used my words to ask her to stop." I nodded. That sounded good. I'd point out that I'd used my words, and not my fists, first. "She didn't like me sticking up for her victims and tried pushing me into my locker."

That sounded like a winner. But, enough to keep me from being locked up in the house for a week while suspended? Probably not. I ran harder. If I could make it home before Mom, I could delete the messages the secretary had left on the answering machine.

She was yet another person I'd like to punch in the face, and not just because of her condescending tone when she'd spoken to me today. Something about her had rubbed me wrong from day one, and it had only gotten worse during the month I'd attended Parkerville High.

Not even winded from the sprint, I stopped in front of my house, only seven blocks from school. Like the omen of ill fortune it was, Mom's shiny red sports car sat at the curb. I swore and touched the hood. Cold.

I was so screwed.

Rubbing a hand over my face in frustration, I stared at my reflection in the glossy paint. Wisps of brown hair, escaped from my ponytail, framed my angry face. I took a deep breath and tried to relax my expression into something that could pass as pleasant. My brown eyes softened just enough to not look like I wanted to rip someone's head off, which I totally did. I hated that I couldn't shake that feeling.

Working hard to keep my relaxed expression, I turned to the house and slowly started up the walk.

"I was upholding the school's anti-bullying policy," I repeated under my breath before opening the door.

My ready excuse fled my mind at the sight of boxes lining the hallway and stacked on the dining room table.

"Come on, Mom! Seriously?" I threw my bag off to the side and stalked toward the kitchen where I could hear the clink of dishes.

"Is that how you address me?" she asked calmly as soon as I entered.

My temper snapped. I needed a Mom, but she'd been fighting that role for years now.

"Okay, Paxton, pain-in-my-ass birth giver. Two little fights in one week don't warrant another move." Hopefully, she wouldn't point out that it was only Tuesday.

She set the coffee cup down slowly. I swallowed the curse I wanted to mutter. I'd pushed her too far. Again. I stood still, waiting for her to lash out at me. Instead, she stood there, gripping the cup as if it were my head and she wanted to smoosh it. A red flush crept over her flawless and naturally tanned skin. My imagination spiked because I could swear I actually felt the heat of her rage radiating off of her. Sweat beaded my brow.

"Paxton, I'm sor—"

The cup shattered.

"You think you know so much, but you don't. I've given you everything, and you throw the few rules I have back at me. Go to your room. Pack. When you're done, come help me. We leave in the morning."

I wanted to say something more, but the cold blue in her eyes when she finally looked up at me sent me scurrying to my room like a good little girl.

Not that I was little anymore. At seventeen, I stood only a few inches shorter than Mom. Paxton. I rolled my eyes in the safety of my room. She'd had no problem with me calling her Mom until I turned fourteen and started sprouting boobs. Then, suddenly, I had to call her Paxton because she didn't want her boyfriends to know she was old enough to have a kid my age. I didn't see why it mattered. She didn't look old. Not in the slightest. We looked more like sisters than mother and daughter. As long as she looked good, why did she care about her age? Vain.

I started shoving clothes into one of the boxes on my bed and hoped I didn't warp into a vain middle-aged woman like Mom.

After an hour of packing up my room, I went back to the kitchen. A note waited on the table along with a plate of food.

Went to deal with Darren. Eat and finish up the packing. We leave at 2.

I looked around the house. Most everything was already packed. We lived light because we moved often. Sometimes due to my fighting, but mostly due to Paxton's failed relationships. Although, lately, that balance had been tipping more in my favor. I didn't know what was wrong with me. Why did I have to be angry all the time?

I didn't use to be like this. The last therapist I had thought it might be due to a hormone imbalance brought on by puberty. Given my age, I had a hard time believing his prognosis. But my belief, or lack of it, didn't change the fact that I had anger issues and no one could figure out why.

Sighing, I sat and ate my plate of spaghetti then packed what remained. When I finished, I went straight to bed. Two in the morning would come early, and my temper got worse when I didn't get enough sleep.

THE SOOTHING VIBRATIONS of tires over pavement stopped, waking me. I opened my eyes and blinked at the dimly lit semi-rural road in confusion. Waist-high grass occupied the space around the house in front of which we'd parked.

"Why'd we stop?" I asked, trying to clear the fog in my head. Even with going to bed early, waking up to Mom's "let's go" had been rough.

"We're here."

"It's still dark? Why did we have to leave at two in the morning?" Even as I asked it, I knew why. A quieter road meant less reason for me to lose my temper.

She opened her door and got out without answering. Not yet done questioning her, I fumbled with my door to follow. Outside the car, my disbelieving gaze locked on the faded, white two-story house hiding in the overgrowth. Paint flaked off the wide boards in not so tiny peels. Within cloudy windows, half-torn curtains dangled, giving the house a creepy, abandoned vibe.

"What do you mean we're here?" I asked. "Where is here?"

"Home," she said, wading through the grass to the front porch. The boards held her weight and didn't send her plummeting straight to hell like I'd hoped.

This had to be a joke. Mom preferred furnished, trendy places, which she always talked her boyfriends into renting for her.

"This isn't a home. This is a fire waiting to happen."

"Hurry up and get inside, Megan," Mom said softly, unlocking the door. "I'll bring the boxes in myself."

Torn between anger and frustration, I stomped through the grass to the wide front porch while Mom disappeared inside. A light came on, then another, so I wasn't walking into the seventh ring of hell blind.

The musty stink of neglect filled my nose, and a sneeze ripped through me a moment later.

"Seriously, this place is a dump," I said, looking around.

The old bulb cast a weak glow in the living room that Mom had lit up. Old furniture coated with dust sparsely decorated the space. The next room, a small kitchen, didn't look much better. The larger room off to one side looked like it wanted to be a library when it grew up. Barren bookshelves and a fireplace played host to long-vacated spider webs.

"I am so not sleeping here," I said under my breath.

"Don't be a baby," Mom said from right behind me, making me jump. "There's a decent room to the right at the top of the stairs. Go back to bed. When you wake up in the morning, things will be different."

I shook my head.

"Yeah, daylight is going to make this all look way worse."

"Go!" Mom's angry yell sent me scurrying up the dark stairs.

A light at the top led the way to a bedroom that didn't look quite as bad as the rest of the place. A full-sized bed with a white, dust-free quilt tempted me. Ignoring the pull to go back to sleep and pretend this was all still a dream, I looked around the rest of the room. Dresser? Check. Creepy, empty closet decorated with more spider webs? Check. A good view from the room's single large window? Nope. Just a crap ton of towering pines.

"Lovely." I turned and face-dove into the mattress. No plume of dust greeted me, so I closed my eyes and let myself pretend.

However, when I opened them again hours later to way too much daylight, I knew I couldn't pretend any longer and trudged down the now dust free stairs. I frowned and poked my head into the library. That looked cleaner now, too, and it had a few more books.

"Come eat," Mom said from the kitchen.

I turned and saw a plate of food for me on the table. Eggs, bacon, toast with jelly. The works.

"Wow. Thanks. Did you sleep at all?"

"No. There's a lot I need to do yet. I went to the store and stocked the cupboards. It was too early for the bank or school so I'll need to leave again in a bit."

"Where are we?"

"Maine."

"I figured that since we didn't drive very long. Where in Maine?"

"This house is on the outskirts of the village of Uttira. Population of about one thousand, but most people only live here part-time."

"Are you trying to say this is a vacation home?" I couldn't keep the disbelief from my voice.

"Don't be smart. While I'm running errands, I want you to try to mow the lawn in back." She turned to look me in the eye. "Only in the back."

"Fine. Geez. You might want to power nap before you go."

She took a long, slow breath and continued her study of the backyard.

"I'll sleep later, once you're settled. Behave and stay inside once you're done with the lawn." She turned and left the room. A minute later, I heard the front door open and close.

I rolled my eyes and quickly finished my breakfast. She'd been trying to keep me inside and away from people for as long as I could remember. Couldn't blame her. I rubbed people wrong because they rubbed me wrong. Yet, I loved being outdoors.

After I washed my plate and put everything away, I strolled outside. The back deck was sad in comparison to the front and looked out over a sea of waist-high grass gone to seed. I didn't know of a lawn mower on earth that would tackle this job.

Parting the grass, I made my way to the weather-worn shed. The right door opened easily. The left tried to give me a hard time, but I was stronger than I looked.

With the doors gaping wide, I studied the variety of rusted lawn care implements. The mower sat off to one side, the pull-start rotted and hanging in two pieces. Even if I could have gotten it to start, it would have done little good.

From the wall, I grabbed a golf club looking thing with a serrated edge at the bottom and gave it an experimental swing over the grass. It neatly sheared the top of the blades from the bottom on the first swing and the return.

Grinning, I stepped out further and set to work. By the time Mom returned, I was in the kitchen, sipping some iced tea. The backyard looked like a farmer had cut hay.

She placed a bundle of papers and a plastic bag with several boxes in it on the table and went to the back door.

"The mower didn't work?"

"The pull cord's broken, and there's no gas. I used that thingy against the door. It worked okay."

"Feel better?" she asked, her voice actually motherly for a change.

"Yeah. I do."

"Exercise always helps with moods. Don't forget that."

How could I? She raised me saying it. I used to jog to help with my moods. But, when the people I passed started pissing me off by just existing, I'd had to stop. After that, Mom suggested I try getting a boyfriend. She'd claimed the right one could help with moods, too. At fourteen, I'd gagged and locked myself in my room, trying not to visualize how she and her boyfriends exercised to help her stay calmer.

"I'll set up a service to cut the front yard."

"What's the point? It'll maybe need to be cut twice before it stops growing for the season. I can do it."

"People will want to stop you to talk."

9

I sighed and quit arguing. I didn't talk to people; I snarked at them.

"I'll see if someone can deliver a new lawn mower or fix the old one so you can do the back," she said.

"Okay."

She turned and nodded toward the stack of papers and the bag.

"That's for you. The school system here is a little different than what you're used to. They cater to the needs of the students. Because of your issues with fighting, you'll learn on your own at home with required weekly check-ins. If you ever reach the point where you can go to classes without wanting to remove someone's teeth, their doors will be open for you."

I indifferently picked up the first folder. It read Girderon Academy. These people had vacation homes and private academies that catered to individual students? That screamed money. We didn't have money. The men in Mom's life usually did, though. Maybe we were here so she could hook up with a new guy.

"Are we in some low-income part of an elitist community?"

"Something like that. I'm going to go upstairs and sleep. Don't answer the door, and stay out of trouble."

As she went upstairs, I reached for the bag. She'd bought me a new laptop, phone, cable modem and wireless router. I started setting everything up, made myself lunch, then picked up the phone. I wasn't sure why she'd gotten it. Friends weren't my strong suit. Who did she think I had to call?

Setting it aside, I went outside and started weeding

around the base of the pine trees. By dinner, Mom was up and had a plate of food on the table for me.

She sat next to me with her own plate.

"There's no TV in this place. I ordered one, as well as cable hook up, so you won't go stir crazy."

All this outpouring of niceness was making me suspicious. For once, though, I kept my snark to myself and just said thanks.

"You're welcome, Megan." She reached out and gave my hand a squeeze.

That was the last time I saw my mom.

CHAPTER TWO

My opinion of our new house hadn't improved any by the time I opened my eyes on the second morning.

"Still looks like hell."

I peeled back the covers and made my way downstairs. Expecting to see Mom in the kitchen, I frowned at the note waiting on the table and looked around for my plate instead. She always made me breakfast.

"Dammit, Mom. You can't train me like Pavlov's dog and then not deliver."

With a scowl, I snatched up the note and started reading. After the first sentence, I sat down heavily and started again.

This is your home, now, but never again mine. You're more special than you know. Learn what Girderon Academy can teach you. You'll need it. There's a checkbook in the kitchen drawer to the right of the sink. The account has enough to start you out with whatever life you choose. I'm sure you'll catch on quickly how to make your own money before you run out.

*I loved you, Megan. Never doubt that. Leaving was the best thing
I could do for both of us. I already held on too long, and I'm sorry
for that.*
Take care,
Mom

She left me? That didn't make any sense. If she was tired
of dealing with me, why go through all the trouble of
moving us here? Why not just take off from the last place?
And why sign the note as Mom? She hadn't acted like a real
Mom for a long time.

Her words from the day we'd left echoed in my head.
*I've given you everything, and you throw the few rules I have
back at me.*

"What bullshit," I said to the kitchen. "She's still pissed
because of the fight. You know what? I don't care. I can
make my own dumb breakfast."

I tossed the note on the table and went to the cupboards.
Mom hadn't lied when she said she'd gone shopping. Food
crammed each inch of storage space in the kitchen. There
was enough food to last me weeks. I tried to ignore the tiny
ball of dread building inside of me.

Box of cereal under one arm and a bowl and spoon in
hand, I went back to the table and sat down. The note
captured my attention again.

I could easily believe that Mom was still pissed at me for
what had happened at school. Actually, for what had been
happening with increasing frequency over the last few
months if I were being honest with myself. My head was
telling me that she was just taking off for a few days to
teach me a lesson about respect or some other load of crap.

But, my gut continued to tug my thoughts in a different direction. What if the note wasn't a way to get back at me?

Instead of pouring milk, I looked around. This wasn't Mom's normal style of house. I'd thought that right away. Mom liked fashion, attention, and town-living. Nothing we'd packed from the prior place was here, only the boxes full of my things, which now sat in my room. Yesterday, I'd figured a moving company would show up. Now? I wasn't as sure.

Looking around, I only saw more evidence that she'd moved me, not us. I didn't know what to do or believe. I couldn't call her to ask what was going on or when she'd be back. She never had a cell phone that I knew of. Men would always just stop by when they wanted her attention, or she would go to whomever she was seeing at the time to get his. I didn't know more about the last boyfriend than his first name. She never let any of them hang around me too much.

Numb with the realization that I had no way to contact my mom, I poured my milk and clung to the belief that this was just a punishment. She'd show up again after a few days. This would be just like those weekender trips she'd been taking with Darren. She'd come home, exhausted and wanting to sleep for a day.

After I cleaned up breakfast, I went to the second bedroom upstairs and opened the window after removing the tattered curtain. Fresh air circulated the dust-clogged room. If I were Mom, I wouldn't want to live here either if this were my room. I got to work dusting, cleaning, washing, and de-webbing the entire space. Since it wasn't big, it didn't take long.

Satisfied that when Mom came back she'd have a place to crash, I went to shower in the house's single, first-floor bathroom tucked into the tiny space between the living room and the kitchen. Like the rest of the place, the bathroom needed updating. And more room. Every time I reached up to wash or rinse my hair, I hit my elbow on the wall or knocked something off the narrow ledge near my shoulders.

"Vacation home from hell," I said under my breath. If I were lucky, Mom would be ready to move again in another month.

Just when I thought the place couldn't get any worse, the faint, off-key melody of "My Darling Clementine" reached my ears.

"That's seriously messed up." I switched off the water and wrapped a towel around myself as I left the shower. The sound grew in volume when I opened the bathroom door. The source of the noise, a newish white box mounted just above the front entry, was hard to miss. I needed a chair and a hammer.

First, though, I needed to tell off the person still pressing the damn doorbell.

I yanked the door open and startled two uniformed men having a discussion on the front porch. Instant anger flared up inside of me, and I tried to slam the door shut.

The police officer moved too quickly and stopped my attempt with his foot.

"Is there a reason you're trying to run?" he asked.

I quit trying to close the door and let him swing it wide again.

"Are you kidding? I'm standing here in a towel. Of course there's a reason."

His eyes narrowed at me slightly.

He's a cop, Megan, I reminded myself. You don't want to piss him off when you're only seventeen and have no way to reach your mom.

"Were you expecting someone else?" he asked with a smirk.

The instant need to punch him in the face had me curling my fingers, around my towel and the doorknob, in a death grip.

"Obviously, I wasn't expecting anyone or I would have been dressed already."

My gaze shifted to the delivery man.

"Can I help you?"

The man's eyes swept over my towel-clad torso and wet hair while a light blush crept into his cheeks. My temper cooled a little, and I gave him a small, encouraging smile.

"I have a scheduled delivery for Megan Smith," he said. "A TV, and it looks like the cable company is here to hook you up as well." He motioned over his shoulder to the three vehicles parked on the gravel shoulder in front of my house.

"Yeah, sure, bring in whatever."

The man fled the porch, leaving me alone with the cop. I itched to do or say something to piss him off as much as he had me.

"You know the rules; all outside visits need to be approved before you can schedule anything."

"Sorry. I didn't know that. My mom and I just moved in yesterday. She set all this stuff up. Not me."

"I know. That's why I'll let it slide this time. But, I'd like to talk to her."

"Yeah, me too. She left this morning on a business trip and was a little vague on when she'd be back."

"I bet." There was that damn smirk again.

"You'll need to get used to how things work around here real fast or you and I will have problems. Welcome to Uttira, Megan." His voice seemed anything but welcoming as he handed me a pamphlet with the words "Welcome to Uttira," printed in bold yellow on a blue background.

When I looked up, the officer was already walking off the porch, and the delivery guy was wheeling a large TV box through the tall grass.

Leaving the front door open, I jogged upstairs and pulled on some clean clothes. Dressed in a pair of jeans and a t-shirt, I felt better equipped to deal with whatever new hell Mom had brought down on my head. Not the TV and cable install, which the guys wrapped up quickly, but the town in which she'd temporarily left me.

Barely an hour after the interruption to my day, I closed the front door on the installation guy and went to the kitchen. As soon as the sound of the delivery engine faded, I walked outside and took in a lungful of late summer air. The second week of a new school year never smelled so good. If Mom wanted to take off, so could I.

Grinning to myself, I started around the house and down the overgrown gravel driveway.

A vast field occupied the space directly across from the house. Beyond that, trees stretched as far as I could see. The twisty road to the right didn't look much different from the road to the left. Nothing interesting either way except distant mailboxes marking the presence of a few scattered houses.

Listening to my gut, I turned to the right and started walking. However, it soon became apparent that we lived nowhere close to town. Trees began to hug both sides of the narrow, twisty street, and roads split off at frequent intervals, creating a web in which I quickly became lost.

When the bird noise around me quieted, my steps slowed.

The hair on the back of my neck lifted with the sensation of being watched a moment before something darted through the trees to my right. The flash of light color low to the ground disappeared too quickly for me to see it clearly.

A soft growl came from behind me, and I twisted to look that direction. Another flash of movement, there and gone. A logical part of my brain said I should have been terrified. The growl had belonged to an animal. With trees this thick, who knew what roamed. Yet, I didn't feel fear, only impatience that whatever hid in the trees seemed to want to toy with me before attacking.

I waited.

A howl rose from within the trees, followed by another, and a third, until five voices blended into one mournful call.

"Just hurry up already," I said. "I have to get to Grandma's house."

A choked laugh came from behind me. I turned and found myself looking into an incredible pair of brown eyes that belonged to a tall boy close to my age. His longish shag of light brown hair fell around his amused face.

Surprisingly, he didn't annoy me at first glance. Not in the slightest.

"Wolves are howling, and the first thing you can think to say is that you need to get to Grandma's house?" A teasing smile played around his lips.

"I slipped into the role," I said with a shrug of my red hoodie-clad shoulder.

He laughed and held out his hand.

"I'm Fenris."

I shook his hand with ease.

"Megan."

"And behind you are my bitches," he said with a glance over my shoulder.

I looked back and found four wolves standing on the other side of the road. Something about the lead dog poked my temper. Probably because it had its teeth pulled back in a silent snarl. I returned the favor. The wolf added volume and started crouching. It was strange. I usually didn't mind animals, but something about that one made me want to kick her in the teeth.

"Aubrey," Fenris said. "That's enough."

The wolf immediately quieted.

"Wow. She's well trained. You probably should still have her on a leash, though."

He burst out laughing.

"Yeah. That'd be quite the fight. Based on the direction you're walking, you're coming from town. You staying at the inn?"

"From town? No. I thought I was walking toward town. I just moved here yesterday."

"And you're already lost. Come on, I'll walk you home."

The lead dog behind us growled low. Fenris might like me, but his dog sure didn't.

"If you just point me in the right direction, I'll be fine."

He continued to grin at me.

"The way you smell, I doubt you'd be fine. It won't take long for every male within a mile to track you down. I'll walk you. You girls can go home," he said looking at his dogs. "We're done running for the day."

The first one snarled and barked then pivoted and raced off into the trees. The other three followed her lead. This guy was crazy to have pet wolves.

"I think someday they're going to turn on you."

"Nah, they love me. They're just moody sometimes. Especially when a pretty girl distracts me."

I rolled my eyes.

"So, which way is home?"

He tilted his head the direction from which I'd come, the obvious first step. I wasn't sure we'd find our way back once we left the current road, though. I'd been walking for almost an hour, and I'd taken too many forks that led to other narrow roads within the trees.

"Tell me a little about yourself, Megan. Any heroic acts of bravery, life missions, or prophesized destinies hiding behind those pretty brown eyes?"

"Nope. Not really."

"Then what brings you to Uttira?"

"My flighty mother, who changes boyfriends as frequently as she does her favorite brand of mascara."

He made a sound between a laugh and consolation.

"What about you? How long have you lived here?"

"All my life. Born and raised in the overprotective circle

of my smothering family. Unlike you, my parents have hammered my life's mission into my head since birth."

"Oh? And what's your life's mission?"

I glanced at him as he looked right then left at the T in the road. He inhaled deeply and looked at me.

"To help damsels in distress. We need to go right."

I grinned and walked beside him as we veered the direction he'd indicated.

"That's quite the life mission."

The sound of an engine from ahead had us stepping off the road just as a cop cruiser came around the bend. It turned on its lights without sound and stopped beside us. The man from earlier today rolled down his window.

"Afternoon, Trammer," Fenris said. "Something wrong?"

"Depends. Why are you two all the way out here?"

"The girls and I were out for a run. We found Megan headed the wrong direction, and I offered to walk her home."

"Wrong direction? Right."

The sarcasm in his voice made my skin tingle with the need to hurt him.

"They were out of hicksville roadmaps at the gas station," I said.

He narrowed his eyes at me for the second time that day. But, his obvious dislike didn't bother me like it probably should have.

"Get in. I'll take you back to where you belong."

"We'd love a ride. Thanks, Trammer," Fenris said, opening the door and sliding in.

I hesitated. I did not want to get into the car, but without an idea of where I was and my guide already in the backseat, I didn't have much of a choice. I got in and closed the door. The locks engaged, and I met Trammer's eyes in the mirror before his gaze shifted to Fenris.

"What would your parents say about this?"

"Good job, son. We're so proud you're finally helping out the community." Fenris shrugged. "There might be a few joyful tears with that, too. It's hard to tell sometimes."

Trammer's face flushed, and he turned the car around. The drive back to the house only took a few minutes, which annoyed the hell out of me. I had to have been walking in circles.

When Trammer stopped the car in front of the house, we had to wait for him to let us out of the back. He frowned at me the entire time, making my efforts to control my temper a real struggle.

As soon as we stood in my overgrown front yard, he took off.

"What is his deal?" I asked.

"The usual. Underpaid. Underappreciated. Has a very small—," he held his forefinger and thumb an inch apart near his waist, "—amount of self-esteem."

I snorted a laugh, enjoying myself and surprised that I'd found someone who didn't make me angry for a change.

"He's not too bad when you take all that into consideration," Fenris said with a shrug. He then looked over my house. "Huh. I don't think I've ever known of anyone living here."

"From the looks of it on the inside, I'm not sure anyone ever has."

A car came whipping around the bend and screeched to

a halt in front of my house. The three female passengers in the convertible and waved our direction. The driver, a blonde, didn't release her tight grip on the wheel as she glared at me. From the corner of my eye, I noticed Fenris wave toward the car.

"The girls and I are going to the Roost for a party tonight. Want to come? It's a good way to get to know everyone."

I tore my gaze from the blonde to look up at Fenris.

"I'll pass. Thanks for the invitation, though."

"If you change your mind, just take a left out of your driveway. The road will take you right into town. You can't miss the Roost."

"I won't change my mind."

He grinned, leaned close like he was going to kiss me, but instead inhaled deeply by my face.

"Too bad." He licked the tip of my nose, and while I stared at him in shock, he turned and walked toward the waiting car where he jumped into the backseat and slid down between the two girls already there.

"See you Monday," he called as he waved.

Without a doubt, Fenris was a player. Not in a cocky way, though. A fun one.

Unable to help myself, I lifted my hand in return.

The blonde gave me another glare, pressed down on the gas, and cranked the wheel to send a spray of gravel my way.

CHAPTER THREE

I LET MYSELF IN THROUGH THE BACK DOOR AND WANDERED around the house. Other than the TV, there wasn't much to do. So I binge-watched shows through the rest of the day, made myself dinner, and went to bed early.

The next morning, no plate waited for me on the table. I didn't let that bother me as I poured myself a bowl of cereal and moseyed to the living room for more TV time. Another day of no responsibilities and no school sounded like heaven. However, knowing that sitting around for too long would start to get under my skin, I eventually got off the couch and went in search of a more physical activity.

By dinner, I'd washed all the windows in the house in my desperation for something to do. The layer of grime that had kept a good portion of the daylight out had taken a fair amount of work to remove. Work that I'd needed. The results made the house feel less depressing. However, the clear view of nothing but towering pines outside my bedroom window didn't really inspire any happy thoughts.

I was still alone and wondering how long it would take my mom to get over her anger.

Through the branches of the pines, a distant glow on the horizon caught my attention before I left the room. Town. I stared at the light like a moth to a bug zapper, drawn but knowing it would only cause pain. That's where my similarities with the moth ended. Going to town wouldn't result in my pain but someone else's.

After running into Dudley Do Right twice, I knew I should avoid any situation that might lead me to trouble. My tendency to get into trouble was the whole reason Mom moved us here and took off, after all. Getting into more wouldn't bring her back any quicker. But, I couldn't hide in this house, waiting forever, could I?

Not giving myself time to second guess my decision, I changed out of my dusty clothes, washed my face, and put on my jacket. Outside, I tipped my face to the light of the full moon and breathed deeply. The cool night air kissed my skin and eased some of the tension that had taken hold of my heart the moment I'd read Mom's note.

"She'll be back, right?" I asked, softly.

The moon didn't answer.

Before I looked away, something large and dark flew across the sky. I shivered and blinked. What I'd thought I'd seen was already gone.

"Country living is making me crazy," I said to myself since I was sure I'd just seen something that couldn't possibly exist. Something with wings large enough to block out the light of the moon. Something with four legs, not two.

The shape appeared in the sky again then dove into the pines to my right. Branches snapped as it landed.

Not a minute later, a naked man, close to my age, walked out of the trees. Blonde hair and dark eyes glinted in the moonlight, along with a whole hell of a lot of beautifully tanned skin. I forced my gaze to stay above the shoulders no matter how much my curiosity was demanding it dip below the waist.

As he strode toward me, the remnants of his wings disappeared behind his back.

This was, by far, the weirdest and best dream I'd ever had. I just wished I could remember falling asleep. I'd probably passed out because of the fumes from cleaning the windows and boredom.

"You're not real," I breathed. Yet, despite the fact that he stood there naked as a baby and had only minutes ago sported massive wings, talons, and a beak, something about him seemed very real.

"Fenris said you seemed naive. Aubrey thought it was an act." His gaze swept over my face. "Which is it?"

The mocking curiosity in his eyes annoyed me as much as the fact that he actually seemed to be waiting for an answer. Instead of replying, I balled up my fist and slammed it into his face. He grunted, his head moving slightly with the impact, and he caught my wrist before I could fully pull back.

"What was that for?" he asked. Anger had wiped out any hint of mocking curiosity from his tone.

I could also feel the throb in my fist. He had a hard nose.

"To see if you were real."

"Most people pinch." He sounded a bit more nasally than he had before.

My imagination was sure good at adding the little details needed to make this all feel real. I didn't let it distract me from the moment, though.

"Most people don't walk around in someone else's backyard while butt naked." Not that I actually minded that part. His biceps were clearly defined, and his thighs were thicker than my head. Realizing where my gaze had wandered, I quickly looked up again.

He shook his head and released my wrist.

"Where were you going?" he asked.

"To town. Do you own pants?"

"It would be better if you stayed here."

"For who?"

"You."

"Stay in a house where a guy shows up naked in the backyard? Yeah, that's not sounding like a good option."

"It's the safest one."

"Of course you would think that. But since this is my dream, I'm going to see how many more naked men are frolicking around this place."

He stayed quiet for a moment, studying me. I was just about to turn and walk to the front of the house when he spoke again.

"The people in this town are going to eat you up and spit you out."

Without warning, he scooped me up and walked into the house with me. In the light of the kitchen, I studied his face. He looked mad, his jaw hard and a frown tugging his lips. Very nice lips. High cheekbones and a strong nose. His gaze flicked down to me just before he started up the stairs. Deep blue eyes. I had amazing taste in dream men.

When he turned to my room, my heart skipped a beat. Was I really going to dream this? A naked man carrying me to bed? I knew where this was headed.

"I think this needs to stop here," I said.

"Oh, it will."

He tossed me so hard, I landed on the mattress with a double bounce.

"If you're smart, you'll stay. You've been warned."

By the time I looked up, I only caught a glimpse of his bare backside. Flopping back down onto the mattress, I closed my eyes and forced myself to relax, the only way I could think of to wake up from a dream.

I woke up, not in a pile of used paper towels and high on cleaner, but in my bed, dressed as I'd been to go to town. Frowning, I sat up, rubbed my face and looked at the daylight pouring in through my window.

There was no way that had been real. Obviously, I'd finished the windows and changed with the intent to go to town, but I'd laid down, instead, and just couldn't remember that part. The stress of the idea that my mom actually abandoned me had probably caused some kind of weird mental snap where my dream had replaced those real events.

But to dream a griffin, of all things? I could totally understand why the dream man had mentioned Fenris. In the little bit of time I'd spent with him, I'd actually liked

Fenris. No doubt, that's the same reason his dog's name had made a cameo in my dream, too.

Yet, I couldn't shake just how real the dream had felt. The way the dream man had looked at me when he'd carried me upstairs...

My stomach churned with that same "oh-oh" sensation I got whenever I had to tell Mom I'd gotten into yet another fight. I didn't think it was because I'd punched the dream man, though. He'd been annoyed by it but not really hurt.

Thinking of Mom, I got out of bed and checked the other bedroom upstairs. Nothing looked changed, and my anger with her started to outweigh the hurt. So I'd gotten into a fight. She'd raised me. I always got into fights. Taking off like she had wasn't cool.

I turned away and went downstairs. A nice, long shower helped the weirdness of the dream fade.

Feeling a little better, I made a breakfast of eggs, bacon, and toast and sat down at the table. Alone. Before I could stop myself, I wondered what Mom was doing. Did she miss me? Probably not. I wasn't the easiest person to get along with. Even though she'd ditched me, I missed her. How messed up was that?

Suddenly the eggs didn't look as good. I sat there and wondered why I was playing along. Why stay here? I was almost eighteen. Okay, not really. I still had six months. But still, why stay?

I stood, went to the kitchen drawer, and grabbed the checkbook the note had mentioned. The register showed fifty thousand dollars. I snorted and rolled my eyes, doubting the number was real. Hopefully, there'd be at least five hundred in there, or at least enough for a night in a motel while I hoofed it back to our old place. I didn't doubt for a second that Mom was either still there packing or having alone-time with Darren.

Tucking the checkbook into my back pocket, I quickly devoured my breakfast then took care of the house. Once I had the trash out and everything put away or closed up, I shrugged into my jacket and stepped outside.

Early morning light shifted through the trees as I walked down the road heading out of town. After paying better attention during the car ride home yesterday, I knew where to turn. Before long the twisty roads opened up to a long stretch of nearly treeless pavement ahead.

Smiling to myself, I imagined Mom's reaction when I showed up at her front door. I'd tell her that I was done playing her stupid game and that she'd need to Mom up for a few months before I'd be out of her life for good, like she obviously wanted.

Lost in my thoughts, I didn't notice the waver that looked like ripples of heat rising off a summer-baked blacktop. I did notice, though, when the hair on my arms stood at attention. My pace slowed. Not because I wanted it to but because my legs grew so heavy that each step took a considerable amount of effort.

"What the hell?" I muttered, looking down at my feet.

Due to the direction of my gaze, I didn't see how close I'd gotten to the weird waves until a bright light flared and sent me flying backward. I landed hard on the pavement, my head connecting with a hollow thud.

I didn't know how long I laid there, but the bitter smell of burnt hair and the taste of blood in my mouth roused me. I opened my eyes and blinked up at the clear blue sky above. It took a second to recall why I lay on my back in the middle of the road.

Given the stench filling my nose, I sat up and patted my head in panic then exhaled heavily when I felt a full head of hair.

"It doesn't actually burn anything," a voice said from beside me. "Just smells like it."

I turned my head and found the man from my dreams squatted down nearby. This time, he wore jeans. My eyes still feasted on his broad bare chest, though, as my scattered thoughts tried to form an explanation for what was happening.

How could I have dreamed an actual person? I doubted I had psychic abilities. If I did, I would have seen myself getting knocked on my ass. And, I doubted I'd seen him somewhere around town because I hadn't left my house. Even as I thought it, I recalled stepping out the back door in my dream and how he, a winged creature, had swooped down and stepped out of the shadows as a man.

There was only one answer. He still didn't exist. The fall had caused me to hit my head harder than I thought, and he was now the result of a concussion.

Sunlight glinted off his blond hair, clearly defining strands in vivid detail. Detail I couldn't possibly dream up.

"This isn't real," I whispered with growing desperation.

"Not that again." He stood and leaned down to offer me a hand, which I ignored. As soon as I got to my feet, he took a step back.

"If you feel the need to test reality, pinch your arm," he said.

I shook my head, not to answer him but in denial of the

whole thing. However, the strength of my denial faltered when I looked down the road and saw the shimmering waves.

"I wouldn't try it again. In fact, if you were smart, you would start running through the trees to get home before Trammer reaches the barrier." I tore my gaze from the waves in time to see my dream man nod toward the woods to the left.

I understood what he was telling me. Run before I get caught. But caught for what?

"Barrier?" I asked.

"Yeah. You really have no clue, do you?" He sighed. "Parents do that sometimes. Keep us in the dark then ditch us. Do yourself a favor and run home. Don't try to leave again. No one leaves until they prove they can handle themselves around the humans."

I opened my mouth to ask what the hell he was talking about when I caught the sound of an engine. His warning about Trammer echoed in my mind. I couldn't afford another run-in with the police. Without waiting, I sprinted into the trees.

"Smart girl," he called from behind.

His high-handed superiority was starting to annoy me.

The thought had barely formed when I heard a huge whoosh behind me. The heavy beat of wings had me looking up as I ran further into the trees. Through the multi-colored canopy, I saw the creature soaring above. It flew in the direction I was headed, its speed quickly making it disappear from sight.

He was real? It was real?

The sound of the engine quickly faded. I didn't slow. I

was freaking out too much. As I wove through the trees, my mind raced. What was really real? All of it? Where had my mom brought me? As much as I wanted to think the hit to my head was the cause of the big griffin flying above, doubt kept me from believing it. I hadn't hit my head last night.

Not more than a minute after the thing disappeared, it circled into view again and repeated the path as if pointing the direction. I veered slightly to the left. It made a deep sound like a rumble of thunder and swooped lower toward the trees before turning again. It circled back around and repeated the move until I corrected my course.

Yep. Definitely leading the way. I was so preoccupied watching the sky that I didn't at first know where I was when I burst through the trees into a clearing. The hacked-up lawn gave it away before the house or leaning shed. While I looked around, wondering where to run next, the griffin circled once then took off toward town. Staying where I was became the safer option.

I quickly let myself in and locked the door. The back of my skull throbbed, and I still tasted blood.

"What the hell is this place?"

I had no answer and no one I trusted to ask. At that moment, I hated my mom. But, I hated myself more. If I could have just learned to control my temper, none of this would have happened. I would still be back home, where I belonged, not in this crazy town.

The computer on the table caught my eye. I sat down and booted it up before tapping out a quick search of Uttira, Maine. A page of the town's activities, which included an upcoming Fall Festival and a reminder to be neat and orderly citizens, pretty much summed up the message on the town's pathetic website. It wasn't any more helpful than the stupid pamphlet I'd gotten the day before.

Giving in to the growing headache, I kicked off my shoes, shed my jacket, and went to the bathroom cabinet to take two pain relievers. Thinking to add to the numbing effects, I ambled to the living room and turned on the TV.

Before I could even get comfortable on the couch, the doorbell rang. I cursed myself for forgetting to rip it from the siding. It rang a second time just as I reached the entry.

I yanked the door open, already scowling. My temper frayed further at the sight of Trammer.

"Going somewhere, Megan?"

I looked pointedly at my bare feet before meeting his gaze.

"Yeah, the beach."

He narrowed his eyes.

"Stay where you belong or we're going to have problems. Do you understand?"

"That you like harassing minors for no apparent reason? Yeah. I understand. If that's all, I'd like to get back to my nineties re-runs."

I slammed the door in his face, too angry to care about the consequences. I didn't belong here, and we both knew it.

CHAPTER FOUR

DESPITE MY CERTAINTY THAT I DID NOT BELONG IN UTTIRA, I had no clue how to leave. Every time I thought about trying to walk beyond the township's limits again, the smell of burnt hair surrounded me so intensely that I struggled to breathe. However, as soon as I stopped thinking about leaving, the smell would immediately disappear.

I could no longer delude myself that what I'd seen, felt, and smelled was a dream. Yet, admitting that there was a magical barrier being used to keep people and creatures inside Uttira sounded completely crazy.

So, I spent the rest of my weekend on the internet, researching plausible explanations. Nothing more turned up on the town than what I'd already discovered. A search on griffins was a joke. Not a single bit of information matched what I'd seen. Magical barriers proved mildly entertaining. People had videos of themselves doing incantations or spells that didn't prove anything. Yet, their complete certainty that they'd performed and documented an act of magic had me looking for medical conditions that would make a person smell burnt hair.

By Monday morning, I hadn't found anything to support that what I'd experienced was even possible, and my non-life in Uttira once again felt like one long bad dream, which worried the hell out of me. Last time I thought events were a bad dream, reality bitch-slapped me. I had the bruise on the back of my head to prove it.

Frustrated and lost, I considered my options. Reaching out for help from anyone official was impractical. What would I say? Help me; I can't leave Uttira because of a magical barrier. At best, it would land me in foster care and at worst, a padded room. I had no one to turn to but myself. And the only way I'd understand what to do was to leave the house again and learn more about this place I now unwillingly called home.

So I showered, dressed, and ate breakfast like a normal person while my mind came up with a ton of weird possibilities regarding what I'd find when I reached town.

A sudden, loud pounding on my front door brought me to my feet. Any triumph I should have felt at disabling the doorbell over the weekend sunk to my toes at the sight of Trammer on my porch. Since he was staring at me through the now clean glass of the door's side windows, I had no choice but to answer.

"Good morning, Trammer." I tried for pleasant. I really did. But, it came out more sneer than anything. What was wrong with me?

"Let's go," he said, motioning to his car.

"Go where?"

"Girderon."

The name sounded familiar, and I quickly recalled how I knew it. It was the name for the preppy Academy here. The school that Mom had given me the paperwork for. The very one she said wouldn't require my actual attendance.

"Why do I need to go there?"

"It's Monday check-in. If you refuse, they gave me permission to arrest you. Are you refusing?" He set his hand on the device hanging from his duty belt.

"Check-in? I have no idea what you're talking about."

"Get in the car or I'm taking your procrastination as refusal and arresting you."

I focused on breathing and not the increasing need to cause him physical harm.

"I'd like to grab my jacket if that's all right with you."

"Hurry up, and keep the door open."

I turned and went to the kitchen where I grabbed my phone and the Academy paperwork, all of it untouched since the day Mom left. Trammer stood in the same spot when I returned, and he waited as I locked up.

The ride in the back of his cruiser gave me a few minutes to thumb through some of the Academy papers. The welcome letter gave instructions on how to get to their special website to review the courses offered. They stressed that Girderon specific courses would not be available online for security reasons. Instead, they would be covered during the required attendance Mondays. The dress code, code of conduct, and internet safety policies seemed pretty standard at a glance.

Wondering what I was in for, I neatly stacked the papers once more and watched out the window. The curvy road on which I lived led straight into town. The place had a lot of buildings but seemed dead. No one walked along the street or moved from shop to shop. A bad feeling settled in the pit of my stomach. Where were all the people?

Trammer turned onto a boulevard lined with stately trees. Not far down the drive, he stopped the car at a gate and pushed the button beside a mounted speaker box.

"Yes?" a voice asked from the speaker box.

"I'm delivering Megan Smith as requested," Trammer said.

"Enter."

A buzzer sounded, and the gate rolled open.

He drove around a slight curve that revealed a huge stone building at least a mile ahead. The thing rose three stories high and sprawled out to the right and left, consuming more space than any one building should.

The cream stone shone pale in the morning light, giving the whole place a clean, new appearance. Yet, the date beside the grand, double-doored entry clearly stated the building had existed for over two hundred years.

Some part of me registered Trammer stopping the car and coming around to open the door.

"Thanks, Jeeves," I said, not looking at him as I continued to stare at the building. Preppy didn't begin to accurately describe the grandness of Uttira's school.

I walked straight up the steps toward the woman waiting there.

"Megan Smith?"

"Yeah."

She gave me a kind smile before she looked over my shoulder.

"You should leave, Trammer. Thank you for your service."

She didn't look at me again until the sound of the car faded, which gave me a moment to study her. Her long, dark hair fell loosely down her back. A plain grey business suit, white top, and grey pumps gave an air of authority. I waited for my infamous irrational anger to grip me and drive me to do something that would ultimately get me kicked out on my first day. Instead, I didn't feel anything but curiosity for the school, the locked gate, and the personal greeting.

"Welcome to Girderon Academy. Allow me to give you a brief tour and an explanation." She held out her arm, indicating I should lead the way inside.

The grand entry rose the full three stories. Glass windows on the roof domed the ceiling and provided light. Potted plants filled the space and created imaginative walkways to the dual staircases leading up.

"My name is Adira Grenald. I'm the studies coordinator for all the students at Girderon."

I tore my gaze from the impressive entry to look at her.

"What's a studies coordinator?"

"The person who tells you what sessions you need to take to graduate, follows your progress, and makes recommendations based on your performance and skills."

"So you're a guidance counselor?"

"Something like that." She flashed me another kind smile and started down the hallway to the left. I followed.

"We strive to make Girderon a safe place to learn for all of our students. As you can imagine, it's not a simple task.

Certain safeguards are in place to prevent death on Academy grounds, but you can still be hurt."

I'd been trying to see through the narrow windows set into the classroom doors we'd been passing when her words registered. My steps faltered. The recent blow to my head must have messed with my ears. There was no way she'd said what I thought she had.

"Did you just say death?"

She stopped walking and met my worried gaze.

"I did. Like you, not all of the students have yet learned to control their impulses." She turned and continued down the hallway. "Most of the general studies are located along this corridor. If you test sufficiently in the core requirements, you will likely spend little time in this area."

She turned a corner to a wider hallway with fewer doors.

"Time between assigned sessions can be spent in this section doing independent, voluntary studies. Each room has an occupancy schedule, which I manage. If you would like to book a time, come see me. The rooms are warded so no one can come to harm and nothing inside can be destroyed."

"Right," I said, drawing out the word.

At the end of the hall, she turned again.

"These are the administrative offices. We'll pause the tour here so I can become more acquainted with your aptitudes." She opened the door to a spacious room with an executive desk and a chair set before it.

"Have a seat." She waved me toward the chair as she moved behind the desk. A maroon folder on the surface caught my eye. She noted the direction of my gaze and set her hand on the folder.

"I'll update your file after each aptitude review, which we will conduct every Monday. Now, Megan, tell me what you know about yourself."

"There's not much to tell except that I'm pretty sure I don't belong here."

She sat back in her chair and considered me for a moment.

"Why do you think that?"

What could I say that wouldn't make me sound as crazy as she'd sounded on the way here?

"Look. You said this place is warded. What does that even mean?"

"That magic protects the Academy and the students within it."

"Exactly. Magic. Something I don't believe in."

"Even after your run-in with the barrier?"

My eyes rounded.

"Yes. I know you tried to leave. I wouldn't have expected anything less, but I do discourage you from trying it again. Without the mark of Mantirum, the barrier will repel you."

"And the mark of Mantirum is…?"

"The mark you receive upon graduation to signify you are a full member of the Mantirum, the world of magic."

I snorted and grinned. "Right."

"I see," she said. "Doubt will not help you learn what you must."

She stood and held out her arms. As I watched, her clothes changed to wisps of material and her skin lost its pinkish hue, turning pale and almost translucent. Light moved just under the surface. Instead of looking creepy, I found it beautifully mesmerizing.

"Do you see me, daughter of Paxton? Do you see the magic pulsing in my veins? Magic is real. The world you knew has been kept blind to this fact. It's time for you to see our world for what it really is. It's time for you to see yourself for what you really are."

"And what am I?"

She dropped her arms, and her clothes and skin returned to normal. Well, what I considered normal.

"What you are is for you to discover in your own time," she said. "Now, tell me about yourself."

"Besides questioning my sanity for even considering to believe any of this, I have a problem keeping my mouth shut and my fists to myself."

She smiled slightly. "You're sane, Megan. And, with time, you will find the truth about this place and yourself. I think, for now, letting you acclimate would be wiser than continuing with your assessments."

She stood and motioned for me to join her. Not sure what else to do, I did as she wanted and followed her out of the room and up a flight of stairs to the second floor. At the third door, she paused.

"I will talk to you again soon."

She opened the door and stepped in. Through the opening, I saw a room full of desks like school back home. In the sea of faces, one winked at me. My gaze stayed locked on Fenris as Ms. Grenald spoke.

"Good morning, Lucas. This is Megan Smith. Please make her feel welcome."

"Hello, Megan.

I tore my gaze from Fenris' grinning face and looked at the older man at the front of the room.

"Good morning."

"Please take a seat."

I looked back at Fenris and the body of occupied desks. The her-herd from Friday surrounded him, including the bitchy blonde driver. Ignoring her glare and the itch of annoyance creeping just under my skin, I moved further back in the room toward the only open desk. The teacher started speaking again as soon as I sat.

"Your very natures will tempt you. The Gods created you and gave all of you purposes that center around the humans. Whether to defend or devour them, you must learn to blend and avoid exposing your true selves."

I didn't care if I was being mentally redundant, but this couldn't be real. Who were these people? Magic? Gods? Devouring people? No, thank you.

Before I could fully form the thought to stand, the person to my left moved. I glanced over and met the calm gaze of the guy from my not-dreams. He was wearing clothes this time. A whole outfit, not just pants.

His deep blue eyes held mine for a moment while I struggled to believe he was actually real.

Ever so slightly, he shook his head then returned his focus to the teacher.

He was telling me not to leave? Why? Was something going to knock me on my butt again? Frustrated, I stayed in my seat through the duration of a lecture about keeping who we were secret while fulfilling our purposes.

When the bell rang forty minutes later, everyone stood.

"Megan," the teacher called before I could do the same. "If you wait a moment, I can explain your schedule."

I stayed in my seat and watched the rest of the students file out. Fenris' girls gathered around him, touching him on the shoulder or arm, all vying for his attention. He glanced back and winked at me while responding to a comment about someone's new hairstyle.

If all the kids in here were some kind of creatures that needed to blend, I had no idea what Fenris was supposed to be. Other than a girl magnet, of course. When I glanced to the left, that seat was already empty, too.

Lucas grabbed a stack of papers from his desk and came to me.

"Your mother indicated that you've been in the human public schools until this year, which should mean that you've already met the general requirements needed for Girderon. However, you'll need to complete the assessment tests in the core classes to verify that. Since you're choosing to homeschool, I've included a packet for English, Math, Social Studies, and Biology that you can use as a study reference if you feel the need. When you log into your Girderon account, you'll see an assessment test link. Whenever you're ready, you can take the tests."

Overwhelmed by everything that had been happening to me so far, I automatically took the papers when he handed over the packet.

"Until then, you will be required to attend History of the Gods, Human Studies, which is this class, and Self Discovery. Standard curriculum for your age."

He handed me another sheet. This one had a schedule with the names of the classes he'd just mentioned. It took a few seconds of silence to understand he was done speaking and waiting for a reply.

I had no idea what to say, though. I'd already tried to tell Adira I didn't belong here, and it hadn't helped me any.

He set a hand on my shoulder and gave me an understanding look.

"I know you must feel lost right now. Living out in the human world without knowing who and what you are for as long as you have might make this seem unreal. I promise it is very real, and you do belong here. The sooner you accept that, the easier your transition will be."

"Transition?"

"Yes. To the life you were really meant to live. Welcome to Girderon, Megan. If you ever need someone to listen, you can knock on my door or seek out any other instructor here."

"Uh. Thanks."

"You're welcome. You better hurry. Self-Discovery's on the first floor."

CHAPTER FIVE

I LEFT THE CLASSROOM AND STEPPED INTO A SURREAL CHAOS IN the hall. It wasn't the level of noise, but the crowd of students, that stunned me. Slowing to a stop, I yet again questioned my sanity and tried to make sense of what I was seeing.

Like any school between classes, the majority of students hurried to some unknown location while a few lingered in small groups, talking and creating congestion. However, unlike any normal school, less than half the student body appeared human.

Dwarves, whom I could easily mistake for normal short people if not for their excessive display of jeweled rings and necklaces, mingled with giants. Where their diminutive counterparts moved briskly with each step, the giants languidly made their way through the crowd. Some stood so tall, the tops of their heads almost brushed the ten-foot ceilings. They weren't the most impressive sight, however. Elves walked gracefully beside minotaurs, centaurs, and cyclopes.

I took a moment to watch a centaur prance past, the clop of his hooves rising above the sound of so many voices. He caught my gaze and nodded at me, the movement slightly terse. Probably because I was staring at him with my mouth open. Closing it, my sweeping gaze made another pass over the creatures in the hall.

My disbelieving heart stuttered in my chest. There were even more creatures, but I didn't have a clue what they were. While most of them seemed human, a few looked anything but. This had to be real. I didn't have the kind of imagination, awake or sleeping, to make this sort of stuff up.

"Hey, newbie," a girl said, stopping in front of me. "Come to the pool with me, and I'll sing for you." She tilted her head slightly, exposing thin lines just behind her ears.

Gills? Were those gills?

"Ah, no thanks."

"Some other time, then." She shrugged playfully and walked away.

I should have been freaking out and running for the door. Instead, I found I couldn't tear my gaze from the bizarreness of the individuals around me. Across the hall, a group of girls wore skimpy tops made to showcase their green-hued skin. They preened at whoever would look at them, and one went so far as to grab a guy's butt as he walked past.

What was this place really? Sticking to the side of the hall, I began to make my way toward the stairs.

"Oh, new meat!" a high-pitched voice squealed.

Turning toward the main body, I briefly met eyes with the source of the squeal, a cute little redhead with fangs.

She smiled at me hungrily. Before I could decide how to react, someone stepped in front of me. I looked up at the back of a shaggy head of dark hair.

"No you don't, Belemina," Fenris said. "You promised I'd be the only boy you'd put under your spell."

"She's not a boy," the girl said with a laugh. "But I'm sure I could be persuaded to look the other way if you walk me to my next class."

"If I walk you to class, Mina, you'll never look anywhere but at me ever again," he said, smoothly offering his arm. A slim pale hand looped through it, and they started away.

He glanced back at me and mouthed, "You owe me."

I wasn't sure what, exactly, he'd just saved me from, but I nodded, relieved. A boyish smile played around his lips before he turned his attention back to his companion.

Released from the fixation that had gripped me the moment I stepped from the door, I glanced down at my schedule. It was easier to think about getting to the next class than the strange world I found myself in.

Unsure how long I had, I turned toward the stairs once more only to be blocked by Fenris' her-herd.

A surge of irritation rose up inside me as I locked eyes with the blonde driver. It wasn't because she was tall, curvy, or insanely gorgeous. Half the females in the hall met that criteria. And my reaction to her had nothing to do with the sneer on her face, although it probably should have. Most people set my temper off for no good reason whatsoever.

"Aubrey, let's just go," the blonde to her right said, tugging Aubrey's sleeve.

"Aubrey," I said, recalling the wolf and the way Fenris

had commanded it. I looked at the rest of them. They didn't all glare at me like Aubrey did and weren't nearly as irritating.

"Man, Fenris really has a thing for blondes, doesn't he?" I said, meeting Aubrey's gaze.

"He does. So stay away from him."

I rolled my eyes.

"He doesn't seem like a guy who can be stolen. He seems more like the guy who does the stealing."

In a rare show of restraint, I tried to step around her, but she shadowed my move.

"Seriously, furball? Go pee on someone else's tree."

One of the girls groaned as Aubrey snarled at me.

I grinned and made a fist. If she wanted a fight, I'd give it to her.

"Bring it, bitch," I said, embracing my anger.

As soon as she launched herself at me, I swung hard toward her face. My fist connected with a satisfying thwaump that encouraged my temper.

Aubrey screeched as she flew backward. Unfortunately, the crush of bodies still coming up the stairs stopped her from toppling down. I launched myself at her, more than ready to pummel her face so she wouldn't be able to snarl for a week.

Mid-swing, I found myself lifted up and away from Aubrey. Unable to stop the punch in progress, my fist bounced off the cheek of the largest man I'd ever seen. At least eleven feet tall to my five foot six, he dwarfed me. His peeved gaze pinned me as I dangled from his fingers by the back of my shirt. I tried to quell the anger boiling under my skin.

"I call Mulligan on that last one," I said, softly.

The giant lifted his free hand and made as if to flick me in the face. Since his fingernail was the size of my nose, I knew it was going to hurt and braced myself.

A voice cut through the commotion around us.

"That's enough."

I turned my head a bit to see Dream Guy standing behind me, his head nearly level with my stomach.

"Put her down, Finnegan. I saw the whole thing, and we both know hitting you was an accident."

"Hitting me was. But what about hitting Aubrey? New girls shouldn't hit people they don't know," the giant said, in a deep voice.

"You're right. And, people they don't know shouldn't try to pick fights with them on their first day either."

The giant nodded and set me on my feet just as a bell rang. The hall around us immediately cleared, and the giant ambled away, ducking slightly to enter the room I'd just left.

Aubrey continued to glare at me. The increasingly red mark on her cheek and the slight swelling of her upper lip let me know I landed a solid hit with the first punch. I wondered if a second one would knock the glare from her face.

"Aubrey, we both know that Fenris flirted with her, not the other way around. It wasn't necessary to try to establish your claim with her. You need to establish it with Fenris. Do you want someone to look at your face?"

"I'll look at it for her," I said before I could stop myself.

"Why are you so angry?" Dream Guy asked, studying me.

"Mommy issues because she left you here?" Aubrey's attempt at a snide smile ended with a wince. It didn't make me want to hit her any less.

I clenched my fist and stepped forward. Dream Guy blocked me.

"Class or home?" he asked.

He'd better not be toying with me.

"If I seriously have a choice, home."

"I'll take you. Jenna, let Adira know."

The blonde beside Aubrey nodded, and the quad walked off. Dream Guy motioned me down the stairs.

"You going to fly me home?" I asked.

He glanced at me but kept walking.

"Was she right?" he asked.

"About my mom? Yeah, she left. So what?"

"Is that why you're angry?"

"Pft. I was angry long before that," I said.

We reached the first floor and started down a long hall that looked just like the one we'd left.

"Why?"

"How am I supposed to know? What about you? Why are you always so bossy?"

"Daddy issues," he said.

His comment didn't make me angry. In fact, it defused the lingering tension under my skin.

We reached the main atrium, but he didn't head toward the main door. He passed through the space toward the right wing.

The smell of salt water tickled my nose before the lilting sound of singing reached my ears. Instead of keeping straight on the main hall, I turned left, following the sound.

I didn't walk far before I reached a section of windows set into the hallway to view two giant swimming pools.

Girls and boys swam in the water or sat on the edges. Some sang. Some played with the next person's hair. All of them had tails. None of them wore clothes. Thankfully, the girls had very long hair.

"How does that make you feel?" Dream Guy asked quietly.

"Watching them play with each other? Slightly pervy."

"I meant their music."

I shrugged and focused on listening.

"A little calmer maybe. Why?"

"A siren's song can be very alluring."

"Alluring? Who are you? Are you really my age?"

"I am. Come on."

We trekked back to the main hall and out through a side door to a parking lot.

"Please tell me you have a car here."

"I do."

He led me to a red sporty thing in a line of sporty cars.

"Way to be unique."

He shrugged and opened my door for me. I slid in, more than a little jealous of his car. Not because it was red or sporty but because it was a car.

When he got in, he caught me petting the leather seat.

"I thought you weren't a fan," he said.

"I'm a fan of anything that will get me to where I want to go without walking."

He started the engine and eased out of the parking spot. I looked out the window and stared up at the towering height of the school.

"I'm still not sure I believe any of this is real," I said. "Giants. Sirens." I looked at him. "Griffins."

His expression remained neutral, as it had been every time I saw him. Except for when I hit him.

"It's real," he said.

"How is it real? And why doesn't anyone know?"

"You were in Lucas's class. We blend. Look at you. You lived in the human world for how many years?"

"Seventeen, and I wasn't blending. I'm human." A thought occurred to me. "What's going to happen to me when they figure that out?"

He glanced at me and tapped the wheel for a moment as he slowed by the gate. It swung open without him needing to use the button.

"If you're here and enrolled in Girderon, you're not human, Megan. They don't make those kinds of mistakes."

"They?"

"The Council. The governing body that oversees the Academy, the town, and our community."

I shook my head slightly, realizing I was actually believing everything. It was hard not to believe after almost being flicked by a giant.

"Okay. I'll bite. What is this community really?"

"A home for the children and creations of the gods."

"Gods?" I couldn't keep the disbelief from my voice.

He glanced at me once more, his expression still neutral, then focused on the road. We drove the rest of the way to my house in silence. If I'd offended him by not buying into his beliefs, he was good at hiding it.

When he pulled over in front of my house, I caught a

subtle, judgmental change in his expression after a glance at my front yard.

"The lawnmower's broke," I said, feeling the need to defend myself since the responsibility of the place fell on me now. That thought triggered the memory of what Aubrey had said in the hall. She'd known my mom had abandoned me. Did they all know?

"Thanks for the ride." I quickly got out and started toward the rear of the house. I didn't look back at the sound of his car slowly pulling away.

The idea that he'd stepped in to help me at school and gave me a ride home because I was the town's charity case sat like lead in my stomach and increased my hatred for this place. Yet, I knew it wasn't Uttira's fault. It was my mom's. She'd brought me here with the sole purpose of ditching me. If what everyone kept telling me was true, she had to have known what this place was and had withheld so much information from me. Why hide the truth from me? Why bring me here? Was it because I actually was something more than human? If so, what was I?

I let myself in through the back door and placed the Girderon papers on the table. After fixing myself a snack, I sat down and logged into the Academy's website. A list of interactive sessions and tests waited on my student home page.

More curious about the school itself than my course list, I clicked around and read what little there was. A page simply titled "Origins" caught my eye. The article, written by Lucas Flavian, contained a fair number of links to Greek and Norse mythology sites. While I munched on some veggie chips, I read how Mr. Flavian proposed "we" were descendants from the gods, some of us direct offspring between human and immortal, and some creations of those godly immortals. He went on to outline the ebb and flow of each god's reign.

To me, the article didn't have a point. It wasn't announcing, reviewing, or summarizing. It lacked persuasion of any kind. It was more a bunch of speculative opinions or the start of a lecture that might eventually lead to a point if it were ever finished.

I continued my random clicking through the website but didn't unearth anything useful to help explain what the school truly was. Deciding to look at the assessments that Lucas had mentioned, I went back to the main page and opened the first interactive session. It followed the standard "watch a short video then answer some questions" format.

The sound of a lawnmower starting up in my yard pulled me from my aptitude review of high school English. Frowning, I went to the front door and looked through the window. There was indeed someone trying to push a lawnmower through the waist-high grass.

Dream Guy.

I yanked open the door.

"Hey!" I called from the porch.

He didn't look up.

I jogged down the steps and waited for him to turn and see me. When he did, he cut the engine.

"What's your name?" I asked.

"Oanen."

"What are you doing, Oanen?"

"Cutting your lawn. Your mom made arrangements for

it to be cut on Wednesdays. When I saw it, I figured waiting wouldn't help."

"You're the lawn service?" I asked in disbelief.

He shrugged and continued to look at me.

"Is there something else you want to ask?" he said after a moment.

"No. Nothing."

Confused and frustrated, I turned and went back inside. Outside, the lawnmower started up again.

I wished more than ever I understood Mom's motivation for leaving me here.

With each passing day, it was getting harder and harder to tell myself that she'd be back.

CHAPTER SIX

"BIG, HAIRY MONKEY BALLS," I MUMBLED UNDER MY BREATH.

Sitting at home with nothing but internet and cable TV to entertain me when I didn't feel like doing any online work sucked.

I idly flipped through channels, trying not to acknowledge that my outside-of-school pastimes were no different in Uttira than back home. Once a recluse because of anger issues, always a recluse.

A fight on the first day at the Academy had only reaffirmed my need to keep my crazy to myself. Granted, the incident hadn't been completely unprovoked. That didn't change the fact that I'd almost gotten face-flicked by a giant, though. Fighting at the Academy would be more dangerous than fighting in real school. It had been better to stay home the rest of the week and just do my school work online. Yet, after so much time sitting home with no outside contact at all, I was going stir-crazy.

Turning off the TV, I went to the kitchen and opened the fridge to stare blindly at the dwindling contents. I wasn't hungry. I was bored. No amount of snacking would cure that. Outside, the sound of the wind caressing the trees called to me. I closed the fridge and moved toward the door. My jacket hung on a peg just to the side, but I didn't grab it or move any further.

Staring into the darkness, I listened. For whatever reason, Oanen told me to stay put that second night. And, deep down, that warning still kept me inside. Why? Was I honestly afraid of anything that might be out there after seeing the possibilities at the Academy? I thought about it for a second and knew I wasn't. So why hadn't I already gone outside and found something to do? Because a bossy, shape-shifting boy my age told me not to.

"What the hell was I thinking?"

I grabbed my jacket and went outside. The heavy sound of Oanen's wings remained absent from the other night sounds as I locked the door. I breathed in deeply, savoring the taste of fresh air and freedom, and set off.

The uneventful walk to town took a considerable amount of time in the dark. The infrequent street lights liked playing peek-a-boo with rural mailboxes on the shoulder of the road. After the second run-in, I walked on the pavement where I felt safer.

Before long, the country shadows faded away with the brighter lights of town living. If you could call it living. Once again, not many people moved about on the sidewalks or from shop to shop. To be fair, most of the shops had closed signs turned in the windows already.

I checked my phone. It was only 7:30 p.m. This town seemed overly dead given the time.

The sound of an engine coming up from behind had me

stepping onto the sidewalk. Instead of zipping past me, it slowed. I looked over my shoulder and tried to suppress the spike of anger knifing through me. The her-herd pulled up beside me in the shiny convertible. Their lead bitch grinned at me from behind the wheel.

"Look, Jenna, the Council decided we needed to add a vagrant to keep the town looking authentic."

"Wow, Aubrey. I'm impressed you know what the word vagrant means. Dogs usually only understand like fifty words, tops."

Her face turned red.

"Enjoy the walk, Orphan."

She peeled away with a screech of tires and a cloud of acrid smoke. Resuming my apparent vagrant shamble, I watched their taillights as I continued on. Of course, they stopped at the only lit up, interesting looking building in town. Sighing, I debated turning around and going back home. However, the idea of walking this far just to give up right at the end didn't sit right with me, even if I knew going home was the smarter choice.

As I drew closer, I noticed the sign on top of the two-story building. The big, bold letters of "The Roost," outlined in neon tubing, took up the front section of the roofline and cast the back half in shadow. This was the place that Fenris had invited me to go hang out, which explained Aubrey's presence.

While I was still looking at the sign, something on the roof moved. Given my experience so far with Uttira, something probably was up there.

The door opened as someone went inside, and the soft

thump of music drew my attention. How could an almost dead town like this have a club?

It didn't take too long for me to reach the unguarded entrance. Some might think I didn't have a ton of experience with clubs, being a self-imposed recluse and all, but my temper had led me into one in New York. That had been two years ago. The last big city Mom and I had lived in. At fifteen, I'd ripped into the bouncer, beating him bad enough to put him in the hospital. I'd never reached my original target, some guy I hadn't even known who I'd spotted walking in.

That no bouncer stood by the red double-doors to prevent underage entrance, and the fact that the her-herd's car sat at the curb, meant this place welcomed underage derelicts of all kinds. I grinned to myself.

"Perfect."

Grabbing the long gold handle, I let myself in.

High school aged kids filled the open space of the dimly lit main floor. No one turned to look as the door closed behind me. They continued to talk in groups while unusual music played in the background. I couldn't exactly call it pop rock, even though it had that thumping beat, because of the soft, lilting voice that sang a song without apparent words. It had a slightly soothing quality, much like the singing I'd heard at the Academy by the pool.

Moving away from the door, I studied my surroundings. A wide loft wrapped around three of the four sides of the building and created a second floor that overlooked the first floor. Some kids hung around up there, sitting on stools along the red, iron rails and sipping drinks. Since couches and chairs outlined the open space of the main floor and a large, empty stage covered the back, the source of the drinks had to be up the stairs to my right.

I didn't make it more than a step in that direction when a small, dark-blonde almost ran into me. The look of panic in her eyes robbed me of any annoyance. I grabbed her by the arms to steady her.

"Is everything okay?" I asked.

"Not really. I need to get out of here."

I looked around at the people behind her. No one seemed to be paying us any attention.

"Is someone bothering you?" Please say Aubrey, I thought.

"No. I'm just really, really hungry." She leaned into me and inhaled deeply. That a girl two inches shorter and about twenty pounds lighter thought she'd make a meal out of me had me grinning.

She caught sight of my smile, pulled back, and blushed scarlet.

"I'm so sorry." I could barely hear her soft apology over the music. "I shouldn't have come here, but Adira said I needed the practice. I'm Eliana, by the way."

"I'm Megan."

"I know. New girl."

Her gaze shifted from my face to something just over my shoulder.

"Oh, we get to watch the mating rituals of the unwanted and pathetic," Aubrey said from behind me.

I curled my fist, ready to turn, but Eliana's hand on my arm stopped me. Some of the anger that had welled up at the sound of Aubrey's voice seeped away. I frowned at Eliana, and she immediately removed her hand.

The anger boiled forward again. Interesting.

I turned to Aubrey and cringed.

"This lighting is not kind to you at all," I said. "I bet the boys you're with have a lights off rule."

Eliana made a choked sound behind me while Aubrey's eyes narrowed.

"You know what I don't like?" she said. Her low, threatening tone, likely meant to intimidate me, just egged me on.

"Wow," I said with a laugh. "You must really like it when I piss you off."

"What are you talking about?"

"Offering to tell me what you don't like. Go ahead. Tell me. I'll be sure to write it down so I know what to do next time we meet like this."

She glared at me with so much malice, I thought she'd sprout claws then and there to rip my face off.

"I don't like you." Her clipped words were little more than growls.

I smiled sweetly.

"Perfect. I'll be sure to stick around then."

The door opened behind her, and she looked back. Her expression of anger changed to simpering desperation at the sight of Fenris. She rushed toward him to cling to his arm. She wasn't the only one. The other girls quickly surrounded him as well.

"Hey, Megan," he called with a wink.

Aubrey glared at me. I ignored her and smiled back at Fenris.

"Glad you finally found your way here," he said, he and his group moving closer to us.

Aubrey bared her teeth at me in silent warning. That girl needed another punch, or seven, to the face, and I itched to deliver them.

Eliana reached forward and wrapped her hand around my fist. Unclenching my fingers, I held her hand, relieved when some of the anger once again melted away.

"Oh, you two are so pathetic," Aubrey said, missing nothing.

Even Eliana's presence couldn't totally smother my desire to pummel Aubrey at that moment.

"Be nice, Aubrey," Fenris scolded.

Aubrey's haughty look turned to hurt. I didn't feel an ounce of pity for her, though. In fact, the inexplicable dislike I'd had since meeting her only intensified with her next words.

"Fenris, there's no need to give either of them social charity tonight. Let's go dance."

At the sound of heavy footfalls on the stairs behind us, I glanced over my shoulder, not ready to discover how it felt to be flicked by a giant. However, no giant descended the stairs. Just Oanen, putting a shirt on. Even in the dim lighting, I could clearly see each ridge of his six-pack. A very nice six-pack that I wouldn't have minded staring at for just a few seconds longer.

When his head cleared his shirt, he looked right at me before shifting his gaze to Fenris' group.

"Hey, Fenris," he said after he reached the bottom.

"Oanen," Fenris said in acknowledgment, his welcoming smile steady.

Oanen glanced at Eliana's hand holding mine. I thought

he might try to give us crap, too. Instead, his expression infinitesimally softened.

"You should have gotten me if you were hungry," he said, focusing on Eliana.

"I'm not hungry." Her quick reply made him scowl slightly. His deep blue gaze flicked to me.

"Can we go dance now?" Aubrey part whined and part cooed, drawing his attention and probably making glass shatter all the way in China. She needed to work on the cooing.

"Yeah," Fenris agreed with his usual smile. "See you later, Oanen, Megan."

Oanen waited until they walked away before speaking again.

"Do you want me to take you home?" His gaze stayed locked on Eliana.

"No. I'm okay. Really. I thought, maybe, I'd hang out with Megan for a bit?" Her fingers lightly squeezed mine, and I realized she wanted me to support the idea.

"Yeah. Sure."

Oanen glanced at me before addressing Eliana again.

"Okay. Come get me when you're ready to go home."

What was with the boys here? Were they only allowed one facial expression? I liked Fenris' easygoing smile better than Oanen's deadpan.

Eliana tugged me across the room to a couch tucked in the shadows. Since I'd only been headed up the stairs to explore, I didn't mind the change of destination. As we passed people, I could feel my bitchometer twitch, but nothing compared to what I felt for Aubrey.

"Let's sit here," Eliana said, releasing my hand and plopping on a couch.

The bitchometer immediately started climbing. I sat next to her and looked out at the groups.

"It's a lot like human school," she said. "There are cliques and groups. Fenris and his girls are kind of in their own group, but they get along with most others."

"Most?"

"Yeah. Aubrey," she said with a shrug. "Once you start looking at the groups, they're pretty easy to figure out. Oanen would be part of the jocks. Aubrey is the leader of the mean girls' club. There are those who are serious about excelling at the Academy, and those who are just there, riding it out while looking for a good time."

"Why are you telling me all this?"

"Because I know what it feels like to know absolutely nothing about them or yourself. But it doesn't last long. The mentors at the Academy really will help guide you to the answers."

I looked at her, trying to believe she was telling me the truth because I had so many questions. Like why she'd tried running out of here then changed her mind.

"Are you still hungry?"

She blushed slightly.

"Not as much. You helped when you looked at Oanen."

"Huh?"

She blushed darker.

"Never mind."

"So who is Oanen to you?" I asked since she brought him up. The way he'd seemed concerned about her hinted that she meant something to him.

Eliana scrunched up her cute, pixie-like face before answering.

"Keeper? Pretend brother?"

"Pretend?"

"We're not the same kind," she said with another blush. "Can we change the subject?"

"Sure."

"How old are you?" she asked.

"Seventeen. You?"

"Sixteen. My mom brought me here when I was twelve. And immediately took off. I know it probably doesn't feel like it, but it's cool yours at least left you with a place to stay. I can't wait to graduate and get back out into the human world. I miss gyros. What was your favorite food?"

And just like that, I knew I had a friend. It wasn't because both our moms ditched us or because we had a similar love of gyros. It was because, when she'd mentioned her mom taking off, she'd noticed my hand curling into a fist and had changed the subject.

"Gyros are up there," I said, answering her question, "but so are tacos and Hawaiian pizza."

She groaned. "Why is it so impossible for the Academy to serve that kind of food?"

"What do they serve?"

"Nothing processed. They don't understand that's where all the flavor is. And it's not like we can get sick from it like the humans." She grinned at me, but the grin faded quickly when her gaze shifted to the right.

I turned my head, following the direction of her gaze, and found Aubrey glaring at us.

"What is her deal?" I asked.

"She's territorial." Eliana slapped her hands over her mouth and looked at me with wide eyes.

"I'm guessing that's not nice to say because she's a dog?"

Eliana snorted laughter behind her hands.

"I won't judge," I promised. "I think I've said worse to her."

Eliana folded her hands in her lap and smiled at me.

"Yeah, I heard about what happened at school. I kind of wish I would have been there to see it."

"It wasn't that impressive. Now, had that giant actually head-flicked me, it might have turned into something more."

"Finnegan is really nice. He just has a small crush on Aubrey."

"I don't know that there's anything small about him. Even his crushes."

She grinned.

"So tell me about Uttira. Is this the only place that's open after seven?"

She laughed and shook her head.

"You just caught Uttira at the wrong time. Everyone's prepping for the Fall Festival."

"I read about it online. Is it fun?"

She shrugged and made a face that said it was anything but fun.

Someone walked over to our couch. I looked up and found Oanen standing over us.

"We gotta go," he said, looking at Eliana.

"Okay." She looked at me. "Do you need a ride?"

CHAPTER SEVEN

IF IT HAD BEEN OANEN ASKING, I WOULD HAVE SAID NO.

"Sure," I said instead. "The walk here was a little long."

"You walked all the way from your house?" Disbelief laced her words as we stood. "You should request a car. The Council will bring in something for you to use since you're outside of town."

"That's okay. It's safer if I walk."

Oanen led the way out of the front door, nodding to people and saying goodbye as he went. A few waved to Eliana. She shyly waved back without pausing. No one seemed to notice me. And I was okay with that.

When we got outside, I saw Fenris leaning over Aubrey's car, his hands braced on the passenger door. It wasn't a she-lost-her-purse-and-I'm-looking-for-it kind of pose. It was an I-want-to-hit-something pose. A pose I knew too well.

"Keeping it together?" Oanen asked.

Fenris straightened, saw us, and smiled his flirty boyish smile.

"Yeah. I'm good. Better get back inside." He walked toward the door but stopped a moment to look back at me. "Maybe I'll see you tomorrow, Megan." He disappeared inside before I could respond.

Eliana cleared her throat slightly. I quickly pulled my gaze from the closed door to find her watching me. Oanen was already halfway down the block.

"We'd better catch up," she said quietly.

We jogged.

When she and I reached the car, Oanen silently held out his hand without looking at either of us. Eliana saved me from any confusion by dropping a set of keys into his open palm.

"You can have the front," she said, already opening the back door as he walked around to the driver's side.

Since Oanen seemed in a rush, I got in without arguing about the seating arrangement. He started the engine and told us to buckle up as he pulled out from his spot.

As soon as I buckled my seatbelt, Eliana passed me her phone.

"Send yourself a text from my phone so we have each other's numbers."

I took her phone and opened the text app. Her message list consisted of four conversations. Oanen, Adira, her mom, and Mom2. I didn't ask, just started a new conversation thread with my number and updated the contact information to Megan before handing it back.

"Maybe when you're done with Fenris tomorrow, we can hang out some more," she said.

"Sure."

The rest of the ride home passed in silence. Instead of

stopping in front, Oanen pulled into the driveway and drove around to the back of the house.

"Thanks for the ride," I said, getting out.

"See you tomorrow," Eliana called.

I'D ONLY MANAGED two bites of my breakfast when someone knocked on the front door. I looked down at my milk stained t-shirt and shorts, shrugged, and stood. It wasn't like I was out to impress anyone.

Tugging open the door, I interrupted Fenris mid-knock. He grinned at me, his gaze sweeping over my body from head to toe.

"Wow. You look amazing."

"Shut up and come in," I said stepping aside. "When you said you might see me tomorrow, I didn't think it would be before eight."

"That's when a woman shows her natural beauty," he said smoothly.

"If you're attracted to this look, I really don't understand your fascination with the bitch brigade."

While he laughed, I closed the door and led the way to the kitchen.

"I'm going to use that. They'll love it."

"Will they really?" I asked, sitting down to resume my breakfast. "Because if they do, they have issues."

"No thank you. I already ate," he said as if I'd offered him something.

I rolled my eyes.

"Apparently, I'm an orphan. That means I'm not equipped to feed guests."

He sat beside me, a small smile still playing about his mouth.

"Then this is your lucky day. I wanted to take you to town so you could see what Uttira's like when all the shops are open. Including the grocery store, Moonlight Market. It's open twenty-four seven."

I drank the milk remaining in my bowl and took everything to the sink to wash it.

"I'd like that. But, I need to shower first," I said over my shoulder.

"Please tell me that's an invitation."

I shook my head and laughed. As soon as I set the dishes in the drying rack, I ran upstairs to grab some clean clothes.

Fenris still sat in the kitchen, looking completely at ease, when I returned.

"The bathroom door doesn't have a lock. And, that's not an invite but a warning. Stay out."

He pretended to pout as I closed myself in the bathroom. After quickly showering and dressing, I threw a load of my laundry into the washer just off the kitchen.

"Does it bother you?" he asked. "Being independent already?"

"Not really. I mean, I did a lot of this stuff before Mom left me here."

I turned and found him leaning against the counter, studying me. He wasn't smiling for a change, and I didn't like it.

"Don't pity me."

"Not possible when I envy you so much."

"How so?"

"There's no one telling you what to do, where to go, who to hang out with. That's freedom."

I snorted and grabbed my jacket.

"I'm still getting told all that stuff, just not by a parent."

He waited while I locked up the house, then we walked together to the front where an older car was parked.

"Wow. I thought everyone under the age of eighteen owned a sports car in this town."

"I do." He grinned. "I just thought I'd treat you special."

He opened the door for me, and it groaned in protest. That sound should have forewarned me. Instead, I clapped my hands over my ears at the noise the engine made when he started it.

"Holy crap," I yelled to be heard.

"She gets all the stares. Just wait and see," he yelled back.

We didn't talk on the way to town.

As he'd predicted, actual people moved about on the sidewalks when we reached the shopping district. Most of the early risers looked our way as Fenris pulled over into a parking spot and cut the engine. My ears rang.

"This is Uttira," he said with a sweeping gesture. "Come on. I'll take you on a walking tour."

After considerable effort opening and closing the ancient door, I joined him on the sidewalk. We walked down the length of the street then back up the other side. The unique little shops offered a diversity of items from handcrafted jewelry to paints to custom clothing. Tucked in with the boutiques, casual shoppers had their choice of three cafes in which to sit and rest their feet.

"Come the festival, the road will be blocked for stalls with food, beverages, and games. The streets will be packed with humans."

"When is that happening?"

"It sounds fun, right?"

"No. It sounds awful. I need to know when to avoid town."

"No chance for that. It's mandatory attendance."

I stopped walking and looked at him.

"The town mayor is going to try to make me have fun?"

He chuckled.

"No. Adira and the rest of the Uttira Council. Our attendance is required in order for us to be considered for graduation. Remember Lucas's lecture about blending? That's what they're going to be watching for. That we can blend."

"I go to the weirdest school ever."

He opened the passenger door for me this time.

"I've heard there are a few weirder," he said with a grin.

I got in and waited for him to join me and start the car.

"Where to now?" I yelled.

He pointed down the road then, with a burst of grey smoke from the exhaust, eased out of the parking spot. We didn't talk for the short ride from the touristy downtown area to the commercial retail area.

Fenris parked in the grocery store parking lot and turned off the car again.

"There's the bank," he said, nodding toward the brown

building. "The hardware store, post office, and bakery. The place next to it is where a lot of locals go for lunch."

"We have people who aren't local?"

"A few. Some human spouses who know the truth and chose to live here."

"And they aren't considered local?"

"Nope. Ready to shop?"

"I need to run to the bank first." He didn't question why and hung back when I quietly spoke to the freakishly goblin-looking teller to verify the checkbook and associated account were real. The woman assured me the account was real and the listed amount accurate. I couldn't believe Mom had left so much money for me. The guilt over ditching her child had probably helped her generosity.

After withdrawing some cash, Fenris and I went to the grocery store. I'd run out of the fresh food but still had plenty of dry goods. So, I shopped light. Fenris marveled at the idea I could pick my own food and, on the way home, begged me to make him something for dinner one night soon.

"What about Aubrey?" I asked.

"What about her?"

"I'm not sure she'd like me making you dinner. She's pretty into you, like she's already staked a claim."

"That's just part of who Aubrey is."

"And what is that?"

He glanced at me and grinned.

"That's like asking humans their sexual orientation. It's personal. Some might even consider it rude."

"Are you telling me this so I don't ask you questions or so I do?"

"I'm telling you this so you'll know not to ask someone you just meet this question, but to also let you know I'll try to answer any questions about anyone if I know the answer."

There were two people I really wanted to ask about, but I debated if I should.

"I'm straight, by the way," he said. "All into females, in case you were wondering."

I grinned.

"I'll keep that in mind."

"If you don't want to ask, that's fine too. If you pay attention, you'll figure out what most of us are. I just wanted you to know you have someone you can trust if you need me."

Someone to trust sounded kind of nice. Along with someone who seemed to calm me with a touch.

"Do you know what Eliana is?" I asked.

His smile slipped just a little before recovering.

"A succubus. But before you go grouping her with the rest of her kind, she's different. She's not a threat."

"Um, keep in mind that I don't know anything about anyone's kind. Are succubuses normally a threat?"

"Succubi. And some can be. They typically feed off of human sexual energy. If they can't control their hunger, feeding can kill their partner."

For whatever reason, he'd lost his smile with that explanation.

"Why do all topics lead back to sex with you?" I asked, trying to tease him into a better mood.

He grinned once more.

"Because it's the most interesting topic on your mind? Because I'm a male and you're insanely attracted to me?"

I laughed.

"I can see why you have your own following, now. So, what about me?" I asked, changing the subject. "Do you know what I am?"

He shook his head. "Not yet."

"Will you tell me if you figure it out?"

He nodded.

"All right. Then, I guess my last questions are what would you like me to make you for dinner, and when do you want it?"

He grinned widely.

"Something you ate a lot of in the human world."

I thought back to the dinners Mom had made.

"Spaghetti?"

"Yes. That."

He pulled into the driveway of my house and went to the back. After he parked, he helped me carry in the groceries and set them on the table. It wasn't even ten yet.

"Thank you for letting me take you to town," he said. He held out his hand, and I automatically offered mine, thinking he meant a handshake. Instead, his fingers closed around mine and brought my knuckles to his lips. The feel of his warm mouth against my skin sent a zing through me.

Before I could decide if it was pleasant or not, he released me.

"I'll see you soon, Megan."

With a wink and a flash of his boyish smile, he left.

I took my time putting away groceries then sat down at the table, wondering what to do next. TV didn't sound appealing at the moment, and it seemed too early to check in with Eliana. So, I opened my laptop and logged into my homeschooling page.

LEANING ON THE POLE SAW, I surveyed my work and grinned, glad I'd given up on schoolwork hours ago. Several of the pines boxing in the yard had died. Thanks to the handy pole saw I'd found in the shed, I'd trimmed back all of the dead lower branches. It didn't make the yard look any better. In fact, it left gaping holes in what had been a natural fence. However, I felt better after doing something physical.

With the sun touching the treetops, I put the saw away and stacked the last tree's branches on the large pile I'd created before going inside. Although the activity had cured some of the growing restlessness crawling under my skin, it hadn't purged all of it.

After I showered to remove old, dried pine bits from my hair, I listlessly walked to the kitchen for my phone and sent Eliana a text.

I'm home and bored. Have any plans?

Her reply was immediate.

I'm on my way!

Less than fifteen minutes later, I heard a car pull up outside and went to the front door.

Eliana parked the car Oanen had driven last night to drop me off. She saw me, waved, and got out. Instead of heading my way once she rounded the car, she went to open the passenger door, and I watched her grab several bags from the front seat. She turned to me with a wide smile.

"What is all that?" I asked, returning her grin.

"Snacks. I didn't want to come empty-handed."

I stepped aside to let her in. She kicked her shoes off by the door then followed me to the kitchen where she began emptying the snack bags onto the table.

"Where'd you find all this stuff? I was at the grocery store and didn't see this much variety."

"I asked someone to bring it in. That's the only way to get anything good here. I heard you have cable. There's a new movie I've been dying to see. Should we watch it?"

In short order, we popped some extra buttery popcorn and got comfy on the couches. Fenris' explanation of what Eliana was had me looking at her in a new light. Not judging, just more curious. Thanks to his little talk, though, I knew not to ask about it.

We watched the first movie in companionable silence until the credits began to roll.

"So what do you do out here all by yourself?" she asked.

"Not much. It's kind of boring. If not for you and Fenris, I might have died of boredom already."

"You can tell me to shut up if you don't want to talk about this...but you and Fenris. Are you really interested?"

I smiled and nibbled on my popcorn for a second.

"Fenris is nice. I like his smile and his easy-going personality. If I were in the market for a boyfriend, he could be an option, minus Aubrey."

She laughed and nodded. "Minus Aubrey is a given. But, you're not in the market? Why? Do you have a human boyfriend?" Excitement lit her eyes, and she leaned forward, eager for details.

"No. I had one once. Almost two years ago. I learned my lesson after that failed attempt at a relationship. It's fine to look at the opposite sex, but that's it."

"Why? What happened?"

"It ended abruptly when I punched him in the face for no apparent reason."

"Like Oanen?"

I made a face. "No. I thought I was dreaming when I did that. When I hit the other guy, I was pissed. Beyond pissed. I felt so horrible afterward. Then, the next day, I found out he'd cheated on me the night before anyway. I didn't feel so bad after that."

"That's actually really good," she said encouragingly.

"How so?"

"You lost your temper when you were wronged, even if you didn't know you were wronged at the time. It might be a trait, like how a banshee cries to announce a death."

"I thought we weren't supposed to talk about what we are."

Her face fell a little. "It's not polite to talk like this to people you don't know well. But, with friends, it's different. I'm sorry if I overstepped."

I reached over and clasped her hand. A subtle calm crawled its way under my skin, spreading out soothingly.

"We are friends," I said. "And, since we are, can I ask why I sometimes feel calmer when touching you?"

She tugged her hand from mine and blushed hard.

"I'm sorry."

"No, it's okay. I like it. I'm just wondering what it is. If you don't want to talk about it, that's fine."

"Well, I'm supposed to feed on sexual energy. But the idea of what I need to do to feed that way freaks me out. I end up getting so hungry that I'll feed on just about any emotion."

"Is it bad for you to feed on other emotions?"

"No, not really. It just doesn't give me what I need. It's like a human going on one of those weird diets where they only eat one low-calorie food. All lettuce or all watermelon or something like that."

"Are you telling me you're the succubus version of an anorexic?"

"Yeah, I guess. Adira is trying to help me overcome my hang-ups." She shrugged. "It's not easy."

"Well, any time you need an anger snack, you let me know. I'm more than willing and have plenty to go around."

CHAPTER EIGHT

I ROLLED OVER WITH A GROAN AND TUCKED MY HEAD UNDER the pillow to hide from the sunlight. At the second beep from somewhere in the direction of the nightstand, I re-emerged in search of my phone.

It took four blinks to focus on the text from Eliana thanking me for last night. I shook my head and put the phone back on the nightstand without responding.

Hanging out with someone who didn't piss me off by just existing had been nice. That she hadn't left until after two hadn't bothered me until now. Whatever type of creature I was, I liked my sleep. However, the sun and my brain had other ideas. Within fifteen minutes, I gave in and got out of bed.

Another long day stretched before me. Out of the blue, I wondered what my mom was doing. It felt weird thinking about her, now. Even though she'd only been gone a week, so much had changed in my head since she'd left. I didn't miss her like I probably should have. It was hard to miss someone who had lied to me and didn't want to be around me anymore. Mom was so unlike Eliana.

Thinking of Eliana, I picked up my phone and sent her a quick text back.

It was nice having the company.

Her reply came almost right away again.

Do you want a ride to the Academy tomorrow for check-in?

That'd be great.

I'll see you at seven, then.

Sighing, I grabbed some clean clothes and went downstairs to shower before breakfast. Not that I needed to bother. No one came knocking on my door, and I spent the day focusing on assessments again.

By the time I finished, I was looking forward to going to the Academy in the morning. Anything was better than sitting at home, studying alone.

Heading upstairs for the night, I changed into my pajamas and turned off the lights. The brightness of the waxing moon lit my room as I made my way to the bed and curled under my blankets. I really needed to get curtains. Shutting my eyes on that thought and how I'd get to town to buy said curtains, it didn't take me long to fall asleep.

ANGER WOKE ME. I opened my eyes, my gaze sweeping the room. The moon's light had moved from my bed to my floor, letting me know I'd been asleep for a while.

My temper was a pain in my ass during the day, but this was the first time it ever bothered me while I slept. I exhaled slowly, trying to relax, and closed my eyes again.

A noise reached my ears. The soft brush of footsteps. I held my breath, trying to hear more. The sound came again. Downstairs. In the kitchen. Someone was in my house.

"Hell no," I said, flipping back the covers.

I flew down the stairs, the thump of my steps loud in my rush. Not loud enough to block out the sound of my quarry escaping out the kitchen door, though. I almost swore as I rounded the corner and mashed my hand on the light switch. The sudden burst of light illuminated the room just in time to catch the screen slamming shut. I raced out onto the porch but saw nothing. Whoever had been in my house had neatly fled.

Going back inside and flicking on lights, I went from room to room, checking everything. Nothing looked out of place. Who had been in my house and why?

I studied the kitchen again. A tuft of white hair on the latch of the screen door caught my eye. I plucked off the fur and held it between my fingers, my anger flaring. Since arriving at Uttira, I'd only seen one pale canine.

"Bitch," I breathed.

Aubrey was a dead dog walking.

WHILE I LISTENED for the sound of Eliana's car, I paced the entry and continued to plan what I would do or say to Aubrey when I found her. Currently, I was leaning toward the doing rather than the saying. But, I would need to be smarter about exacting my revenge within Girderon's halls. I couldn't just attack the moment I saw her.

Controlling my temper wasn't my strong suit, though.

Not even for the few seconds it would take to look around for giants who might take offense at me punching Aubrey in the face. Chances were I'd end up face-flicked before the day ended.

The sound I'd been waiting for cut my plotting short. If you could call seven hours of plotting short. I hurried to the kitchen to grab my jacket and my bag before returning to the entry. I yanked the door open just as Eliana got out of her car.

"Let's go," I said, rushing toward her.

"You don't need to bring a school bag," she said. "I promise. There's never any notes to take and everything's online homework-wise. It's an either-you-know-it-or-you-don't kind of system."

I opened the front passenger door and got in. A large shadow moved across the hood, and I leaned forward to look out of the windshield at the sky. A griffin circled high above.

Eliana got in and noticed what held my attention.

"Yeah, sorry. He's following," she said with a shrug.

"Whatever. Let's just go."

She started the engine and gave me a hurt look as she pulled away from the house.

"Are you mad at me?"

I took a calming breath.

"Nope. Aubrey broke into my house last night, and I need to get to school so I can punch her face in."

"What? Are you serious?"

"Yeah. I did it once already. I just need to make sure there's no giants around to stop me this time."

"Not that. About her breaking in. Did you see her?"

I snorted. "I found white dog hair on the door after I came running downstairs, and the chicken fled."

Reading doubt in Eliana's lack of response, I launched into a defensive explanation of what I considered a logical and foregone conclusion.

"Think about it, Eliana. Aubrey's the only one who's had an attitude toward me since the moment she saw me. I mean, who else would sneak into my house in the middle of the night and snoop around my kitchen?"

The shadow passed over the car hood again.

"Megan, maybe we should talk about this later," she said hesitantly.

"Why? There's nothing to talk about. I missed seeing who was in my house by half a second because I wasn't sure what had woken me up, and it made me a little slow getting downstairs. But when we get to school and I confront her, you'll see."

A scream, very much like an eagle's, cut through the sound of the engine before the griffin sped off in the direction of the school.

"What's his deal? Does he follow you everywhere?"

Eliana made a face.

"Pretty much. Um, you should probably know his hearing is crazy sharp."

"What? You mean he was listening to us?"

"Yeah. And, I don't think he liked what he heard."

"Big deal," I said. I wasn't letting Oanen stop me this time.

"What do you do when you don't like something?"

"Punch it in the face."

"Exactly."

"Wait, are you saying he's going to punch me in the face?"

"Of course not. I'm saying he's going to react like he typically does."

I frowned and thought of the time Oanen did more than just impassively watch me.

"He's going to throw me on my bed?" I guessed.

"What?" Eliana squealed, half in shock and half giggling.

"I don't know. How does he normally react?"

"When did he throw you on a bed?" she demanded, grinning like a crazy lady.

"When I first met him. I thought I was dreaming and punched him."

"In the face?" she asked in disbelief.

"As you just pointed out, it's my typical reaction."

She shook her head and slowed down, having reached town.

Even though she wasn't scolding me or wearing a judgmental expression, I felt the need to defend what had occurred.

"He was fine. Maybe a little annoyed with me. He picked me up, carried me inside, tossed me on my bed, and told me to stay where I belonged."

"And you did?"

"Again, I thought it was a dream. I went to sleep and figured out it wasn't a dream the next day when I saw him again by the magical barrier that sent me flying."

"Ouch," she said sympathetically.

"Yeah, it wasn't fun. Now, about his reaction?" I asked

as she turned into the Academy drive. The gates opened as soon as she approached.

"Lectures. Long, boring lectures about safety, responsibility, you name it. He likes to lecture."

"And I like to ignore, so it'll be fine," I said with a grin.

Eliana turned to the right, pulling around to the side of the Academy. Not many students had arrived yet, so it was easy to spot Oanen in the mostly vacant parking lot. With his arms crossed and a scowl on his face, he stood waiting for us in Eliana's chosen parking spot.

"Told you," she whispered.

He stepped back as she pulled forward and turned off the car. Through the windshield, his gaze remained locked with mine. Did he honestly think he had any right to lecture me on anything? He unfolded his arms, the material of his shirt pulling tight across his chiseled chest for just a moment, and moved toward my side of the car.

As soon as I opened my door, he was there, crowding me.

"You heard someone in your house, and you went running downstairs? Where's your common sense?"

I shouldered my bag, mildly annoyed.

"Hold on. I never claimed to have any common sense. I have anger issues. The two usually don't work well together. And what difference does it make to you?" Gravel crunched behind us as another car arrived. "Now, if you'll excuse me."

His gaze flicked behind me a second before he clasped my arms.

"Keep your hands to yourself," he said with a low warning.

"I was about to say the same thing." I threw off his hold moments before my anger reared its head. Not at Oanen, though. I turned and faced Fenris and his group of girls.

"Why'd you break into my house last night?" I demanded.

Fenris scowled. Jenna and the other girls' gazes darted to Aubrey.

"I don't know what you're talking about," Aubrey said. She reached for Fenris' arm and snuggled close to his side.

"How did you know I was talking to you, Aubrey? I was looking at Fenris."

The girl's face flushed scarlet, and her lips curled back to show her teeth.

"Stay away from him. He's mine," she snarled.

A hand slipped over my clenched fist, calling attention to the fact that two strong arms gripped me, and I was struggling to get to Aubrey. Eliana's small hand on mine did wonders to ease some of my anger. Enough to hear what Oanen said next, anyway.

"You need to take care of this."

Fenris sighed and pulled off his shirt. The view wasn't as nice as when Oanen removed his, but it still elicited a yearning whine from Jenna as she looked at Fenris. With a snarl, Aubrey turned on the girl and lashed out. Her claws left red welts on Jenna's cheek. Despite Eliana's hold, my temper surged again.

Fenris unzipped his pants, turned before showing anything interesting, and collapsed into a wolf. He sprinted away with a howl, leaving behind a pile of clothes and his girls.

Aubrey turned on the other girls, snarling as she slipped

from her sundress and stood naked in the parking lot without an ounce of inhibition. I wasn't a prude, but I wasn't an exhibitionist either.

Collapsing into wolf form, Aubrey howled and ran after Fenris. A moment later, the other girls stripped where they stood and chased after the pair.

Oanen's hands released me.

"What the hell was that?" I asked, my anger fading to confusion.

"Desperation. Aubrey knows Fenris' mate run will happen soon and is doing everything she can to keep her scent foremost in his nose."

"Eliana, you know better," Oanen reprimanded her softly.

"If they don't want people to talk about it, they shouldn't make it so public."

"A mate run? What's that?" I asked Eliana.

"When his kind reaches a certain age, the urge to run out and mate hits hard. Overwhelmingly hard, I've heard. And, it's nothing like when the human boys get horny. Fenris can't just go out and have a good time. Fenris' kind mate for life. Whoever he picks in his moment of weakness is who he's stuck with forever."

"Ugh." The idea of him stuck with Aubrey for the rest of his life sent a surge of pity through me.

"Yeah," Eliana said in an equally sympathetic tone.

"Are you two done?" Oanen asked.

"Almost." I walked over to Aubrey's sundress and thoroughly stomped it into the dirt. Adjusting the weight of my bag on my shoulder, I turned back to the pair waiting for me.

"Now I'm ready to go inside."

"Seriously, you don't need your bag," Eliana said, not commenting on the dress.

"I might." I took a step toward the school.

"What's in it?" Oanen asked.

"A change of clothes in case I get bloody."

He plucked my bag from my shoulder and tossed it back into the car.

"No fighting today." He stood, arms crossed and biceps bulging, before the door so I couldn't pull the bag back out.

"Who do you think you are? You can't tell me when not to fight. I fight all the time. Why do you think I'm here?" I said, exasperated.

"The clothes stay in the car," he said.

I narrowed my eyes at him.

"Fine, but if I end up needing them and don't have them, you're going to be on the receiving end of my temper next."

A howl cut through the air followed by four more.

"Come on. Let's get inside before they come back," Eliana said with a tug on my hand.

I gave Oanen one last glare and followed her inside. A few students already walked the hall, and I heard singing coming from the pool.

Adira waited for us in the main entry.

"Good morning, Megan. I was hoping I could talk to you before your first session."

I shrugged and said goodbye to Eliana before following Adira. It didn't escape my notice that Oanen stared after us a moment before following his ward.

As soon as we reached Adira's office, she went behind her desk, and I took a seat.

"I saw you completed all your assessments. I must say, I'm impressed. It usually takes more time for students in your situation to gain the focus needed to see what needs to be done."

"What's my situation?"

"Alone in a strange, new world."

"Ah. Yeah, well, I have no car to go anywhere and was bored." I shrugged.

"Regardless, you did very well. You've mastered the requirements to graduate from human high school. That means we can focus specifically on your Girderon requirements."

"Which are?"

"To master your control of yourself around humans."

"Perfect. Considering where I lived before coming here, that shouldn't be a problem."

"As you pointed out to Oanen in the parking lot, you have little self-control."

"Wait a minute. I pointed out I had a problem with common sense because of my temper. I never said anything about self-control."

We both knew it was a weak objection to the truth. When my temper flared, I didn't have control or common sense.

"Fine. What do I need to do? And if your answer contains the words 'visualize,' 'find your center,' or 'breathing technique' forget it. Been there. Done that. It doesn't work."

"The humans were trying to help you with something they couldn't begin to understand."

"I don't know, some of them gave my anger their best efforts."

"It's not just anger. It's part of your abilities."

"Hold up. My anger has something to do with what I am?" My mind raced, trying to think of any mythological creature known for anger issues or general grumpiness. Trolls, giants, brownies, dark elves...there were more grumpy ones than not. I'd need to do some research and compile a list.

"Stop trying to guess who you might be. It will distract you from who you are," Adira said, interrupting my thoughts.

"You're talking in circles."

She smiled serenely. Instead of calming me, it had the opposite effect.

"And, you're annoying me," I said flatly.

"I know. But, I'm not making you angry. Do you see the difference?"

"Not really. I still kinda want to wipe that smile off your face."

The natural abrasiveness I channeled when annoyed didn't faze her.

"Pay attention to your emotions. Break them down and ask yourself why you're feeling the way you do in any particular situation. By analyzing each feeling, you can start ruling your emotions instead of letting them rule you. Gaining that level of control, before your true form emerges, will—"

"True form? You mean this isn't what I really look like?"

I could feel panic welling up inside me. Everything else they'd thrown at me, I'd taken with a grain of salt. But this? Hearing that I would physically look different melted a sane portion of my brain.

"Breathe, Megan. I showed you my true form on your first day here. Yet, here I sit in the form you find the most familiar. The fact that you will have another form doesn't mean you must use it."

I stood and gripped the back of my chair.

"I don't want to be late for class."

Adira sighed. "Very well. Run away, Megan. It doesn't change a thing. I will see you at the Fall Festival."

"I'll pass. I don't do well in crowds."

"Attendance is required. Unless you're not interested in leaving Uttira. Ever."

"Why did I ever think you were nice?"

She smiled, not cruelly but as if she thought I was the funniest thing ever. We'd see how funny she thought me at the festival.

Turning on my heel, I stormed out the door and came to an abrupt halt at seeing Fenris leaning against the wall in the hallway.

CHAPTER NINE

WHEN HE SAW ME, FENRIS STRAIGHTENED AWAY FROM THE wall and ran a hand through his already mussed hair, a look of guilt on his unusually serious face.

"I'm sorry about Aubrey," he said.

The door closed behind me. Apparently Adira didn't much care about our drama.

"Don't sweat it. Eliana told me about your mate run thingy. Are you considering Aubrey?"

"Not if I can help it."

"Then, why don't you tell her that?" We stayed where we were in a quiet corridor without other students.

"I've tried. You saw how she treats the others. It's worse when she doesn't think she has a chance."

He'd just given me more reason not to like her. I hated bullies.

"Is that why she has a problem with me? She thinks I threaten that chance?"

"She knows I hung out with you and that I'd like to do it again."

As much as I liked the idea of continuing to piss Aubrey off by just existing, because it was nice to know someone else lived in my hell, I didn't want to lead Fenris on.

"Look, I like hanging out with you, Fenris, but—"

"Aubrey won't be a problem. I have a plan to keep her distracted this time."

"Um, that's not what I was going to say."

The bell rang.

"We'll talk about this tonight. Okay? I'll swing by your place after school. Eliana's taking you home, right?"

"Yeah."

"Perfect. I'll catch you later."

He turned on his heel and jogged down the hall to the stairs.

Wondering why I'd been crazy enough to want to come to school, I followed. Slowly. When I reached the end of the hall, Oanen stood there. His expression wasn't neutral this time. Disapproval tugged at his brow and lips.

"What'd I do now?"

"You're late for your first session."

"I know. I'm going." I grabbed the railing, intending to start up the stairs. His hand closed over mine. The heat of his skin distracted me.

"Do you even know where you're supposed to be?" he asked.

I pulled my hand out from under his.

"Second floor. First hall. Third door on the right."

"No. Principles of Human Integration is your second session. Introduction to Self-Discovery is your first session. I'll walk you there."

I rolled my eyes and gestured for him to lead the way.

Instead of taking the steps up, he turned and went down the wide hall that Adira first showed me and stopped at the second door.

"This is it. I'll see you in Lucas's session."

"You mean you don't have this one?"

He studied me for a second.

"I already know what I am," he said quietly.

"So this class is about figuring out what I am?"

"I don't know. Never had to take it."

"Why do you know my schedule?"

"Because I knew you wouldn't." He turned and walked away, leaving me at the door.

I stared after him a moment, wondering what his deal was. Was he really like this with all the girls or was I getting special treatment because of my association with Eliana?

Pulling my gaze from the view of his retreating backside, I entered the room and interrupted a woman mid-sentence.

"Megan," she said. "I'm LuAnn. Come in and take a seat. Adira said you'd be joining us today."

I looked at the students and immediately saw Eliana's smiling face and the empty seat beside her.

After almost ninety minutes, I understood that Self-Discovery wouldn't give me a straight up answer about what I might be. Instead, it was just like it said. Meditative self-discovery crap.

With a promise to find me during our lunch break, Eliana said goodbye in the hall. In the crush of bodies, I kept my eyes on the floor and found my way to Lucas's Principles of Public Integration session without incident.

Most of the desks were empty, except the group at the

front. I openly smirked at Aubrey's dirty sundress. She scowled at me. Ignoring her, I winked at Fenris. The soft rumble of her growl filled the room. Satisfied, I took my seat and waited for the bell to ring.

"Why must you purposely annoy her?" Oanen asked from beside me.

"According to Adira, pissing people off is my superpower."

"Don't you take anything seriously?"

I thought about it.

"Not really. That must be another superpower."

He exhaled slowly and sat back in his chair, not talking to me again until the bell rang ten minutes before eleven.

"I'll walk with you to the cafeteria," he said, standing.

It wasn't an offer; it was an order. Oddly, though, it didn't annoy me. I had no idea where the cafeteria was anyway.

"Ok. Eliana said she'd meet up with me there."

We stepped out into the chaos. Only, this time, I didn't have to hug the walls and avoid eye contact. With Oanen beside me, people moved out of the way. Even Finnegan nodded to Oanen and gave him wide berth.

I glanced at the guy beside me, wondering what hold he had over everyone. It couldn't just be his incredibly good looks because his hold wasn't only on the students. The faculty all treated him with respect, too. Instructors nodded to Oanen when they passed him in the halls. And, when we reached the cafeteria on the ground floor, the lunch lady gave Oanen a wider smile and an extra helping of grilled trout and fried greens. She offered me the same because I was with him, but I politely declined.

I'd have enough trouble finishing what was already on my tray.

Turning away from the extremely bland but nutritionally packed lunch line, I spotted Eliana already at a table. She waved at me, and I quickly started across the crowded room.

Mid-way, my temper flared. I froze, the tray dropping from my stiff fingers. Sniggers erupted around me. I clenched my fists and started to turn, already feeling the location of the object of my rage.

Before even seeing the person, arms wrapped around me.

"I don't think so," Oanen said. He lifted me off my feet and strode toward the side door. As soon as the door closed, I felt fine.

"Was it Aubrey?" I asked. "I could have taken her."

Oanen set me on my feet, his head bent as he looked down at me disapprovingly.

"Sorry to disappoint you, but Fenris and his followers always go for a run at lunch."

"I liked you better when you were still trying to figure me out and didn't scowl at me all the time," I said.

The door opened, and Eliana rushed out.

"Are you okay? Do you want a hug?"

"I'm fine. A hug isn't necessary." Did she think I was embarrassed over dropping my tray?

"Because, I could, you know, take some of that anger, if you wanted."

"Oh! Sure. Hug away." I opened my arms, and she shyly wrapped her arms around my torso and laid her head on my shoulder.

Eliana's hugs rocked. The anger lingering inside me immediately melted away, leaving me with an uncommon mellowness. It felt weird but oh so nice. Knowing I had Eliana to thank for this new feeling, I hugged her in return. The embrace turned into more of a snuggle, but I didn't care.

"I think that's enough, Eliana. She's starting to smile," Oanen said from beside us.

I was, and realizing it made me smile more.

"You have my permission to hug me anytime I look like I'm going to lose my temper," I said before Oanen pried me off of her.

"Only if I'm not around to stop the fight myself," he said. "Stay here, and I'll get you a new lunch. We'll eat outside."

Again with the bossiness. I stared after him, noticing the way his shirt hugged his shoulders and the way his jeans rode low on the curve of his tight—

"Can I come over and talk to you tonight?" Eliana asked, interrupting my thoughts.

I wrinkled my nose.

"I'd say yes, but Fenris is coming over. He and I need to talk."

"Oh?" she said with a teasing grin.

"Not that kind of talk. Although I enjoy doing anything that will piss off Aubrey, I don't want to lead Fenris on. I'm not healthy for a relationship. Especially one of my own."

Her playful smile fell, and she looked at me rather sadly. Before she could say anything more, Oanen returned with two trays, and we finished our lunch period in relative quiet.

My second and third sessions, General Living Skills and Advanced Human Studies, were a joke. The fight that I almost caused during the free time between the two sessions was just as sad. I didn't land a single decent punch thanks to Oanen.

Eliana met me in the hall after Advanced Human Studies, which was on the third floor.

"Oanen's already on the roof. He told me to tell you, no fighting."

I rolled my eyes and followed her down the stairs. No one moved out of the way for us this time.

"What gives? When Oanen's with us, everyone moves. When he's gone, people try to push us into the walls."

One of the passersby snorted and kept going. Eliana didn't say anything, but I caught her smirky grin.

Outside, people mingled by their cars. Fenris stood near the sporty red car he'd arrived in while talking animatedly with Aubrey. She caught me looking, and I blew her a kiss. Before she could take a step in my direction, Fenris grabbed her arm and pulled her toward their car.

That same eagle cry we'd heard on the way to school echoed around the parking lot.

"We better get going," Eliana said.

I glanced at the top of the building and saw Oanen perched there. His golden gaze pinned me.

"No one likes a bully, Oanen," I said softly. "I should know."

I got into the car and buckled up. A shadow fell over the hood, circling.

"Is he always like this?" I asked. "How has he not smothered you, yet?"

Eliana shrugged as she backed out of her spot.

"Do you think you'll come in tomorrow?" she asked.

"Not if I can help it. I thought I missed people, but today reminded me why I'm better off at home, reading the notes and watching the videos. Why do you go?"

"I didn't, but Adira talked to Mr. and Mrs. Quill and told them it would be in my best interest to attend."

"Mr. and Mrs. Quill?"

"Oanen's mom and dad. My guardians."

"And has it helped?"

"Not really." She glanced up at the sky then took the turn out of the Academy.

For the rest of the drive, neither of us spoke. When Eliana pulled up in front of the house, I thanked her for the ride.

"Let me know if you want company tomorrow after school," she said before she drove away.

I waved then looked up at the sky for Oanen, but he'd disappeared.

A single day of school should have cured me of my boredom; yet, now that I was home, loneliness surged again. Probably because I'd found someone I actually liked. Not just Eliana, either. Oanen, too, even though he could lighten up a little. And Fenris. I sighed, thinking of him and the upcoming talk. Usually I liked making people cry.

Shaking my head, I walked around to the back and let myself in.

Over an hour later, Fenris knocked on my front door. With a smile, I welcomed him and waved him to a seat in the living room.

"As promised, Aubrey is conveniently distracted," he said with a small bow.

I chuckled, unable to help myself.

"Good to know. Is that why she came here? Because she'd found out that you took me to town?"

"Yeah. Even over the stink of the exhaust from that old car, she caught your scent when she saw me. Our noses are a pain in the ass sometimes."

We sat on the couch, and I turned toward him. He continued to watch me with that open, attentive look he gave everyone.

"Fenris, I need to be straight with you. I'm not interested in being anyone's girlfriend. My life is too complicated." I shook my head. "My issues have issues. I'm more likely to spontaneously hit you than kiss you. Hanging out like this, although really awesome for me, is just going to cause you more trouble."

He grinned a smile that would have melted the coldest girl's heart.

"You're adorable, and that is my favorite rejection, by far."

I rolled my eyes. "Like anyone ever rejects you."

"You'd be surprised," he said with increasing seriousness. "What did Eliana tell you about the mate run?"

"Not much really. Just that, like most teenage boys, your hormones will get the best of you; but whatever willing girl you find yourself with, whenever that magical moment occurs, you're stuck with for life."

"Willing? She doesn't know as much as I'd thought."

"Willing was my addition. Would you actually force someone?"

"No. I hope not." He rubbed his hand over the back of his neck, his frustration clear. "For us males, when our biological clock goes off, we're a slave to our instincts. Or, so my father has told me. The first female we smell, we want, and we tend to chase her down. That's the mate run. Chasing her until she stops and gives in. My father says it's a playful chase." He exhaled slowly.

"So Aubrey is sticking to your side in hopes that your clock will go off when she's near, so you can playfully chase her down, have your way with her, and make her your wife for life." I gave him a sympathetic look. "That's rough."

"Not just Aubrey but all the rest of the girls in my pack who are around my age."

"Aren't there any other guys?"

He shrugged and sighed.

"Thank you for being honest about not being interested in me. I'd still like to hang out, though, if you don't mind the occasional evil eye from Aubrey."

"I think I can handle that."

He looked toward the foyer a second before someone pounded on the door.

"Be right back," I said, already moving to answer.

I opened the door to Oanen. Bare-chested with jeans riding low on his hips, he stood barefoot on my porch. Sweat glistened on his chest, right between his pectorals. I licked my lips and tried not to stare.

"Oanen?"

His gaze barely swept over me before settling on something over my shoulder. I glanced back at Fenris.

"She's on her way here," Oanen said. I knew he meant Aubrey when Fenris groaned.

Fenris looked at me apologetically.

"I'm sorry." He stepped in and hugged me, breathing deeply next to my hair.

It didn't quite feel like a platonic hug. Awkwardly, I hugged him back.

"You know she'll smell you on her," Oanen said. "Knock it off."

When Fenris pulled away, his pupils looked a little too dilated, like he was high or something.

"I'll see you soon," he said. He leaned in once more to smell my hair then slipped past Oanen and jogged to his car.

Fenris quickly peeled off down the road.

"Can I come in?" Oanen asked.

"Sure." I motioned to the kitchen and closed the door behind him.

Instead of going to the kitchen, he went to the living room and sat on the couch. A position he kept just long enough to eye the length of his chosen seat before he lay down on it. His feet rested on one arm and his head, the other.

"Okay. Make yourself at home."

He stood and strode toward me. Before I knew what he had planned, he pulled me into his arms and buried his nose in my hair. Having Oanen do what Fenris had just done shocked the hell out of me. Oanen's hands smoothed over my back, pulling me firmly against his front, and I shivered at the full body contact. This was nothing like what Fenris had done.

Just as soon as Oanen had hugged me, he released me.

While I still reeled from having that bare, chiseled chest

pressed against me, he strode outside, leaving the door wide open. The sound of a car pulling up in front drew my attention. Oanen stood on the shoulder of the road, shaking his head at the slowing, shiny red car.

Anger bubbled up inside me at the sight of Aubrey. I fisted my hands, ready for her to try something. She didn't stop, though. At seeing Oanen, she continued by.

Oanen waited until Aubrey was out of sight then looked back at me.

"Behave, Megan." He walked into the pines and took flight not long afterward.

I closed the door and leaned my head against the panel.

"Monday from hell," I whispered.

CHAPTER TEN

TUESDAY, THANKFULLY, GAVE ME A REPRIEVE FROM LIFE-DRAMA until Eliana called me after school.

"Please say I can come over," she said.

"Sure. You can save me from boredom. I finished Academy stuff before lunch."

She cheered and promised to "be there in just a few."

The sound of a car pulling into the driveway only seconds after we'd hung up made me smile as did Eliana's playful knock on the back door.

"I'm so glad you said yes," she said when I invited her in. "You're not going to believe what happened today."

She launched into her story before I managed to close the door.

"Aubrey went ballistic because Fenris didn't show up for first session. And since you weren't there either, Aubrey naturally assumed his absence was due to you, even after Adira told her that Fenris' father called to excuse him. Rumor is Fenris answered the call of the trees, which means he's on his mating run. Which made Aubrey even crazier. You should have seen it. Adira barely stopped her from coming over here. So?" she said, looking at me expectantly.

"So, what?"

"Was he here today?"

I rolled my eyes. "No."

"Aubrey was telling everyone who would listen that she'd tracked his scent here yesterday but that Oanen stopped her from checking the house. She would have come straight here after school today, but Oanen made it very obvious that he was tailing her. So, she went to Mr. and Mrs. Quill to complain about Oanen's interference in pack matters. That's why I came here. I couldn't stand listening to her whiny, desperate voice anymore."

She barely breathed before continuing.

"What happened yesterday? With you and Fenris?"

I gently steered her toward the kitchen table as I answered.

"Nothing. I told him I wasn't girlfriend material and, as much as I liked annoying Aubrey, I didn't want to make his life any more difficult. He seemed okay with it, but said he still wanted to hang out anyway."

"Hmm. Hang out because he's desperate to get away from Aubrey? Or because he's interested and is subtly not taking no for an answer?" Eliana sat in a chair and tapped her chin in thought. "He's always struck me as a player because he seems to thrive on keeping his little group of women around him. And, every time I see him with his swarm, he always reeks of sexual energy. I think he's interested. Better watch out for him."

I grinned at her.

"Yes, ma'am." I went to open the fridge. "You staying for dinner?"

"Can I?"

"Of course."

While I started getting out ingredients, she filled in more details around the Aubrey drama.

"After Adira threatened to magic her into a two-week coma, Aubrey started sniffing everyone. Looking for even a hint of a trace of Fenris' scent. You should have seen her face when she smelled Fenris on Oanen. Get this, he looked at her all calm like and said, 'I'm a hugger,' and shrugged. Half the kids in the hall busted up with laughter. That's just another reason she's bitching at the Quills right now."

Hearing that clarified the reason behind yesterday's spontaneous hug. Oanen had done it to cover up Fenris' scent. I couldn't help but feel a little disappointed about that.

"I wouldn't be surprised if she comes straight here when she's done ranting at the Quills, though," Eliana continued. "She said she could smell you on Oanen, too."

Eliana grew suddenly quiet. When I looked at her, her hands were flat on the table and she was pale and shaking.

I tossed the ingredients for lasagna aside and quickly moved to her.

"What's wrong? Eliana?"

When she looked up at me, her eyes were black.

"Don't touch me," she whispered. "Go upstairs and lock your door."

"Not a chance. Tell me what's happening."

"I had a bad thought. I'm so hungry now."

I turned to the cupboard where I'd stashed a bag of

double chocolate dipped cookies. Before I could grab it, the back door clicked, and I found myself alone in the kitchen. I ran out the door and took a running jump, neatly clearing the hood of the car and blocking Eliana's escape.

"I'm not letting you leave like this," I said, studying her still black eyes.

Eliana feinted to the right then left. I kept up, not letting her set more than a finger on the door handle. The sound of an engine and the sudden scream of tires braking on the pavement at the end of the driveway stopped our little dodge game.

A car door slammed

"Bitch!" Aubrey yelled.

The sound of her voice hit me hard. Rage ignited in my blood, and I turned away from Eliana, completely focused on a new objective: piss off Aubrey then punch her in the face.

She was making it easy on me by stomping her way up the driveway. Her blonde hair snaked around her head in a windblown mess from her drive here. It added to the crazed look in her eyes as she snarled at me.

"Heard you finally figured out Fenris isn't interested in you," I said. My hands ached with the need to hurt her, and I took a step closer.

Something slammed into my back, knocking me forward. The weight of whatever had hit me stuck tightly and wrapped around my arms and legs as I fell face first toward the ground. The anger that had flooded me vanished, replaced by a disgruntled calm and a mouth full of grass.

I turned my head and spat.

"Time to get off, spider monkey," I said.

Eliana made a hesitant sound near my ear, and I knew she wasn't going to let go just yet.

I lifted my head and found Aubrey towering over us, only a step away. Her lips twisted in a vicious, triumphant smile as she took a picture of us on the ground.

"Fenris is smart enough not to want succubus seconds." She flounced her tangle of hair, turned on her heel, and marched back to her car.

Eliana got off me as soon as she pulled away.

"You gave me permission," she said. "Any time you were mad, remember?"

I slowly got to my feet, brushing myself off. When I looked at Eliana, her eyes were back to normal.

"Inside, now," I said, sounding stern.

Her bottom lip protruded slightly, but she listened and began a sulky pace toward the house. I spat out some more dirt and followed. When we were back inside, I poured us both a drink of water and sat at the table with her.

"I'm not mad about the hug. But I am mad about you trying to leave. What happened? I thought we were trying to be the kind of friends that could," I shrugged uncomfortably, "talk about stuff."

Eliana sniffled and nodded. "We are. It's just hard. You know what I am. But you don't know who I am. I'm Eliana Magdalene Margarete Howland, daughter of a piously religious man. That was who my mom seduced.

"For a year, she kept him under her spell feeding on his passion for her. After she gave birth to me, she left. He raised me, believing my mom some form of demon who tempted him from his path. He was right. The moment she walked through the door again, he fell to his knees and begged her to let him 'worship at her temple.'"

"Oh, geez. I think I just threw up a little."

"I know. I was there, and I definitely threw up a little. The point is, what I am and who he raised me to be doesn't mesh together well. Sometimes, it feels like I'm being ripped in two." She looked down at her glass, turning it in slow circles.

"And that's why you're not feeding. Because you feel guilty?"

"No. Because the way I need to feed feels so wrong."

She sounded so guilty when she said it that I quickly changed the subject away from her feeding.

"Maybe my mom was like yours because she thought sleeping around was great, too."

Eliana smiled slightly and looked up from the glass.

"I don't think so. We can sense our own kind. It's weird. Like seeing someone on the street and somehow knowing they're your brother or sister."

"That would be cool."

She shook her head. "You're thinking Brady Bunch, but it's more like Cinderella."

"Oh."

"And I don't necessarily need to sleep around. Being near people who are making out works, too, but it's kind of awful. It's like I am a peeping Tom on their emotions."

"Okay. But what happened just before you tried to leave? Why'd your eyes go black?"

She went back to looking down at her glass before answering.

"Thoughts pop into my head. Sexual ones. And they

make me so hungry. I don't know why I think them. It's not who I am."

"We all think things we might not want to think. It's nothing to run from."

"It might be," she said softly.

"Spit it out. What thought did you have?"

She took a deep breath.

"We were talking about how Oanen smelled like you and Fenris, and the image of the three of you on—"

"Okay, I get the picture. It's not that big of a deal. I bet loads of people our age have weird sexual thoughts. I mean, look at what Fenris is dealing with, right? It'll pass. But, you don't need to run. Not from me. I won't judge you if your eyes go all black."

She nodded, flashing me a watery smile.

"Thank you."

"No problem. Now, let's make some food and binge eat a package of cookies."

AN INSISTENT DREAM about a snoring beaver woke me to the sound of a lawnmower running in my front yard. I lifted my head and looked at my clock.

"Seven? He is not sane," I grumbled, tossing back my covers.

I stomped down the stairs, almost falling, and yanked open the front door. The bright light of the early morning sun blinded me, but it didn't stop me from speaking.

"Why do you hate me? Is it because I hit you? Because I'm friends with your sister from another mister? Or do you just hate everything that's good in this world?" I leaned limply against the doorframe, too tired for a righteously indignant stance as I tried to blink him into focus.

Oanen, who'd turned toward me at the first sound of my voice, turned off the mower.

"Too early?" he asked.

"Yes! Eliana didn't leave until two. Again."

I blinked him into focus and caught his lips twitching along with the fact that he wasn't wearing a shirt. The sight of his sun-kissed chest and the steam rolling off of it as he stalked toward the porch perked me up better than a cup of coffee. Where was his shirt? Wasn't it too cold to be mowing without one? Not that I was complaining. How could stoic, lecturing Oanen look so good? All the sexual-thought talk with Eliana must have messed with my head.

"Did you get in trouble?" I asked, mostly to distract myself from the way the light played on his abs.

He stepped onto the porch and gave me a puzzled look.

"For what?"

"For keeping me from tearing Aubrey a new one at school? For stopping her from coming here and getting her butt kicked?"

He studied me.

"You're very sure of yourself."

"Yep. Aren't you going to be late for school?" I gave the truck parked on the street a meaningful glance. As good as he looked without a shirt, I wanted sleep more.

"Is sass a superpower, too?"

I couldn't help the smile that curled my lips. I liked his wit.

"Maybe. Can I bribe you with a toaster waffle to come back and finish this after school?"

"Maybe. If you let me keep my things here so I can fly."

"Deal. Come on in. Don't forget your shirt."

I turned and shambled to the kitchen. The freezer surrendered its lone box of organic waffles, the only kind the store in town had offered, with very little struggle.

When I closed the door, Oanen was already sitting at the table. He once again wore his shirt, which clung to his sweaty skin. I wasn't sure covering wet muscle with a thin shirt was any better than just skipping the shirt.

He leaned forward, bracing his forearms on the nicked wooden surface, as he watched me work my culinary magic with the toaster.

"Want syrup?" I asked.

"Yes, please."

I got out a plate and a fork and put them in front of him before going back to the fridge.

"You're not going to eat?" he asked, watching me.

"It's barely seven, and there's no one here to stop me from sleeping until noon. I'm not eating breakfast until I'm ready to face the day." I set the syrup on the table just as the waffles popped.

"Breakfast is in the toaster. See you after lunch, lawn boy," I said over my shoulder on my way out the door.

"Megan, wait."

I stopped and groaned, removing the one foot I'd managed to place on the stairs. When I stepped back into the kitchen, he already had two waffles gone and a quarter of another on his fork. Chewing, he held out my phone. The play of his jaw muscles mesmerized me, and it took until he swallowed for me to take the phone from him.

"Text me if Aubrey shows up again, like she did last night. I already put my number in there."

"Uh, okay."

I quickly fled upstairs. Not long after I flopped on my mattress, I heard the water run then the door close.

"My life is so weird," I said to the ceiling. I thought of my estranged mother, wondered if that was why she'd left, and closed my eyes.

I crashed hard. When I woke up again and went downstairs to fix my own waffles, I found Oanen's dishes washed and in the drainer and his pants neatly folded on a chair. A note lay on top.

I'LL BE BACK for these this afternoon. Try not to kick them in the dirt.

I GRINNED THEN FROWNED. Was he planning on walking inside naked again? My pulse picked up at the thought. Setting his pants down, I ran back upstairs for my phone and a clean set of clothes.

Before getting into the shower, I sent Oanen a quick text.

Your pants are on the back porch.

I tossed them onto the old wood planks then went back inside to get ready for the day. By lunch, I was eating my cereal and feeling pretty all right.

CHAPTER ELEVEN

"Is there any chance I can sleep over tomorrow night?" Eliana asked.

I held the phone to my ear while muting the T.V., the current device to fend off boredom.

"Sure. Why? What's up?"

"Humans are going to start coming into town for the Fall Festival first thing in the morning. I'd rather not be anywhere near that mess until the last minute. Plus, if I stay over, we can drive together. We need to show up around three."

"Ah. Yeah, it's fine if you come over. I'm running low on food, though. Would you mind taking me to the grocery store for some food after you get here?"

"No problem. Talk to you after sessions tomorrow."

I set the phone next to me and blindly stared at the TV. Nothing about the festival appealed to me. I knew myself well enough to know I'd end up getting into trouble somehow. Yet, the restless boredom that kept crawling under my skin had me almost looking forward to it, trouble and all.

"Obviously, I have issues," I said before turning up the TV volume.

After I finished watching the current show, I shut everything off and went to bed. Just as I started to drift off, I heard something. It sounded like it came from above rather than below. I waited for it to come again, but the house remained quiet, and I eventually drifted off to sleep.

In the morning, I dusted the spare room, removed webs from the corners in the upstairs hallway, and washed the steps. Everyone thought having their own place was glamorous because no adult told them what to do. They didn't stop to think that meant there would be no adult taking care of the crap jobs like cleaning, laundry, yard work, and paying bills. The reality was...adulting sucked.

When I had the upstairs clean enough for Eliana to stay over, I started in on the downstairs. The kitchen didn't take much time because I kept up with it daily. Nothing had really been deep-cleaned in the living room, though. I pulled the couch into the entry along with the two chairs, the old oil lamp, and side tables. With the room mostly clear, I wiped the baseboards and mopped the wood floors. For the first time, the house took on a completely fresh scent. Rolling with it, I opened the windows.

Doing all that work helped cure a little of the restlessness and brought back Mom's words about exercise. I needed some kind of daily activity. A routine that would help keep me from going crazy. The money Mom had left could easily buy a treadmill, but I hesitated to use any of it for more than the basics. I had no idea if there were house payments I'd need to make or what other bills might come with this place. Which was also why purchasing a car seemed like a bad idea. Not only would it be a chunk of money, it would also take me to places where there were people. Hitching rides with Eliana seemed smarter, for now.

Finishing the task at hand, I moved the furniture back into the room and went to read lecture notes for the current week's sessions.

The restlessness was back by the time Eliana pulled into the driveway, and I had my coat on before she reached the door.

"Ready?" she asked when I met her.

"Yep. I'm going crazy here and have come to the realization that, as much as I seem to hate people, I need them, too."

She smiled as she walked back to the car with me.

"It's almost the same for me. As much as I fear what I want to do to people, I need them, too."

"And, what do you want to do with people."

Her blush answered me.

"Oh, you sassy girl," I teased. "I can't wait until you take the plunge and actually make out with someone."

Her flushed face immediately paled.

"Hey, kidding. It will be fine. You'll see."

She nodded, and we both got in. She didn't make any move to start the car, though.

"I'm sorry," I said, feeling guilty that she still looked pale.

"It's not that." She exhaled heavily. "It's this weekend. If I want any chance of leaving this place ever, I need to show some progress. I need to kiss a human."

"Seriously?"

"Yeah. I'm so scared. What if I can't stop at a kiss? What if I jump them and take everything?"

"You won't. I won't let you. I'll tackle hug you to the ground like you did for me."

She turned her big brown eyes on me.

"Do you swear?"

"I promise. And in return for interrupting any possibility of a booty call, I'm hoping you'll do the same for me. Not the booty call part. There's no chance of that. The fighting. Someone's going to piss me off big time, and I don't want to go to jail for kicking some grandma's ass."

Eliana snorted a laugh and started the car.

"I swear to keep you from kicking granny booty."

WE WAITED until the last possible minute to leave for the festival. Even the weather seemed to know it wasn't a day for fun. The overcast sky and cool damp air hinted at storms before nightfall. None of it would stop the festival from taking place, though.

Eliana took her time on the country roads, unlike the day before when we went to town for groceries. I knew she was still terrified of what she needed to do today.

"What happens if we don't go?" I asked.

"We'd fail our human relations sessions. You're in Principles of Human Integration, right? I think they put you there because you've lived outside of Uttira for seventeen years. I had to start with the beginner course, and I'm still there. Trust me when I say you don't want to hear the same lectures for more than one semester."

"Got it. Not showing up is an automatic fail."

"And for me, not kissing a human is an automatic fail." Nervous energy rolled off her with those words.

"Don't think about it," I said. "We have all afternoon. When we get there, let's just check out the booths and not worry about the humans. Okay?"

"Okay."

The town was crawling with people. We had to park seven blocks from the actual downtown area.

Eliana looked pale again.

"It'll be okay," I said. "We'll stick together."

She nodded shakily, and we got out and started walking. The wind toyed with my hair, using the ponytail like a whip.

We'd barely reached the edge of the festival when Adira found us.

"Good afternoon, Megan and Eliana. I wish you luck. Eliana, the kiss isn't as important as much as the way you control your feeding. Do you understand? You must feed the way every succubus is meant to feed. No more denying yourself."

Adira's gaze turned to me.

"Today is about control for you, too, Megan. Remember what we discussed in my office. Examine your anger before you give in to it. Ask yourself why, and see if you can discover a reasonable justification for your reaction."

"And if I can't?"

"We'll try again. I need to find Fenris now. Excuse me."
With that, she walked away.

I turned to Eliana, the snarky comment dying before it reached my lips. Not a trace of color remained in her ashen face, and tears welled in her eyes.

Grabbing her hand, I tugged her behind the nearest vendor booth.

"Breathe, El. You got this. Don't let what Adira said get in your head."

"How? She wants me to feed. I've never even kissed someone without feeding, and she wants me to do it with feeding?"

Color returned, but not the right kind. Her skin took on a greenish hue.

I grabbed her arms before her knees gave out.

"Look at me, El. Look. You know what you are. You know what to watch for. I know, too. I won't let you do anything bad. Okay? Do you trust me?"

She nodded weakly.

"Then pucker up buttercup."

Before she could guess what I intended, I pressed my lips to hers. She immediately stiffened but didn't jerk away. Since I'd only ever had the one boyfriend, and not for very long, my little pool of experience didn't give me much to go on. I relaxed my hold on her arms and lifted one hand to gently cup her cheek. She exhaled softly against me and tilted her head. I felt the moment she started to feed. The ever so subtle stirring of lust in my belly caught me off guard.

"I've died and gone to heaven," a familiar voice said. Fenris. The sound of his voice acted like a bucket of ice water, breaking the spell of her kiss and the lust snaking its way through my blood.

"Shut up," Oanen said.

"How can you not think that's hot? I'm not even sure I can walk right now without breaking something," Fenris said.

I gently pulled back and looked at Eliana. Based on the expression on her scarlet face, she looked ready to bolt. But not sick or ready to hurl. Mostly just embarrassed.

"Are you mad at me?" I asked.

Eliana shook her head.

"Do you feel like jumping me and taking the rest?"

"Please say yes," Fenris said under his breath.

I shot him a look, but he only held his hands up pleadingly. Beside him, Oanen watched me, the intensity of his gaze a contradiction to his impassive expression.

"No, I'm okay," Eliana said, almost sounding impressed.

Focusing on her, and not our unwanted audience, I grinned at her.

"Then go try that with a human."

"Boo," Fenris pouted.

"Adira was looking for you. Why don't you go find her instead of tormenting us?" I asked, arching a brow.

"Tormenting? No way. I'm encouraging. I think it's great that Eliana's embracing what she is."

I glanced at Eliana. She didn't look like she believed him; she looked like she wanted to fall into a hole. I wrapped my arms around her and hugged her close, letting her hide against my shoulder.

"Adira sent us to keep an eye on you," Oanen said.

"She'll be fine," I said. "I'll keep an eye on her."

"Not Eliana. You."

"Me?" I looked at both of them over Eliana's head.

Fenris nodded.

"Why me?"

"Aubrey," Fenris said.

"You like to fight," Oanen said at the same time.

"She'll be fine," Eliana said, pulling away from me. "We're going to stick together. I'll make sure Megan doesn't fight."

Oanen shook his head and glanced at our joined hands.

"That's not going to help you do what you need to do, Eliana. You need to focus on yourself."

An adult poked his head behind the booth. His forehead went from smooth skin to a third, scowling eye in a blink.

"You guys need to find somewhere else to talk. Get going."

Too stunned to protest, I followed Eliana's insistent tug until we found ourselves on the main thoroughfare, weaving our way through the clusters of people. With her hand wrapped around mine, I barely felt the brief flares of anger. Being free of it meant that my other senses actually had a chance to work.

"Do you smell that?" I said, tugging her in a different direction.

"Pumpkin pie?" she asked.

"Is that what that is? It smells so good." I found the vendor booth where the ladies were taking slices of hot pie and putting them into to-go cups topped with a generous amount of whipped cream.

"Oh, I need some of that," I said.

Eliana's chuckle died almost as quickly as it started.

When I looked to see why, I found her staring hungrily at a guy around our age. The sheer look of torture on his face as he walked behind his parents begged for rescue. However, in a single glance, I knew he wouldn't be a good candidate for Eliana's first feeding.

I tugged her to my side and whispered in her ear.

"Not him. He'd fall hopelessly in love with you and follow you everywhere. You need a player. Someone who'll kiss you and walk away."

She took a slow breath and tore her gaze from him with effort.

"Let's get some pie and walk around. We'll find you someone."

"Here," Oanen said from beside me. I looked down at the pie-filled cups he held out.

"Thank you." I didn't hesitate to snatch mine and take a huge bite. The cup warmed my cool hand, and the pie tasted even better than it smelled. I groaned.

"You've never had pie?" Oanen asked.

"Not that I remember. Mom cooked, but she didn't bake," I answered absently, doing my best to ignore our babysitters.

The crowd flowed around us as I took my second bite. Although there seemed to be a good number of families strolling around, I still spotted plenty of people our age wandering on their own. Eliana would have no problem finding someone with all these people. But, would she be able to feed with our shadows around.

The sudden urge to hit something sent my cup of pumpkin pie slipping from my fingers. Oanen deftly caught it, but I barely noticed. My gaze shifted to the man passing beside us, the source of my anger.

As I clenched my fists, Adira's words came back to me. What about him made me angry?

It took every ounce of control that I didn't think I had to study him instead of fly at him. Older. Physically fit. Neatly dressed. Alone. There wasn't anything that stood out as wrong. He walked far enough away that the anger faded. Instead of letting him leave and taking the non-encounter as a win, I started to follow him.

He made his way to the center square, where people lounged on the benches, and took a seat. Then he people-watched. That was it. I leaned on a pole not far away and scrutinized him.

"Are you okay?" Eliana asked softly beside me.

"No. I want to make that man over there bleed, and asking myself why, like Adira said to do, isn't helping anything. There's no logical reason that I can see. He's just a guy sitting there watching—"

His gaze met mine. He gave me a slight smile, stood, then headed our way.

"Hi, girls. This is something, isn't it?"

I wanted to hurt him so badly my hands shook. Eliana's hand slipped under my shirt, and her fingers touched the skin of my back.

"Is this your first time here?" Eliana asked.

"It is. You two from around here?"

"We are," I said, feeling more in control. "Don't let this fool you. Uttira is boring as hell."

His grin widened. "There's nothing for two, pretty girls like yourselves to do around here for fun? That's no good."

He took his wallet out and gave Eliana a card. It had a number on it. That was it.

"If you're ever bored enough and want to have some fun while earning some serious money, give that number a call."

He moved like he was going to go back to his previous spot. Something told me not to let him walk away.

"I don't think we want to wait. Let's have some fun now," I said, thinking quickly. "My friend and I were taking bets on you."

"Oh?" He looked amused and completely interested in hearing what I had to say.

"We thought you were the kind of man willing to give a girl a kiss in public."

"Megan," Eliana whispered. That single word held so much worry. Her fingers twitched on my skin as I continued.

"Obviously, I thought yes. She thinks no. I know of a quiet spot."

"A quiet spot would be perfect."

"Then follow us. At a distance." I grabbed Eliana's supporting hand and started walking.

"What are you doing?" she whispered harshly. "I can't kiss him. That's so gross."

"Can you feed without kissing?" I asked.

"I don't know. Maybe. I've never done this before. But the sexual energy coming off of him is so disgusting. Please don't make me do this."

"You don't have to. I just figured you could get a hit off someone who didn't really matter before I kicked his ass."

"Why are you kicking his ass?"

"Mostly because I feel like it and partly because he's a pervy old guy."

"He didn't do anything wrong, though. Just talked to us."

"And gave us a card with a number and a promise of good work. Come on, Eliana. Nice people don't do that."

We ducked behind one of the closed shops. Cars lined the back alley but remained empty of people except us.

"What happened to Fenris and Oanen," I asked, for the first time realizing they weren't with us.

"They're close. Watching but staying out of it unless it looks like you need them."

The man walked around the corner.

"Well, girls. What did you have in mind?"

My rage knocked me blind for a moment. I breathed through my nose and fisted my hands.

"What's wrong, Megan? You look upset." He still sounded so calm. "I hope you're not going to try to change your mind now. Guys don't like girls who go back on their word."

Someone stepped in front of me, blocking my view.

"She's mad because I get to go first."

Before I could push Eliana aside, she moved close to him and brought her hand to his cheek.

"What's your name?" she asked. Her voice didn't sound like Eliana anymore, and that broke through the haze of anger.

His gaze heated as he stared down at her.

"Jesse. What's yours?"

"Doesn't matter." She trailed her fingers over his skin.

He groaned and closed his eyes. "What matters is what you want to do to me, Jesse. Tell me."

He proceeded to tell her in great detail how he would use her body then sell her to the highest bidder. Gently used young women were in high demand. He couldn't promise gentle though because he ached for her.

"That's okay. I'll help with that ache." She pulled him down to her mouth. Instead of kissing him, she inhaled. From my standpoint, it looked like a backward attempt at mouth to mouth without the contact, until I saw her eyes.

They'd turned black again. The guy she'd held didn't seem to notice, though. His eyes were rolled back in his head.

"Eliana? I think you might need to stop," I said. "Not that I really care, but he doesn't look so good, and I don't want you to be upset by that."

She immediately pulled away with an "eep!" Like a puppet without its puppeteer, Jesse fell to the ground with a thud.

CHAPTER TWELVE

ELIANA AND I BOTH STARED AT THE UNMOVING MAN. HE LAY in an awkward sprawled position, his legs slightly folded under him. His head lolled slightly to the side, showing his eyes closed and lips slack. A bit of drool started to run from the corner of his mouth.

"Please tell me I didn't kill him," Eliana said in a panicked voice.

I squatted down beside him and felt for a pulse. The wind gusted through the alley, ruffling his hair.

"He's alive." I lightly slapped his cheek, but he didn't respond.

"You don't still want to hit him, do you?" she asked.

"No. Not really." Most of my anger had faded the moment his eyes had rolled back into his head. I wedged my hands under him and gave him a shove to roll him over to his side.

"You don't want to jump him, do you?" I asked.

"Ugh! No. I'm feeling a little sick, honestly. That was the most disgusting thing I've ever done."

"So sexual energy doesn't taste like chicken?" I asked, smirking as I pulled out his wallet.

"Not even close. It'll be easy to stop feeding if it always tastes like moldy cheeseburgers. Although, I'm not sure how I'll ever again be able to start in the first place. Are you robbing him?"

I grinned at her and opened his wallet.

"No. Not robbing him. Though, I'd make a fortune. There's at least a grand in here."

Continuing to look through the contents, I found his pictures. Polaroid's of girls and boys too young to be of age.

"Now, I'm going to be sick," I said. "We need to get Trammer."

"He's on his way," Oanen said. I looked up and saw him standing by the entry to the alley. He had his phone in one hand, and my cup of pie in the other.

"How much trouble are we in?" I asked, standing.

"None. You didn't hurt him, and Eliana did what Adira wanted. Fed without killing."

"I hope I never have to do that again," she said with a shudder.

"Feeding, my dear, is a part of your life," Adira said from behind me.

I yipped and spun around. Adira stood a few steps away, her grey pantsuit matching the stormy sky above.

"When did you get here?"

"Just now. Well done on your first feeding, Eliana. You're free to spend the rest of the day as you'd like."

"What about me?"

"Did you do as I asked?"

"He's not bleeding, is he?"

"Then you are free to do as you'd like, as well."

"That's it? You're not going to tell me what the point of this was?"

"No."

"Seriously? Everyone else knows what they are? So what's the big deal? Why keep what I am a secret from me?"

"We'll talk more Monday."

With a wave of her hand, a portal opened and Adira disappeared through it.

"Way less than helpful," I said.

"Eliana, can you go watch for Fenris and Trammer?" Oanen asked.

She gave me a quick, sympathetic look then left me alone with Oanen and the knocked-out man.

Oanen walked toward me and handed over the cup of pie. However, he didn't release his hold when I gripped the cup.

"Your ignorance is a gift. By not knowing what you are, you don't have to conform. You don't need to be what everyone thinks you should be. You decide for yourself who you want to be. So stop whining about what you don't know and focus on what you do."

Eliana was right. He did like to lecture.

"And what do I know?" I asked.

"That you're not human. So stop trying to act like one."

"What the hell is that supposed to mean?" I dropped my hand from the cup, too annoyed to take it now.

Before he could answer, I heard Fenris' voice.

"Trammer, you might want to lay off the extra portions.

The sound of your heavy breathing is going to let everyone know there's something wrong."

The tittering laugh that followed Fenris' remark spiked my already simmering temper.

"Behave, Megan," Oanen warned softly just before Fenris rounded the corner.

Only a few steps behind Fenris, Aubrey looked at me with narrowed eyes as she walked into the alley but said nothing. Instead, she focused on the man laid out on the ground nearby. Moving closer, she studied Jesse's face.

Behind her, a red-faced Trammer joined us. His irritated gaze swept over me and Oanen as a pale and shaky Eliana entered the alley last.

"Well, that's one less human to worry about," Aubrey said with a laugh.

Because she was facing me, she missed Trammer's angry glare. I didn't care so much about his opinion, but I did care about Eliana's. When she paled further and tears gathered in her eyes at Aubrey's insensitive words, my anger surged.

Without consciously deciding to do so, I balled up my fist and slugged Aubrey in the face. The satisfying sound of flesh hitting flesh brought a smile to my lips as her head snapped to the side. Her growl filled the air, and her face went from human valley-girl to freakishly fur-faced monster from a bad Hollywood movie.

As she changed, Fenris stepped between us.

"Enough, Aubrey." His growl cut hers short. Her face immediately reverted back to valley-girl.

"I don't have time for this," Trammer said. "Just show me the human you think did something wrong."

"We think?" I said, turning the remnants of my temper on him. "We know. Look at his wallet, Trammer. He has kiddie porn pictures in there. And he described in detail how he would sell Eliana after he was done raping her."

He bent down, tapped the guy's face, then looked at his wallet like I had.

"Well, we'll see what the Council wants to do with him after they wipe his memory."

"What do you mean?"

He stood and crossed his arms.

"I can't press charges against him for the photographs because he'd need to go to court. Uttira doesn't have court. That means the two of you would be witnesses out there in the real world. And, what would you tell any law enforcement out there, anyway? My succubus friend was feeling a little munchy, and we decided to go for a pedophile?"

"Trammer," Oanen said, sharply.

The sheriff looked at Oanen, no trace of guilt or remorse on his face.

"It's the truth."

"Seriously?" I said. "A man who admitted to human trafficking is going to be let loose?"

Trammer shook his head at me as if he was disappointed.

"Because the secrets of Uttira could be jeopardized if the Council chose to pursue charges? Yes. Now, get out of here. Fenris and I will get him to the Council for the memory wipe."

I glanced at Fenris in time to catch his look of distaste

before he stepped forward and helped hoist the man to his feet.

I couldn't believe that man would just go free. Rage boiled under my skin. I wanted to hurt him. I wanted to hurt Trammer, too, as if he were the one responsible. But based on Oanen's firm scolding, Trammer wasn't to blame. The fault lay with Eliana and me. My actions let this happen, and I wanted to yell my frustration.

Eliana grabbed my hand and some of the emotion slipped away. Her hand shook just as badly as mine, though. Together, we watched Fenris and Trammer haul Jesse away. Aubrey shot me a look that promised retribution as she followed.

"I need to go home," I said, my voice tight.

"I'll take you both," Oanen said.

I started down the alley, Eliana gripping my hand. Neither of us spoke once we reached the main thoroughfare. She took over and led me in the direction of where we'd parked. The distant car became a beacon of escape from the press of bodies.

Eliana handed the keys to Oanen and insisted I sit in front. Closing the door on the noise of the festival crowd, I buckled my seatbelt as Oanen slid in behind the wheel.

"It's not your fault, Eliana," Oanen said firmly once he'd pulled away from the curb. We weren't the only ones leaving. The dark clouds that looked like impending rain were sending the humans scurrying for their vehicles, too.

I glanced back at Eliana and saw her guilt-stricken face.

"It's not," I agreed.

She gave me a small nod.

"The Council will make sure to manipulate that man's

mind in a way that he'll get caught so he can pay for his past crimes," Oanen assured us both.

"How quickly, though?" I asked.

"It'll most likely depend on the man and what he confesses to them," he answered.

"Not good enough. If we'd been anything other than what we are, he would have raped Eliana and had us in his trunk or something."

Oanen turned into a more spacious neighborhood with well-cared for lawns and took the columned driveway at the end of the street. The pristine tree-lined lane led to a sprawling stone house that looked as old as the Academy.

"Do you want to come in?" Eliana asked.

I gave the house a long look and shook my head.

"I'll see you Monday," I said.

"Okay. I'll pick you up at seven again."

Eliana got out and closed her door, heading toward the front entry as Oanen turned around. I waited until he was on the road again before picking up our conversation from before Trammer's interruption.

"What did you mean when you said I'm acting like a human? What other way is there to act?"

"You aren't human, so neither are your emotions. Stop treating your anger like it's normal. Adira is telling you to pay attention to it because it might be more than just a part of what you are."

"And the part about not conforming, where you called me a whiner?"

"Right now, you can be anything you want to be. Embrace it. Because once you know, they're going to treat you like a tiny gear in a large machine and nudge you into the right place for our world."

"Is that what they did to you?"

His non-answer confirmed the question.

"If you were me, what would you do?"

"Not worry so much about what I am and just learn everything I can about the new world I just discovered."

"Oh, like what?"

"The history of it. The creatures you'll likely encounter. Their strengths and weaknesses. Why they exist."

I had to admit, the topic of conversation piqued my interest.

"And where would a girl learn about all of that? Apparently, it's impolite to just ask people, and I didn't see that topic in any of the lecture notes."

"I'll teach you."

The offer made me immediately suspicious.

"Why?"

"Because of Eliana. Because I understand what it's like to come into this life and not know anything. Because...just because."

Oanen finally left the festival crowds behind and made his way toward the outskirts of town.

"Okay. Fine. Where should we start?" I asked.

"The most important thing for you to know is that the gods are real."

"Which ones?" I asked, humoring him.

"Zeus, Oden, Hera, Frigg, Thor, Loki, Hades. All of them. And, just like an overpaid CEO of a global corporation, they've each had their time in the spotlight. The waning adoration of the humans they so obsessed over brought an end to each reign. While knowledge of them faded into myth, the mementos of their reign, creatures like us that they left behind, have struggled to remain myth as well."

I thought about what he was saying for a moment.

"Why does it matter if I was created or just popped into existence by natural evolution?"

"If something created you, don't you want to know why?"

"Yeah. I guess so. But doesn't that start tying into what I am? I thought my whiner self wasn't supposed to focus on that?"

"You don't let things go easily, do you?"

"Nope."

He sighed.

"The 'why' ties into our purpose and our abilities, which is where you should focus. The gods had their own reasons for creating whatever they left behind. Most wanted to protect the humans. Some grew jealous of the humans' quick, passionate lives and created creatures to hurt them."

Hurting others sure seemed to be another one of my superpowers.

"Ah, crap. Does that mean I'm playing for Team Jackass?"

He snorted.

"It doesn't have to be that black and white. Look at Eliana. Her kind is supposed to feed on humans, use them and leave them in thrall. She won't do that. She can but won't. Even if we have no control over what we are, we can still try to choose who we want to be."

Instead of stopping in front of the house, he pulled into the driveway.

"Try?" I asked, opening my door.

He shut off the car and got out as well.

"Sometimes, like Eliana, it's a fight against your nature. It's a conscious choice every moment." He followed me to the back door. "I've seen you angry. I've seen you attack Aubrey for very little reason."

"Says you. She's a bitch. I consider that a huge reason." I opened the door and went inside, going to the fridge since I hadn't really eaten anything at the festival.

"My point is, I've seen you let your anger take over, and now I've seen you hold back. That means you have a choice. You can resist your instincts if you want. You can try to be who you want."

"I didn't resist my instincts at all. It was just about how I got what I wanted. I wanted that man hurt and figured out a way that wouldn't get me in trouble so I could still help Eliana." I pulled out the leftover lasagna and showed it to him.

"Want some?" I asked.

"Yes, please." He sat at the table and studied me while I got out the plates and heated two pieces.

"Why not hit him right away like you did with Aubrey?"

While I thought about it for a minute, the microwave beeped, and I gave Oanen his food before warming up some more for myself.

"Aubrey's my age. I knew I'd get in less trouble fighting with her because we mutually antagonize each other. Maybe, I've just gotten smarter about targeting adults with my superpowers after my last run-in, which landed me in anger management counseling for three months."

"Sounds less than fun," he commented.

"Yep. It was." But had twenty-four of those hour-long sessions really been enough to bore me out of impulsive fighting? No. I'd gone right back to it. Oanen was right. Why had I acted differently today?

"So what else should I know?"

"The Council was created out of necessity after the last of the gods disappeared. We police ourselves to prevent anything that may expose our existence to the general population."

"Like killing humans." I sat beside him, surprised he hadn't consumed one of the pieces already. He'd waited for me to begin eating.

"This is really good," he said, after his first bite. "And try not to assume anything about Uttira or its residents. We were all created for different purposes. For some, that purpose is to kill humans. We just ensure it's done in a way that doesn't create risk."

I swallowed quickly while he took a bite.

"Wait a minute. You're telling me it's okay to kill humans in this place? Why would any human want to live here?"

"No. It's not okay to kill here or in any other Mantirum town. Killing close to home would be a risk the Council wouldn't ignore."

"Mantirum. That sounds familiar."

"Did Adira maybe mention the mark of Mantirum?"

I nodded, the conversation with her coming back to me.

"Yeah. The mark I'd receive after graduation in order to leave this place."

He nodded, letting me know I had it right.

"That mark doesn't just let you come and go from here. It lets you into any Mantirum location because it signifies you belong to the gods and the world of magic. However, it also signifies you understand the rules of our world and the consequences of breaking them."

Thunder rolled outside and the first patter of raindrops hit the kitchen window.

"And will I learn those rules at the Academy?"

"No. A member of the Uttira Council will schedule a series of meetings with you once Adira believes you're ready."

"They could keep me here forever based on Adira's recommendation?"

"They could, but Adira wouldn't recommend that. Like I said, we all have our purposes. There's no point in trying to keep you from yours."

We finished our meal and worked together to clean up the dishes.

"I don't like you out here on your own," he said when we were done.

"Why?" I set the dish towel aside and met his gaze, waiting for his answer.

Instead of answering, he just looked at me. It normally took a lot to make me uncomfortable. However, his neutral, assessing expression managed to make me squirm in just under a minute.

"You know, it really annoys me when you do that," I said.

"Do what?"

"Look at me like I'm a bug in a jar. On display for detached clinical study."

His lips twitched slightly.

"That's not how I'm looking at you."

CHAPTER THIRTEEN

I OPENED MY MOUTH TO ASK WHAT HE MEANT BY THAT BUT never got the chance. His head jerked toward the hall.

"We have company," he said softly a moment before someone pounded on the front door.

I hurried to answer it, wondering what magic-world drama I was in for now.

As soon as I turned the knob, the door thrust inward. I flailed back at the same time my temper exploded. Oanen caught me mid-fall and pulled me against him, his hands remaining firmly locked around my biceps as Aubrey pushed her way inside.

"Where is he?" Aubrey demanded.

The anger that had welled up at her presence, faded at the press of Oanen's muscled chest against my back, and I struggled to concentrate on Aubrey's words.

"I know he's here," she said, looking around wildly.

"Who?" I asked.

"Fenris."

Oanen's hands slid up to my shoulders until his

fingertips brushed my collarbones, and his thumbs rested on each side of my spine. The heat of his touch bled into my skin, and I shivered subtly.

"Fenris is with Trammer," I managed to answer.

"No, Fenris left with Trammer, the Council wiped the meat bag's memory, and then Fenris went for a run."

Oanen's right thumb smoothed upward, skimming over my shirt to the skin of my neck. My pulse jumped, and I realized what he was doing. He didn't have Eliana's ability to syphon my anger to prevent me from fighting, so he was distracting the hell out of me instead.

"Oanen, cut it out. Aubrey, Fenris isn't here. So why are you?"

Her gaze drifted to Oanen for the first time.

"Aubrey," he said lightly.

"Oanen." She focused on me once more. "I hope this means you've moved on."

"Psycho obsession is a huge turn off. Might want to try to medicate that."

Aubrey bared her teeth, and I fisted my hands, ready to give her the beating she was begging for. Oanen's hands tightened on my shoulders in warning.

"Stay away from Fenris," she said before turning on her heel and marching back to her car. The downpour robbed her exit of any dignity.

"Wonder if she smells like wet dog even when on two legs," I said.

Oanen sighed, reached around me, and closed the door.

"Her hearing works as well as mine."

"I know." I looked over my shoulder and grinned at him.

"I'd better get going and keep an eye on her," he said. "Thank you for dinner."

I ROLLED over in bed and wrinkled my nose at the weak light of a new day. Sleep hadn't come easily and had fled too readily. Why? Because my dumb head wouldn't stop replaying those few moments by the door with Oanen. What had been up with his hands?

Grabbing me to stop my fall, I understood and appreciated. Moving his hold to my shoulders might have been to give him a better means to control me in Aubrey's presence. Given my previous issues with her, I again understood and appreciated the gesture. But that swipe of his thumbs on the back of my neck? Completely unnecessary and in no way understandable. My skin still itched and tingled there, and I couldn't stop thinking about it.

He'd never shown signs of interest. Had he? No, I didn't think so. Although I may have been too busy drooling over his chiseled abs to notice. I had two options. I could pretend it hadn't happened and carry on as usual. Or, I could confront him about it and probably make a fool of myself.

"Pretending it is," I said to myself.

Sitting up, I looked out the window at the still overcast sky. The droplets on my window didn't invoke hope for sunshine anytime soon, which meant another boring day inside.

I decided to entertain myself by making an omelet. Cooking had been Mom's thing not mine. However, since

Mom left, I'd managed a few basic meals. Stuff I'd helped Mom make over the years or I'd learned on my own on the occasions she stayed over somewhere. Now, I used the internet to search out a recipe for a broccoli and cheddar concoction that made my mouth water.

Heating the pan, I whisked my eggs and set about making myself some happy food while listening to the birds. I hummed over the caws and poured the eggs into the pan. While they sizzled, I went to the fridge for the cheese. A crow zipped past the kitchen window just as I turned. It looked way too big up close.

Shaking my head, I added my leftover broccoli bits and cheese. A sudden flurry of crows cawed loudly then quieted.

I frowned and turned off the burner before standing on my tiptoes to look out the window over the kitchen sink. They'd sounded like they were right outside, but I couldn't see anything.

With my face inches from the glass, I almost screamed when another crow flew up, flapping its wings right in front of me before it drifted back out of sight.

"What the hell is going on out there?"

I slipped on my shoes and went out the kitchen door. As soon as the screen slammed shut behind me, a chorus of caws rose from the back corner of the house.

Wrapping my arms around my middle, I shuffled forward slowly, a sense of something bad building inside me. Not so much dread as much as aw-crap-I'm-not-going-to-get-to-eat-my-omelet-anytime-soon.

A half dozen crows took flight when I rounded the corner. With their cries ringing in my ears, I stared down at the very dead body on which they'd been feeding. I'd beaten people to the point of hospitalization, but seeing the waxy color of the man's skin did something to me. I started to shake.

He had been partially eaten by something much bigger than a crow, however. And, although bits were missing, and blood stained much of his clothes, and he lay face down, I still recognized him.

"Shit."

Heart hammering, I turned and ran for the house. When the door slammed closed behind me, I already had my feet on the stairs, racing to get my phone.

My hands shook as I dialed 911. I couldn't unsee the body. Every time I blinked, the image refreshed in my mind.

"Moonlight Market, how can I help you?"

I jerked the phone from my ear and looked at what I'd dialed. Yep. 9-1-1. I put the phone back to my ear.

"I dialed 911," I said

"Oh, honey, Uttira doesn't use that. Tell me what's happened."

I hesitated a moment. Who in the hell decided it would be a great idea to route 911 calls to a damn grocery store?

"There's a dead body outside my house. Crows and something else have been eating him."

"Oh my. I'll send Trammer right away."

The line disconnected, and I dialed my only lifeline.

"Hey, Megan," Eliana chirped. "Want some company?"

"Yes. This town is fucked up."

"What's wrong? You don't sound like you."

"There's a dead body outside my house, and I called 911

and got the grocery store. The grocery, Eliana. Do you know how crazy that is?"

"Holy Mary and Joseph." I could hear her running down some stairs. "I'm on my way. Don't hang up." She covered the mouthpiece, but I could still hear her.

"Megan Smith just found a body outside her house. Yes. I'm going there now."

The muffled sound left the phone.

"Tell me what happened," she said.

"Beyond discovering a chewed-on body being pecked at by crows? Nothing."

"Chewed on? By what?"

"I don't know. Do I strike you as a walking Animal Planet reference guide?"

"No. Sorry," she said quickly. "Any idea how it got there?"

"I'm about three seconds from hanging up on you. Of course, I don't know how it got there."

"I'm so sorry. I'm not good at this. What should we talk about?"

"My omelet."

"Uh, okay. What's your omelet's name?"

"Cold and soggy. Damn body interrupted my breakfast. But that's not the worst of it, Eliana. I know who it is."

"Who?"

"That guy from yesterday. Jesse."

She gasped.

"Yeah. I know."

After that, we didn't really talk about much. I listened to the sound of the car engine and her soft, erratic breathing until she pulled up in front of the house.

"Bye," I said a moment before racing downstairs and pulling the door open.

Instead of Eliana on the porch, I found Oanen. He filled the opening as he looked down at me with concern.

"Are you all right?" he asked. A siren wailed in the distance, the sound growing louder by the moment.

"I don't know. Am I? I don't know." The shaking hadn't stopped. That probably wasn't a good thing. But why was I shaking? I honestly didn't care that Jesse was dead. I think I was more pissed that someone had killed the guy and eaten him.

Oanen took me by the elbow and led me to the couch. The simple warmth of his hold helped calm me. When I sat, I saw Eliana hovering just behind him.

"Where is he?" Oanen asked, drawing my attention.

I shook my head and instead of telling him, stood up to show them. His hand wrapped around my arm to stop me.

"You can stay here. You don't need to see that again."

"No, I can't stay here. I need answers. Why is he dead? And why is he at my house? He was alive when he left that alley yesterday, Oanen. Who killed him?"

Outside, the siren silenced. Instead of moving toward the back of the house, I went to the front door again. The two walked with me so I wasn't alone to greet Trammer. Together, we watched him leave his car and give his duty belt a tug before walking our way.

"Why am I not surprised?" he said. "Trouble seems to like you. Or maybe you like it?"

I didn't respond. Eliana's small hand around mine was the only thing keeping my temper from igniting out of control.

"Well, show me what you found," he said impatiently. I could hear in his tone that he didn't believe I'd actually discovered a body in my yard.

Turning around, I led the way out the back door. When I reached the corner, just enough to see the body, I stopped and pointed with my free hand. Eliana gasped, and her fingers twitched against mine.

"Sweet mother of mercy," Trammer said under his breath.

He stepped around us and looked at what remained of Jesse.

Between the side of the house and the pines, I caught a flash of silver as a car pulled up in front. Trammer exhaled heavily and crossed his arms. Car doors closed. A soft murmur of voices floated to us from around the house.

I turned toward the driveway. A moment later, two well-dressed adults and Adira appeared.

"How are you, Megan?" Adira asked.

"Uh, not good. There's a body in my yard."

"How does that make you feel?"

"Are you serious right now?"

"Not just any body," Trammer said from behind me. I turned and saw he'd rolled over Jesse.

Trammer's hard gaze met mine. "You expect me to believe you had nothing to do with this after yesterday?"

"What? You think I killed him?" I snorted. "This is not what comes to mind when I think home-cooked meal. He's been gnawed on. Who eats people?"

Trammer opened his mouth to say more, but someone cut him off.

"We don't think you did it, Megan. But, we are interested in how it makes you feel."

When I looked at the other adults, Adira was now missing, but a simmering circle remained where she'd stood. Before I could ask why my feelings on the subject mattered, a wolf appeared through the portal. Adira emerged just behind the creature. No one spoke as the wolf trotted forward and sniffed around the body.

One moment I stared at a mottle-colored canine, the next a naked older man. I quickly averted my eyes. That was not the age bracket of nudity I wanted stuck in my retinal memory.

"Based on the feeding, it's one of ours," the man said in a deep somber voice. "But, the rain washed away any hint of scent. I'll start asking around to find out who was on their own last night."

"Might want to check with your boy first," Trammer said.

The man turned his steely gaze on Trammer, who paled slightly. Even I wanted to cower from that look.

"You believe Fenris did this?" the man asked.

"You said you would ask who was on their own. Per the Council's request, Fenris rode with me to return this guy. I left him on this side of the barrier, where he'd wait for a ride back to town, but he wasn't there when I returned."

"Aubrey was out last night, too," Oanen said. "She stopped here looking for Fenris."

The man exhaled slowly, his gaze going to Adira.

"We know that neither of them killed this human."

"We do?" I asked.

His hard, silver gaze turned to me. Eliana's fingers twitched in mine.

"No one without a mark could have left the barrier to kill this man and bring him here. I'll start questioning the pack."

"Thank you for coming, Raiden," the well-dressed man said. "Please let us know what you learn."

"Shouldn't I be there to question them, too?" Trammer said, frustration lacing his words. "It's my job, after all."

"No, Trammer. It would be best if you left this to the Council. Thank you for your services, but all we require is that you burn the body and remove all evidence of the man's return."

Trammer's face flushed.

"I'll go get a body bag from the car then." He stalked off.

"I will return you, Raiden," Adira said before looking at me. "Megan, I'll see you tomorrow."

She and Raiden disappeared into a shimmering hole that vanished quickly behind them.

"Will the two of you stay for a while?" the woman asked.

"If that's all right with you," Eliana said.

I glanced between Eliana and the woman, and the woman caught my look.

"I apologize, Megan. We know so much about you and have forgotten you know very little about us. I'm Anwen Quill, and this is Lander, my husband."

Holy crap. Those were Oanen's parents?

"Hi. Sorry we're meeting because of a dead body in my yard."

Anwen smiled slightly.

"It happens occasionally. Don't worry about it. We'll get it sorted out." She turned her gaze to Oanen. "We'll see you for dinner."

"Yes, Mother."

The pair of them walked away, passing Trammer with his arms full of body bag.

"Let's go inside," Eliana whispered.

I readily agreed, and we escaped into the kitchen.

CHAPTER FOURTEEN

I TOOK MY TIME IN THE SHOWER AND THOUGHT ABOUT THE DAY before.

A dead body.

A weird conversation where adults hadn't seemed overly concerned about who'd made the body dead.

And Oanen.

He'd managed to weird me out again. After Eliana had ditched me in the living room to warm my breakfast, Oanen had sat next to me on the couch and watched TV. Simple. No big deal. Except he'd put his arm behind me on the back of the couch. Still not that big of a deal. Until I'd felt his fingers on the back of my neck again. The soft stroke, up and down, had spread a tingle of something racing under my skin.

I'd bolted. Me. I didn't bolt. I decked people.

I groaned and stuck my face in the spray of hot water, wishing I didn't have to go to the Academy. The idea of skipping Monday check-in bounced around in my head until I remembered how Trammer had come for me the last

MELISSA HAAG

time. If I wanted to avoid a ride in his dead-body car, I needed to go with Eliana.

Turning off the water, I mentally prepared myself for another Monday.

By the time Eliana pulled up in front of the house, I'd talked myself up enough to greet her with an enthusiastic smile.

"Hey, Megan," she said when I got in. "You look much better than yesterday. Headache gone?"

I only felt a tiny bit of guilt that I'd lied about having a headache to get her and Oanen to leave.

"Yep. All better." I leaned forward and eyed the skies. "No Oanen?"

She shook her head slightly. "He's running late, but he'll be there."

I settled back in my seat as she took off and debated asking her about him. He was like her brother. Did that make him a closed topic?

"Can I ask you about Oanen?"

"Sure. But you better make it quick. I'm not sure how long it'll be before he catches up."

"Does he have a girlfriend?"

Instead of the yes I was hoping for, she let out a crazed shriek that nearly gave me a heart attack.

"Oh my gosh! I can't believe I was right. I mean, I saw you checking him out that first day we rode together, but I wasn't sure if it was check-checking him out. He's going to go crazy when—"

"Whoa, whoa, whoa. Timeout. I wasn't asking because I'm interested."

"Right." She drew out the word in obvious disbelief.

154

"I'm a succubus. I know you're interested every time I get a whiff of your l-lust when you look at him."

I ignored her stumble on the word and her beginning blush.

"What? No way."

Her peal of laughter filled the car.

"It doesn't mean anything," I said quickly, denying the possibility of me with Oanen. "It's like window shopping. I might like looking, but I have no intention to buy."

"Too bad," she said. "Because I'm pretty sure he has his eye on you. And he really wants to buy."

"I'm not for sale. Ever. We talked about this. I have way too many issues to be someone's other half. I'm barely my own half. I just need to know what to do."

"Do? What do you mean? Did something happen?"

A distant cry cut through the air.

"Never mind," I said quickly.

She said no more but grinned the entire way to school.

As usual, our flying escort zoomed ahead as soon as we reached the gates.

"Can you let me off at the front?" I asked her.

She did as I requested, and I quickly closed the door on her knowing smile. Once again, Adira waited for me in the main lobby.

"Good morning, Megan."

"Morning."

I followed her to her office, took my seat, and released a slow, calming breath, relieved that I'd managed to escape face to face time with Oanen.

"Is everything all right?" Adira asked.

"Yeah. Sure. I mean, except for finding that body over

the weekend, everything's great." I might have been more convincing if I'd managed something other than a sarcastic tone.

"Yes. The body. A man named Jesse who was into human trafficking. Would you like to talk about him?"

"Not really. He was a scumbag. That much was clear when he detailed how he wanted to rape Eliana then sell her. I can't say I'm overly bothered that he's dead. I am bothered by how none of you seem too concerned about who did it, though."

She smiled slightly. "Good. That should bother you. I'd like to change things up for you, Megan. I think you're ready, and very able, to start attending sessions daily."

Disbelief coursed through me.

"What?" I fisted my hands, already knowing how this would end for me. "I don't think that's a good idea at all."

"Whenever you start feeling angry, I want you to let me know who triggered your anger."

"Before or after I beat them bloody? I mean, that's why I'm in Uttira, right? Because I don't have much control over my temper. Because I want to hurt everyone and everything ninety-eight percent of the time. Adira, I don't have many people in my life the way it is. The few friends I have managed to make, despite my amazing personality, are going to bail when I start getting into fight after fight."

"You're not among humans anymore. You might be surprised by how your friends here react when you do fight. However, I encourage you to come to me before you beat someone bloody. If you can manage."

I sat back in my chair and considered what she was asking of me. Try to control my temper? My gut reaction demanded that I laugh in her face. But I couldn't because, as Oanen had pointed out, I had managed to control my temper with Jesse. However, I'd had Eliana right there. It wouldn't be that way here, though. I doubted Adira would be too impressed with my efforts on my own. I'd probably get into so many fights that she'd kick me out of school. Maybe even Uttira. Two weeks ago, I wouldn't have cared. Now, though, I had a friend. Maybe more than one if I counted Fenris and Oanen. Although I did want to be able to leave town, I wasn't sure I wanted to be banished from it or whatever their punishment would be.

"What happens when I fight here?" I asked.

"You will not be expelled if that is your hope. If it proves too much for you on your own, I will assign someone to stay with you at all times while you're at the Academy. I believe Oanen is already in most of your classes."

The idea of Oanen with me every minute of the day made my insides go funny.

"No, I think I can manage on my own with minimal carnage."

"Good." She stood, and I knew we were done.

Leaving the room, I wandered toward the main halls, lost in thought. Although I had issues here, they were far less than at a human school. I'd get small flashes of irritation, but not full bursts of my true temper. Unless Aubrey was around.

"Hey, Megan," Eliana said when I reached the main hall. She straightened from the spot where she had been leaning against the wall.

"How'd it go?" We started toward our first session together.

"Okay, I guess. Adira wants me to start attending daily."

Eliana's face lit up with excitement.

"That's great. I can pick you up and drop you off every day. There's this new show I've been dying to watch but not alone."

I grinned knowing where this was headed.

"Yes, you can hang out with me after school."

Her smile widened, showing perfect, white teeth.

Further down the hall, a voice rose above the rest and ignited my temper. As my steps faltered, the back of Eliana's hand touched mine. The contact was enough to calm the heat of my anger so I didn't charge forward.

"I don't care what you need to do, just keep her away," Aubrey seethed, glaring at Oanen who didn't look the least bit upset.

"I didn't do it, you know," Fenris said softly beside me, making me jump.

"What?" I turned my head to meet his earnest brown gaze.

"Kill that guy. I couldn't care less what everyone else thinks, but I want you both to know I didn't do it."

For whatever reason, I believed him.

"Okay," I said.

"Good." He gave me his best boyish smile. "You still owe me a spaghetti dinner. What about this Wednesday?"

I glanced at Aubrey, who still spoke in a barely hushed, vehement tone to Oanen.

"I don't know, Fenris. Aubrey already has it out for me the way it is."

"That's exactly why you're going to say yes."

I sighed and playfully grinned back at Fenris.

"I'll see you Wednesday at five."

The bell rang, and Eliana and I headed to our first session.

As the minutes dragged into hours, I couldn't say I looked forward to a whole week of Academy time. Sure, I liked hanging out with Eliana, but as Adira had pointed out, the rest of my sessions were with Oanen.

When I saw him after the first session, he didn't ask about my headache and acted completely normal. He quietly sat beside me in class; and in the hallways, he kept me from losing my cool whenever my temper spiked. I only had to report to Adira twice that day for two separate girls. I didn't bother going to her every time Aubrey set me off, though.

By the end of the day, I was more than ready to escape and beat Eliana to her car by less than a minute.

"How'd you do after lunch?" she asked, backing out of her spot.

"Not too bad. Thanks for making me something, by the way. It was way better than having to wait in line. I'll need to remember to pack a lunch tomorrow."

"I didn't do it; Oanen did. He thought you might want to avoid the crowd in the cafeteria. What's up with you and Fenris? I thought that was just a friend thing."

"It is."

"I don't know. Remember what I said about sensing emotions? There's a whole heck of a lot of lust coming off of him. Although, to be fair, he's always sending off waves of the stuff."

"He knows where I stand. I can't do relationships. I'd be bad for any boyfriend's health."

Overhead, a griffin cried out, reminding me our conversation wasn't exactly private. Neither Eliana nor I said anything else the rest of the way home.

"I DON'T UNDERSTAND why Adira and the Quills are forcing it so hard," Eliana said, gripping the steering wheel tightly in frustration. "I proved that I could feed. Why can't that be enough?"

"I think they're afraid that if you get hungry enough with a ready, willing food source nearby, you'll snap."

"I haven't snapped on you."

"That's because you're not pulling lust or passion from me. I'm the wrong food group."

She sighed and shook her head.

"I don't know what I'm going to do."

"You have time. You said it yourself. Adira's telling you now so you can wrap your head around it. The end of term is a long way off, and you get a break before the new term and your deadline. Plenty of time."

"What about you and Fenris? Ready for tonight?"

"There's nothing to be ready for."

She snorted.

"Every time he's near you, he's sending off waves of sexual energy. I'm betting he's going to make a move tonight."

This time I snorted.

"I'm betting he shows up at school with a black eye tomorrow, then."

She laughed and parked in front of the house.

"We can watch a few episodes of our show before I have to start dinner," I said.

She killed the engine and came inside to keep me company until four. Granted, she teased me the entire time and bailed as soon as I pulled out the pot to start browning the meat.

"Good luck," she said, giving me a tight hug.

"Don't need it. I don't plan on doing anything you wouldn't do."

She laughed and left me to get dinner ready on my own.

I only enjoyed about thirty minutes of quiet before Fenris knocked on the front door. Since I was in the middle of draining noodles, I just called for him to come in.

"It smells amazing in here," he said, walking into the kitchen.

"Thanks. I wasn't sure how much to make and think I overdid it. Hope you're hungry."

"Starving." The husky note in his voice was the only warning I had before his arms wrapped around me, and he hugged me tightly from behind. His hands didn't grip anywhere inappropriate. In fact, other than his arms, and his nose sniffing in my hair, he didn't touch me. Still...

"Er, Fenris? This doesn't feel like just friends."

"Sorry." He pulled away. "I was just really looking forward to this."

I put the noodles in a bowl and drizzled them with oil before setting the dish on the table.

"I bet you were. More Aubrey avoidance time?"

He gave me a sheepish smile.

"Something like that."

"Well, sit down. I think I have everything just about ready."

After his hug, I thought things might get awkward. Instead, dinner progressed in a relaxing stream of conversation. I learned a bit more about the Council's weak investigation into the body I'd found, and Fenris got to hear all about the shows Eliana and I were watching because I didn't have much of a life beyond that. He didn't seem to mind, though. He listened attentively and asked questions as if he was actually interested.

It didn't seem like an hour had passed until he sighed and looked at the clock.

"I better get going."

"An hour is all she gives you?"

He chuckled. "If I'm lucky. Hopefully, she'll leave you alone. It helped that Oanen was here last time she showed up."

I said nothing as I walked him to the door. He surprised me again with a tight hug and his face buried in my hair.

"Thank you, Megan. This meant more than you know."

He turned and left before I could respond. Watching him get into his junkie car, I hoped that this dinner with him didn't mean more than I wanted it to.

"So," Eliana said when I got in the car, "how was dinner?"

"Nice."

"Well? Was I right? Did he try to put any moves on you?"

"I don't think so. He hugged me when he got there and hugged me goodbye, but I think it was mostly just friendly. I don't hug many werewolves so I'm not sure. He sniffed my hair."

She snorted a laugh.

"Are you serious? That's funny stuff."

"It was a little weird; but other than that, he was a gentleman. It doesn't sound like his father is any closer to ferreting out who might have killed Jesse. All the adults are accounted for, and none of the underage wolves had left the barrier that night, not even with adult supervision."

"Honestly, I don't think the Council's too worried about it," Eliana said. "They sent a few guardians to affirm the guy's disappearance wouldn't be questioned. I guess he was into bad enough stuff that no one will really care if he just goes missing. And because of what he meant to do here, he apparently had been pretty quiet about where he was going when anyone last saw him."

"Doesn't it bother you that no one seems to care that there's a human-eating creature here?"

She laughed.

"The gods made us all differently. Some feed off of humans without killing them, like I do. Or like I would do if I wasn't so hung up on feeding. Some creatures, like Oanen, are just here to protect. And some others? Well, they like flesh. They have found ways to satisfy their hunger for it without killing every human they come into contact with. It was hard for me to come to terms with all the different ways we use humans. Obviously, I'm still hung up on a few.

But, I keep reminding myself, no matter how one of us feeds, we all still need to eat. It's not any of our faults we were made the way we were."

"So you're okay with the occasional dead body?"

"If it's humans like Jesse? Yes. His death prevents the death of innocent humans."

She had a point.

When we got to school, Oanen was waiting in the parking lot. His steady gaze swept over me and settled on the bag I clutched in my hands. On Tuesday, he'd packed another lunch for me. I had assured him he didn't need to keep making meals for me, and even though his expression hadn't changed at the time, I'd felt that telling him so had somehow disappointed him. Now, I felt the same thing as he stared at the bag hiding my leftover spaghetti and garlic bread.

"I can smell it!" Aubrey screeched.

I looked to where Fenris and Aubrey stood near their car. He had her arm firmly clasped in his hand to keep her from running this way.

"Calm down," he said.

"You said you had spaghetti at home. Why do I smell it here?"

Something tugged the bag from my fingers. I turned my head forward again and blinked at the up-close view of Oanen's snuggly fitted shirt. He didn't say anything as he looked down at me and slipped a paper lunch bag into my hand.

My pulse increased the longer he stood so close. I opened my mouth to ask what he was doing, but the moment his gaze dipped to my lips, I forgot what I meant to say.

"I should have known it was you," Aubrey said from behind me.

Oanen broke his gaze away first and looked at Aubrey. I turned, ready to confront her, but Oanen quickly anchored me to his side by the weight of his arm settling over my shoulder. My confiscated lunch dangled against my arm.

"Morning, Aubrey," Oanen said.

Her gaze shifted to the bag that hung from his fingers to the brown paper bag that I clutched in my hands. Oanen had once again covered for Fenris. Or maybe me. I still wasn't sure who he was actually helping.

"Hey, Oanen," Fenris said. "I forgot to ask. You guys going to be at the Roost on Friday?"

"Of course," Oanen said.

Fenris looked at me and Eliana for confirmation, too.

"Sure," Eliana said.

Aubrey glared at me. I grinned.

"I wouldn't miss it," I said.

CHAPTER FIFTEEN

"Sessions were boring without you there today," Eliana complained. "How did you get Adira to allow you to stay home?"

We both sat at my kitchen table and munched on some afterschool snacks while I listened to how her day had gone. I'd only woken up and showered a few hours ago. However, I felt zero guilt over sleeping in after putting up with a week of regular anger.

"I told her if she said I had to come in, I'd run for the barrier and keep trying to get out until my hair really did fry off." Grinning, I recalled the brief pause before Adira had surprisingly agreed.

Eliana chuckled and ate another chip.

"I wish I was as brash as you."

"Brash?"

"Yep. And don't even try to deny it. You're passionate about what you think and feel—when you do think, that is—and you don't let anyone stop you from anything."

And that kind of stuff always landed me in trouble, but I didn't point that out to her.

"And if you were more brash, what would you be doing right now?"

"Probably eating something more satisfying than potato chips."

She sighed.

"So do it," I said, stealing a chip.

"Right." She rolled her eyes at me. "We both know it's not that easy."

"Why not?"

She gave me an impatient look.

"Okay. Walk up to Oanen and give him the kiss you know you want to plant on him."

"What? You're crazy. I don't want to kiss Oanen."

She snorted.

"Succubus, remember? I know you're trying not to have dirty thoughts about him. Why fight it?"

"Because I don't want to punch him in the face again. Guys tend not to like that."

"Exactly. Being with someone I don't really know just so I can feed feels morally wrong. And, I don't want to feed off someone I do know because I wouldn't be able to stand their false devotion to me. It'd be like I'd made a slave out of a friend."

"Fine. No boyfriends for either of us. Just the crappy excuse for junk food we can find at the grocery store."

We munched for a minute in silence, wasting time until we needed to get ready for the Roost.

"I think he missed you," she said.

"Who?" I asked. But, I already knew who.

"Oanen."

"Closed topic or I rescind your afterschool invitation."

"Fine. Let's go get ready."

"Get ready?" I looked down at my jeans and t-shirt and brushed off a few chip crumbs.

"Yeah. I promised Anwen I'd wear the dress she bought me, so we need to look at your closet and figure out what dress you'll wear."

I jerked my head up to frown at her.

"I'm not wearing a dress."

"Please?"

It only took three seconds of staring at her pleading gaze to cave.

"If I end up getting in a fight and exposing myself because of my attire, I'm not going to be very forgiving."

Eliana grinned widely.

"It'll be fine. You're with me. I won't let you get angry, remember?"

Thirty minutes later, I sat in her car and tugged at my skirt, a gift from my mother from ages ago.

"I look like a hooker."

"Yep, you do. Maybe this will teach you to do your own shopping."

As Eliana drove, I glared at the cute little sundress outfit she wore, complete with a tiny jacket. Compared to my black miniskirt and flashy top thingy that looked like a giant mouse had nibbled holes in the stomach and chewed off the shoulder, Eliana looked ready to go to church. I looked ready to be branded with the letter A.

"I still think we should switch," I said. "This outfit screams succubus."

"Oh, it screams all right. I can't wait to see everyone's reaction. This is going to be fun." She laughed.

"Yeah, for you."

I zipped up my winter coat and silently swore she'd need to pry it off my cold, dead body.

Eliana pulled up in front of the Roost and parked.

"Why are we here again?" I asked.

"Because you like pissing off Aubrey."

"Oh, yeah."

Suddenly the skirt and top didn't seem as revealing. Getting out of the car, I changed my mind again when a cool breeze brushed way too far up my thighs. We walked toward the door, which Eliana held for me.

"You owe me," I mumbled under my breath.

I walked inside, head held high and legs exposed from mid-thigh down. The crystals on the strappy sandals on my feet caught the flashing lights on the stage. Tonight they had live singers. The sultry melody tugged at my insides, and I knew they weren't human.

"Sirens," Eliana said, answering my questioning look.

"Great."

I glanced up and caught sight of Oanen and Fenris, talking on the second floor. They stood by one of the tables lining the rail. They already had drinks and company. Aubrey, dressed in a skimpy red tight dress, clung to Fenris's arm and played with his hair. It didn't appear that he was enjoying the attention as much as putting up with it. How could Aubrey not see the difference?

"I don't know how he can stand her," Eliana whispered.

Behind them, the rest of Fenris' girls stood in a cluster. None of them approached the trio, but looked at Fenris with longing. After seeing how Aubrey had run them off in the parking lot, I knew she was the one behind their distance.

"She is such a bitch," I agreed, feeling my anger burst forth even at this distance.

Aubrey stiffened and slowly looked in our direction. Her attention drew the notice of the rest of her group. Her eyes narrowed on us when she realized we'd gained Fenris' attention when she hadn't. I grinned and unzipped my coat.

Fenris' lips moved; and based on Aubrey's fierce scowl, whatever he'd said had been complimentary to me. Beside me, Eliana let out a small sound of amusement. I ignored her and shrugged out of my outerwear before blowing Aubrey a kiss. She bared her teeth at me and gripped the railing.

"Tonight's going to be amazing," I said, glancing at Eliana with a smile.

"Should we dance?"

"Yes. We should."

Before we turned away from the group above, Oanen's gaze captured mine. He wasn't grinning in amusement like Fenris. He watched me with a singular focus that made me wonder if I was in for another one of his "behave, Megan" warnings. Probably. However, I chose to carry on as if I didn't care. Which I didn't.

Eliana and I set our things on an unclaimed couch near the dance floor then swayed to the sultry siren songs. Eliana had crazy sexy moves when she let go, which she did in short, infrequent bursts.

"I kinda want to hump your leg when you do that," I teased.

She blushed red but did it again. We laughed and had a good time until she called it quits because she needed a drink.

"You go on upstairs. I think I'll avoid that area for a while," I said.

I sat on our couch and watched her disappear up the stairs. After that, I people watched. Everyone seemed pretty chill; but between one moment and the next, my bitchometer started to spike. It wasn't the level of anger I got around Aubrey, but it still called my attention.

I looked around the room, zeroing in on the source.

In the back corner, a girl sat alone at a dimly lit table. Her strawberry-blonde hair hung loosely around her face as she stared at the open book before her. She reminded me a bit of Fenris because she was doing her best to ignore the girl standing nearby, talking to her. No. Not talking. Based on the look on the other girl's face, the girl at the table was being bullied.

I got up and moved closer in an effort to hear what was being said. It sounded like the one standing was trying to get the one sitting to buy her something to eat.

"Hey, guys," I said. Irritation didn't require a fist before words, but I wouldn't be opposed to dishing it out if I thought it warranted.

The hungry girl looked at me, her eyes sweeping me from head to toe.

"Do you mind? It's my turn with the science project."

I glanced at the girl who hadn't looked up at my approach. Her unmoving gaze remained glued to the book.

"Science project?" I asked.

The hungry one sighed. "The human. You must be the new girl. You can have a turn practicing with her when I'm done."

There were so many levels of "what the hell?" going on in my head I didn't know how to respond.

"It's okay," the girl with the book said, speaking for the first time. "It's my assigned night. It doesn't bother me."

The other girl made a sound of disbelief.

"Of course it doesn't bother you. It's the only reason you're here, human. Now, go order some food so I can try to steal it."

"I have no money," the girl pretending to read said without looking up.

"I'm telling Adira you were being uncooperative."

"Okay." The reader's even, uncaring answer made me grin.

While the angry girl stomped off, I sat at the girl's table.

"Are you going to get in trouble for that?" I asked.

"No. The whole point is that they're supposed to get me to do what they want. She failed, not me."

She sounded bored and relaxed, but I knew better. She hunched forward slightly, her shoulders rounded protectively, and she'd yet to move her eyes from the page she'd focused on since I'd arrived.

"You don't like it here," I said. "Why don't you leave?"

"I'm assigned the Roost until eight. My uncle will pick me up then."

"How does a human get picked for something like this? I thought the only humans in town were the ones married to a non-human."

"Non-human." Her lips twitched, but she still didn't look up. "I like that."

"Is there something else to call them?"

"Them?" She glanced up at me, her hazel eyes full of amusement and confusion. "You're one of them."

I sighed.

"So I'm told."

"I didn't get picked. I was—"

"Megan, what are you doing?" Eliana asked, rushing up to the table with two drinks in her hands.

"Talking to—" I glanced toward the girl. "What's your name?"

"Ashlyn."

"There you go. I'm talking to Ashlyn."

"Unless you were assigned a task by Adira, we really shouldn't be over here," Eliana said.

A girl, who'd been singing on stage when we walked in, strode by and paused to look at the three of us before her gaze settled on Eliana.

"You can't really be so desperate that you need to feed from the science project. That's like sleeping with your pet." The snide tone of voice and the arched brow the girl gave Eliana had me opening my mouth.

"Wonder what you'll sound like after I throat punch you."

She tossed her hair in a huff and moved away from us.

I grinned at Eliana and pointed to the other side of the table. She sighed and took a seat, sliding one of the drinks toward me.

"Sitting here is going to draw attention and trouble," she warned.

"We both know I'd draw attention and trouble no matter where I sit, but why is this such a big deal?"

"Because any human in the Roost is here for testing. Adira assigns students tasks to complete on the human."

"Ashlyn," I said, not liking that Eliana wasn't using her name.

"No. Not just Ashlyn," Eliana said. "The humans take shifts. It's like an afterschool job."

"The pay sucks," Ashlyn mumbled.

Eliana looked at Ashlyn, sympathy in her gaze.

"Can I get you anything?" Eliana offered. "Something to eat or drink?"

"Nah, Uncle Trammer will be here soon enough. He'll have something in the car for me."

"Trammer is your uncle?" I asked, surprised.

"Yes. That's why I'm here."

"All humans are vetted by the human liaison officer to ensure they can be trusted with their assignment," Eliana said.

"That they can be trusted? What about the people in here? And, are you saying Trammer recruits humans so the upstanding youth of Uttira can test their skills?" I had a hard time believing he would actually do that.

"Pretty much."

"How many are there?" I asked.

"Five. Three girls and two boys. The other four are the last liaison's recruits," Eliana said.

The way she said it rose a red flag for me.

"Last liaison?" I asked.

"My father," Ashlyn said. "He was killed over a year

ago. Uncle Trammer took over his position and brought me along so I wouldn't be alone."

"I'm sorry," I said softly.

"It's okay. It was an accident. A bar fight between giants. One tripped. My dad didn't have a chance."

Our moment of silence was disturbed by the pounding of angry high heels on the wood floor. Eliana reached across the table for my hand before I could look up. It didn't matter if I saw Aubrey or not. I knew it was her approaching by the feel of my mounting anger, which Eliana did her best to subdue.

"Quit hogging the science experiment's time," Aubrey said, stopping at our table. "Those of us who actually have a chance at graduating need the practice."

I chuckled.

"Oh, Aubrey, we both know your focus isn't on graduating."

She leaned in. If not for Eliana's hand lightly covering both of mine, I would have snapped and laid into Aubrey. As it was, I just sat there, pretending to be calm.

"I know it was you," she said. "I could smell you on him under the scent of garlic and tomato sauce. He's mine."

I glanced beyond her at the red entrance door before meeting her gaze.

"Are you sure? Fenris just slid out the front door with Jenna. Better run."

She snarled at me before pivoting on her heel and sprinting for the door.

"She's going to be so pissed when she realizes you lied to her," Eliana said after the door closed.

"Yeah. Too bad I won't be there when she realizes it."

With us at Ashlyn's table, no one else bugged her. Eliana and I sipped our drinks over the next hour and talked about Aubrey's obsession with Fenris, my obsession with pissing off Aubrey, and my choice of clothes.

"Those incubi have been watching you for the last fifteen minutes," Eliana said.

"Me? No. Probably Ashlyn. She's the primary practice target."

Ashlyn gave a short laugh.

"I'm not the one showing enough skin to tempt a saint."

"Speaking of saints, here comes Oanen," Eliana said.

I turned my head and saw him striding across the room, his gaze locked on me. The long-sleeved pale shirt he wore stood out in the crowd of jewel-toned colors as did the dark jeans hugging his hips. Something in the way he moved and the way he held my gaze made my stomach do a weird dip, and I recalled Eliana's goading that I should just kiss him already. Now, I couldn't stop thinking about it.

Eliana inhaled audibly, and I knew she could taste what was on my mind.

"I'm going to punch you if you open your mouth," I said softly, without looking at her.

"Ladies," Oanen said in greeting when he reached us. He focused on me.

"You look nice, Megan."

"Thanks." The word didn't sound thankful though. It carried more of a "shut your face" tone.

He looked at Eliana.

"When you're ready to leave, can you let me know? A storm's coming, and I'd rather have a ride tonight."

"Sure thing, Oanen. We'll let you know."

He nodded and walked off again.

"He is so hot," Ashlyn said. "Too bad griffins never go for humans."

"They don't?" I asked, surprised.

"Nope. They watch over humans, but it's nothing like the protective dedication they give their mates."

Something thumped under the table, and Ashlyn winced. I looked at Eliana who was giving me a way too innocent look.

"Did you just kick her?"

"Maybe. Wanna dance again?"

I narrowed my eyes at Eliana then looked at Ashlyn, who'd once again picked up her book.

"Fine. Let's dance."

But I couldn't enjoy myself like before. Eliana's reaction to Ashlyn's information spill and the way Oanen and Fenris watched us from the second story made me edgy. When my phone beeped, I quickly used it as an excuse to leave the dance floor, alone, and find a quiet corner.

Under the balcony, out of sight of Oanen's watchful gaze, I read the message from an unknown number.

Meet me out back in ten. Alone. Mom.

CHAPTER SIXTEEN

ALL SOUND BLED AWAY WITH THE RAPID BEAT OF MY HEART. After abandoning me for three weeks, my mom was back. Excitement coursed through me. Annoyance immediately followed. How could I be excited to see the person who left me without a word? Correction. With the note that didn't explain jack. She had better have a damn good reason for ditching me like she had. And for not telling me about what this place was. Or what I was.

Looking at the message again, part of me wondered if she even deserved my time. She'd hurt me over the years with her insistence to call her Paxton and her increasing distance. But, I also remembered who she'd been before that. She'd been my everything. When no one else in the world had liked me, she had. She'd hugged me and told me she'd always love me.

My chest ached with the memory and with the realization that she'd abandoned me long before leaving me in Uttira. The one person who should have been able to love me unconditionally hadn't been able to.

As much as I wanted to tell her to leave like she'd proven she could do so well, I knew I couldn't pass up the chance to find out what I was. And, to see her one more time.

I tore my gaze from the phone and waited until I caught Eliana's attention on the dance floor. Wiping any trace of trouble from my expression, I motioned that I was going to the bathroom. She nodded and kept swaying to the sultry music, oblivious to the incubus trying to gain her notice.

Ducking into the bathroom, I took a moment to check myself in the mirror. The curls Eliana had coaxed into my hair still framed my lightly made up face. If I just focused on my head, I looked good. Like I'd managed just fine without any parental presence. However, from the neck down made me want to cringe.

"One month without supervision, and suddenly I'm a hooker," I said under my breath. Knowing Mom, she'd celebrate my choice of clothes instead of scolding me for it.

After waiting a few minutes, I slipped out of the bathroom. No one noticed as I made my way to the back door because everyone was focused on Trammer, who was glaring down an incubus at Ashlyn's table.

Closing the door on the music, I took a moment to let my eyes adjust to the dim light that cast shadows in the alley behind the Roost. The rank air from a dumpster that desperately needed to be emptied had me covering my nose as I looked around. Why in the hell would Mom want to meet me out here? I glanced toward the entrance. No one. I checked the time on my phone. One minute early.

Something buzzed to my left. I glanced toward the dark dumpster and caught sight of a faint outline of light on the ground. Someone's phone? I went to pick up the buzzing device, and my fingers touched something wet. I cringed in disgust but didn't drop it.

"Can this get any grosser?" I said to myself, turning the phone over.

A missed call from a private number showed on the screen.

Frowning, I looked at the mouth of the alley again. Was this Mom's phone? Had I already missed her? Why had she dropped it?

Looking back at the phone, I caught sight of the dark stain on my fingers. At first, I thought oil. Then, I brought my hand closer to my face.

Blood.

Fear wormed its way into my stomach, the feeling unfamiliar and unwelcome.

I turned the phone over and used its weak light to illuminate the ground. A puddle of blood pooled near where the phone had lain. More blood dripped onto the ground near the dumpster. Images of mom the last time I saw her filled my head. Slowly, I lifted the light of the phone.

Lifeless eyes of the corpse lying on top of the mounded garbage stared back at me. It wasn't my mom but a girl not much older than me. Exhaling in relief, I took in the dull brown hair that partially covered her neck, but not enough to hide the unmarred skin.

This body hadn't been eaten. I turned the light, trying to figure out how she'd died. When I got to her middle, I struggled to breathe evenly. She'd been gutted.

Trammer's loud voice shattered my fragile control.

"Drop what's in your hands," he barked.

I turned on him, rage heating the blood in my veins.

"Shit," he breathed, fumbling for something at his side.

While he struggled, I flew toward him. Everything inside me screamed to give the man a beating he wouldn't easily walk away from.

Before I reached him, he freed an object from his belt. An instant later, something invisible punched me in the chest. I flew back and landed hard on the ground, convulsing. My anger didn't seize with my muscles, though.

While I lay locked in convulsions, Trammer used his foot to turn me over. I barely felt the cool metal of the cuffs as they clicked into place.

"Not so tough now, are you?" he said.

A moment later the convulsions stopped, and Trammer pulled me to my feet. The probes of his Taser stayed embedded in my flesh just inside my right shoulder and below my collarbone. I rolled my shoulders, feeling the ache.

"Take them out," I said.

"I don't think so. Try anything, and I'm juicing you again."

He gripped my arm and led me toward the front of the building where his car and niece waited.

"Ashlyn, you'll need to ride in front," he said. He opened the door and proceeded to shove me into the backseat.

I met Ashlyn's wide-eyed gaze as he yanked the probes from my chest.

"It's okay. I'll walk home," she said.

Trammer grunted an acknowledgment and shut the door. Ashlyn stayed by the entrance of the Roost as her uncle got in and started the car.

With lights flashing but siren silent, he pulled away from the curb. Ashlyn's pale expression made more sense when I caught my reflection in the glass of the back window. Blood matted my hair and smeared my ear and cheek from when Trammer had rolled me over. Asshat.

When I looked back, Ashlyn had already disappeared. Facing forward, I looked at the guy I wanted to hit.

"Why am I in handcuffs?"

"You tried to attack an officer after being found at the scene of a crime."

"Speaking of the scene of a crime. Don't you think another dead body is a bigger concern than a teenager with anger issues?"

"Yep. That's the other reason you're in the back seat."

"What? You can't be serious. I didn't kill that girl."

"Then why were you in that alley?"

"Because I got a text from my mom."

He laughed. "Nice try. We both know she's not coming back. They never do here."

"I didn't kill that girl," I reiterated. "Do I look like a killer?"

"For all I know, you're just another flesh-hungry monster disguised as a human."

"Nice. Don't be afraid to tell me how you really feel," I said.

"We'll see how smart-mouthed you are after the Council deals with you. Human killing inside Uttira is forbidden."

"I didn't kill her."

"Right. You were just taking in the night air in a dark, back alley that happened to have a dead body in it? Nice try."

He didn't say anything more as he navigated the streets for several minutes. I stared out the window and wondered how long I would need to sit in jail before he actually went back to the scene of the crime and looked at my phone.

The idiot needed to do his job. Although, to be fair, I had tried to attack him. And I still wanted to. In fact, I was pretty sure he'd be feeling some pain as soon as these cuffs came off.

The car started to slow, but I barely noticed the pathetically small building labeled "police station" that he pulled in front of. Instead, my entire focus fixated on the partially clothed Oanen, who stood before the place. With his arms crossed and a frown pulling at his normally stoic expression, he looked wildly fierce.

When his gaze met mine, some of that fierceness softened for a brief moment before Trammer made a sound of annoyance and opened his door. Oanen looked up at the man.

"What do you think you're doing, Trammer? Let her out."

"Not happening. I found her in the alley right next to another dead body. When I told her to drop what she had in her hand, she tried to attack me."

Oanen glanced at me and exhaled in obvious frustration when I gave a slight shrug.

"She can sit in a cell until the Council gets here." Trammer opened the back door. But before I could lurch toward him, Oanen was there, offering me a hand.

"Oanen," Trammer said from somewhere behind the wall of protective muscle helping me from the car.

Oanen's gaze missed nothing, including the two bleeding spots just above my right boob. He turned away from me but kept a hand around my upper arm as he spoke to Trammer. The cocky cop was looking far too pleased with himself.

"Did you call them?" Oanen asked.

"Of course not. My first priority is to secure her. Then, I need to go back and secure the scene."

"Good thing I called for you. They should be here shortly. Would you like to wait inside?"

Trammer's face flushed.

"I'm not waiting. I have a suspect and a crime scene to secure."

Trammer reached for me; but before his hand could close over my arm, Oanen once again stood in front of me.

"I'll help her inside."

With Oanen's hampering hold keeping me from Trammer, we moved as a group toward the tiny building, which looked more like a small-town post office than a police station. A desk sat in the tight space just inside the door. Beyond that, a single cell beckoned.

"She goes in the cell," Trammer said, moving past us to slide open the narrow-barred opening.

Oanen led me forward but stopped just before we reached the cell. I looked up at him, trying to ignore the gentle swipe of his thumb on my upper arm.

"I'm sorry, Megan."

"For what?"

His lips twitched slightly.

"That you're here."

"Don't worry about it. As soon as Captain Duffus checks my phone, which I dropped in the alley when he zapped me, he'll see I was telling the truth."

"Get in the damn cell," Trammer said angrily.

I stepped in and listened to Trammer shove the door closed behind me. The lock clicking into place admittedly worried me. What the hell was going on? Who had texted me to meet in the alley? I no longer believed it was my mom. Trammer at least got that right. She wasn't coming back, and I'd been stupid to think that for even a minute. My stupidity only added to my anger.

Someone had set me up. Who and why?

"I thought you couldn't wait," Oanen said. I turned and found him staring down Trammer just outside my cell.

"You need to leave."

"No. I'll stay and keep an eye on things here while you go bag the body. The Council will want to know what happened to Camil."

"Who?" I asked, unable to help myself.

"Are you sure it was Camil?" Trammer asked, going pale.

"Yes. I looked before flying here. There were no bites like the last time, but pieces were missing. Heart. Liver."

Trammer swallowed hard, and his eyes widened.

"Ashlyn," he said. With that he disappeared out the door, taking a good portion of my anger with him.

I gripped the bars and looked at Oanen.

"Why is he worried about Ashlyn?"

"Camil was human. Just like Jesse. Someone in Uttira seems to have developed a taste for them."

A shimmering hole appeared inside the cell.

"Yes," Adira said, stepping through. "And that someone is very bold leaving a body at the Roost." She looked at me. "How are you, Megan?"

Was she serious?

"Not good. I'm covered in a dead girl's blood, and Trammer thinks I killed her."

"Unlikely or he wouldn't have left in such a concern for his niece." She set her hand on the lock. It clicked softly, and Oanen reached out to slide it open.

"Are my parents here?"

"No. They sent me to release Megan. They're at the Roost. I need to find Raiden before it rains."

A soft rumble from outside punctuated her words.

"You'll see Megan home?" Adira asked Oanen.

"I will."

Another circle opened and Adira disappeared through, leaving us alone. Oanen stepped close and gently moved part of my torn shirt to look at the two holes in my chest. I glanced down at them, too. Stupid Trammer wrecked my shirt.

"Eliana liked this top," I said, annoyed.

The tip of Oanen's finger brushed over the unmarred skin, just above the marks. A tingle of awareness coursed through me and set my pulse racing. However, when I looked up, his expression was once again closed off, making it hard to know what the touch meant.

"If it's okay with you, I'd like to leave before Trammer comes back," I said.

Oanen nodded and moved to hold the office door open

for me. I quickly stepped out, desperate to leave before someone changed their mind about keeping me locked up.

Outside, the wind had picked up, and I shivered slightly.

"Eliana is coming from the Roost," Oanen said as we started walking in that direction. "She'll have your coat."

"Thanks."

"Are you all right?" he asked after a moment of silence.

"Not really. Trammer's convinced I'm capable of murder. And you know what? I have no idea if I am or not. I'm covered in blood and more annoyed about it than grossed out. I've seen two dead bodies in less than a week. Shouldn't I be upset? Shouldn't I be having some sort of an emotional breakdown? If I were normal, I would be. But, as everyone here has made very clear, I'm not normal. I'm not human. So, how can anyone be sure I didn't do it when I'm not even sure what I'm capable of?"

Thunder rolled through the skies, and Oanen paused his barefooted stroll to look down at me. Silent, serious Oanen. The streetlights cast shadows on his bare chest, and I didn't know how he wasn't freezing.

I shivered again.

He stepped closer, his gaze holding mine.

"I think you do know what you're capable of," he said softly. "You're just afraid of facing it."

CHAPTER SEVENTEEN

THE RAIN LET LOOSE, NOT IN A LIGHT SPRINKLE THAT increased in ferocity, but in a downpour accompanied by a flash of lightning and boom of thunder. Frigid water soaked my hair in seconds. I didn't care.

Grateful for a reason to look away from the intensity of Oanen's gaze and to wash away the girl's blood, I closed my eyes, tipped my head to the sky, and ignored my shivers.

I let the rain wash away more than Camil's death. I let it take the remnants of my anger, guilt, and self-pity. Trammer might piss me off to hell and back, but he cared about his niece, which meant he wasn't all bad. And, from the sounds of things, he was the only family she now had. I would need to remember that the next time I saw him. There was nothing I could have done for the girl in the alley. Discovering her body might mean she'd get justice if Adira found Raiden in time. And, who cared if my mom never came back. She had made her choice. It had nothing to do with me. Or my anger issues.

Yeah, right. What mom wanted a daughter who got into fistfights almost daily, swore like a drunk when mad, and—

The rain suddenly stopped touching my face. I opened my eyes and blinked at the canopy of feathers over my head. Slowly, I traced them to their source. Oanen. He watched me closely, his wings curved overhead, a protective shield from the rain.

He lifted his hand and gently moved a wet strand of hair from my cheek. His fingers stayed there a moment, lightly caressing my skin as our gazes held.

"A thousand lifetimes and a thousand dreams could never conjure this," he said.

"What?"

"I should have asked you to dance."

My chest ached as I understood what he was getting at, and this time there was no denying or misunderstanding his meaning.

"Don't." The word came out a hoarse whisper.

"Don't what?" he asked.

"Don't want me. It's not safe."

I recalled the look of hate my last boyfriend had given me as he'd bled from his nose, and I knew I wasn't talking about Oanen's safety but my own. It would hurt more than I cared to admit to have him look at me like that.

Unaware of my thoughts, Oanen smiled slightly, a drop of water falling from his wet hair to his chest. I swallowed hard and followed its trail, wishing more than anything that it was safe for him to want me. Because, I wanted him like I'd never wanted a boy before.

"It's too late," he said.

I looked up again, my questioning gaze meeting his.

"I'll never stop wanting you."

He leaned toward me.

My heart started to hammer in earnest. I should have stepped back. I should have said no. But in the shelter of his wings, I did neither. Instead, I tipped my head up, wondering what it would feel like to finally kiss Oanen.

A blinding light made us both cringe. The honk of a nearby horn shattered the fragile moment and brought back a measure of sense.

"I'm serious, Oanen. Don't." With that, I ducked out from under the protective cover of his wings and raced for the car.

Eliana's worried gaze greeted me as soon as I opened the door.

"Get in quick," she said.

I did as she asked and slammed the door.

"Whoa," she said with a sharp inhale.

"Sorry. Didn't mean to slam it. The rain's cold though."

"I didn't mean the door. I think I just got a contact buzz." She leaned forward and peered out the windshield into the rain a moment before a pair of wet jeans hit the glass.

"Interesting," she said. "I guess he's flying. Reach out and grab his pants then start explaining what happened."

She didn't pull away from the curb until the saturated pants were on the floor of the backseat.

"Well?" she prompted.

"I got a text from someone claiming to be my mom. She said to meet her out in the alley. When I got out there—"

"Not that. I don't want to hear about another dead body popping up around you. Here's your phone, by the way."

She grabbed it from the center console and handed it to me. "I want to know what just happened on the sidewalk back there. Oanen doesn't fly in the rain. It's dangerous. Especially when it's gusting like this. What happened? Did he try to kiss you and you hit him?"

"How'd you get my phone?"

"Mr. Quill gave it to me. Now, what happened?"

I sighed and struggled not to recall the moment just before she'd pulled up or she'd know exactly what had almost happened.

"I didn't hit Oanen. We were talking. Speaking of just talking, what was up with you kicking Ashlyn under the table?" I asked, neatly changing the subject.

"Nothing."

"Don't lie to me, succubus. I will slap this hooker outfit on you and drop you off at the nearest high school dance."

She rolled her eyes at me.

"We're trapped in Uttira, remember?"

"Talk."

"I can't. I promised this was one topic I wouldn't discuss with you. Please, Megan. I take my promises very seriously."

"Who made you promise that?" I asked.

She hesitated then looked up toward the roof of the car, giving me my answer.

I sighed and lay my head back against the seat.

"Sorry for getting your car wet."

"Don't worry about it. It's not mine. It's Oanen's."

The ride home was quiet. When Eliana pulled into the driveway, she got as close to the back door as possible.

"Want me to stay?" she asked.

"Nah, it's okay. I want a hot shower and an early bedtime. I'll call you in the morning. Be careful out there."

She gave me a sad smile.

"I don't think I need to worry. I'm not human."

I nodded and bailed, racing toward the house. As soon as I was inside, I flicked on the lights in the kitchen. Our chips still waited on the table. Opening the bag, I munched a few while I kicked off my stupid sandals.

"Shoulda known the night would end this way for a girl dressed like a hooker." I smirked at my wit and padded upstairs for a change of clothes so I could shower.

A little over twenty minutes later, I lay snuggled under my quilt while listening to the rain pound down on the roof. Thoughts of Oanen and our almost kiss filled my head. Try as I might, I struggled to fall asleep.

I YAWNED and cracked an egg into the pan. Weak sunlight shone through the kitchen window. Mostly because of the clouds but partly because of the early hour. After a long night with little sleep due to noises I kept hearing around the house, I'd decided I had enough and got out of bed two hours before dawn.

My phone buzzed on the table. I shuffled over to it with another yawn and read the text notification.

Call me when you're up. Worried about you.

I dialed Eliana's number and wasn't surprised when she picked up before the first ring.

"Are you okay?" she asked.

"Peachy. Tired as hell because the storm kept me up. It sounded like someone pacing on my roof."

"Oh…that's weird."

"No, what's weird is the way you just said that."

She laughed.

"Want me to come over? We can spend the day watching our shows."

"Sure."

"I'll be right there." She hung up before I could say okay. Shaking my head, I set the phone down and went back to making a mess of my egg.

Eliana pulled into the driveway not long after I finished my last bite.

"That was fast," I said when she walked in.

"I was ready, hoping you'd say yes. You do look like you didn't get any sleep."

"Yeah, I might doze off during the first episode."

I didn't just sleep through the first one; I slept through the first two.

While Eliana looked in my fridge for lunch, I showered and dressed. We spent the rest of the day talking and watching TV. When the sun went down, she asked to stay over. I readily agreed, liking her company more than the thought of another lonely weekend.

Even with Eliana there and the storms long gone, I woke twice to what sounded like someone pacing on my roof. Eliana dismissed the idea with a laugh when I told her about it the next morning.

"ARE WE LATE OR SOMETHING?" I asked when Eliana pulled around the side of the Academy on Monday morning. More cars than usual already crowded the parking lot.

"We're not late, but something's up. Oanen looks mad."

He stood waiting near Eliana's spot. A heavy scowl pulled at his features. Between that and his firmly crossed arms and braced stance, "mad" seemed a bit of an understatement. The sight of his current mood made my rushed breakfast churn queasily in my stomach. It was probably because I hadn't seen him since I'd ducked out from under his wings on Friday, even though I'd thought about him plenty. We needed to talk, but now was definitely not the time.

His gaze locked with mine as Eliana pulled in between the two neighboring cars. He backed up a few steps, making room for her. Dark shadows smudged under his eyes like he hadn't been sleeping well. Because of Friday? Because of the almost kiss? Because I'd run? Crap. We really needed to talk. And, I definitely wanted to avoid that talk.

Before Eliana even cut the engine, he was moving toward my door.

"Why do I feel like I'm in trouble?" I whispered.

"Because you usually are," Eliana answered with a snigger.

Anxiously, I opened the door and stood.

"Morning," I said, forcing myself to meet his eyes.

"Good morning."

I didn't miss the way his gaze swept over my face then landed on my shoulder.

"It's fine," I said. "Well on its way to being healed."

He nodded but didn't step aside.

"Uh, everything okay?" I asked.

"No." He stared down at me for another moment. "But it's getting better."

My stomach went into acrobatic overtime. Ignoring it, I leaned to peek around him at the group of people waiting by the door.

"What's going on?"

His gaze flicked to Eliana, who listened from the other side of the car.

"Nothing much. Just rumors about Camil's death."

I rolled my eyes. "I bet. Are there any leads on who did it?"

"Not yet."

"Okay. Then, maybe we should go inside?"

He nodded and finally stepped aside.

A group of boys and one girl stood near the door. They all looked like they'd had unfortunate run-ins with an ugly stick. The girl's ugly stick must have been smeared with makeup. All of them watched me with a keen interest that gave me the willies. No anger, though.

One of the boys stepped forward as we neared. As soon as he did, the ugly boy morphed into a hideous large... troll? Ogre? I'd need to ask Eliana later. The no-longer-a-boy smiled at me, a show of jagged, broken yellowed teeth.

"Megan," he rumbled. "We should meet up by the rocks some time."

Before I could process his invitation, Oanen stepped in front of me. His wings exploded from his shirt, fanning out in a crazy huge display of feathers.

"Whatever you heard, you heard wrong. She's not meeting you anywhere." While Oanen delivered his warning, Eliana gripped my hand. I didn't understand either of their reactions.

I shook off Eliana's hold, poked Oanen in his bare side, and ducked under his wing.

"You seem to know me, but I don't know you," I said addressing the big man.

"I'm Epsid."

"I'm curious. What did you hear about me, Epsid?"

"That you've killed twice and have gotten away with it both times. No evidence to point to you. We could use some tips. If you have time."

Feeling more than a mild level of disgust, which had nothing to do with his looks, I considered the creature before me.

"Why do you want to know how to kill?"

"We know how to kill. We need to learn how to do it without leaving evidence."

"Why?"

He frowned, looking confused.

"Because the humans can't know we exist."

"So you want to kill humans?"

"Of course." He glanced back at the rest of his group then lowered his voice further. "Not the nice ones like Camil, though. I liked her." The look he gave me was almost censoring. Almost, but not quite.

"I'm sorry to disappoint you, but I haven't killed anyone. Nice or not. Good luck at your rock meeting, though."

Shaking my head, I turned and walked toward the door.

The troll-giant people weren't the only ones waiting for me. The girls with green skin and leaves in their hair swore at me and flicked acorns my way. The mermaids at the pool slapped the water with their tails when I passed. Not sure if that was the equivalent of applause or boos, though.

It seemed the students of Girderon Academy were equally split in support or rejection of me. However, they remained unanimous in their belief that I'd actually killed two people.

By the time I reached Adira in the main lobby, I'd gained quite the following. However, she barely paid any attention to it as she focused on me.

"How are you this morning, Megan?"

"Pissed. Can you please set everyone straight?"

She glanced at the people behind me.

"They have the facts. A body was found at your house a week ago Saturday. You were found near another body this past Friday. Someone fed on both bodies but used two different methods."

"And did I do it?"

"We have no leads at this time to indicate any suspects."

"Why won't you say I didn't do it?"

"Perhaps we can discuss this further in my office."

"Discuss what? I didn't kill anyone." She was starting to annoy me, and she seemed to know it too because one second, we stood in the hall and the next, we stood in her office.

"I understand that, but we would like to let the other students believe you have."

"What? Why?"

"It's better for everyone if those reasons are unknown for now." She moved around her desk, sat, and opened my folder. "I understand that you tried hitting Trammer when he discovered you near Camil. Why were you angry with him?"

I rolled my eyes and sat with a sigh.

"I have no idea. I never have an idea. Why do you keep asking how I'm feeling?"

"Because it matters. This week, I need you to focus on the specifics of your emotions. When you get angry, try to determine why you might feel angry with that person. Before you confront them, come to me. Tell me who made you angry and anything you might have discovered about them or your anger."

What point was there to doing any of that? It felt like a useless task designed to try to keep me out of trouble. Annoyed, I stared at Adira. She sat there so calm, her hand open and loosely set over my folder.

"What's in that folder?"

"Your transcripts from the prior human schools you've attended, the student assessments you've completed online, and my notes on your progress."

"Progress on what?"

Instead of answering, she smiled and stood.

"Remember what I said. Come to me when you feel angry. I want the names of the people who are upsetting you. And think more about why you wanted to attack Trammer. Your main task this week is to gain a better understanding of your anger."

She picked up the folder and walked me to the door.

One of the papers inside slipped as she moved, tipping just enough so I could read the hand-written note in the margin.

Current fourth generation.

Fourth generation what? Even as I shuffled out the door, my mind wouldn't let go of that question.

I needed to know what was in that folder.

CHAPTER EIGHTEEN

I WAVED GOODBYE TO ELIANA, TRYING NOT TO LET MY impatience show, and let myself inside the house with a relieved sigh.

"School day from hell," I said under my breath.

My assessment of the Girderon's student body hadn't changed throughout the day. They either saw me as some human-killing hero or as the devil herself. A few switched camps, but they all consistently remained convinced I'd killed Camil, at the very least.

The whispers and stares hadn't bothered me. But, Adira sure had. As she'd requested, I went to her every time someone ticked me off. She quizzed me endlessly on the level of pissery I felt each time, until I made her a happy-to-mad face chart and gave each face a scale of 0 to stop-asking-these-stupid-ass-questions. After that, I just pointed to the correct, corresponding face. And, each time, she made a note in my damn folder as I left.

While I had tried not to look overly interested in the folder, I had started paying attention. The first few times I went to her occurred after some altercation that either Eliana or Oanen had to pry me out of. Well, Oanen did the prying; Eliana just kept hugging me. Each time, the folder waited on the desk as soon as I opened Adira's door.

Near the end of the day, I'd felt a mild surge of annoyance for a succubus. Other than wearing clothes similar to those I'd worn Friday night, no logical reason had presented itself to explain my anger. Determined to try one last time to discover where Adira kept my folder, I'd gone to her office.

Knocking on her door, I'd received the typical, "Enter."

However, that time, she hadn't been ready for me. She'd greeted me and motioned to the chair as she'd leaned over to open a filing drawer on her desk. I'd ignored the maroon folder she'd withdrawn and launched into an explanation of what I'd felt. To keep it real, I'd laid on the attitude.

During that session, a plan had been born.

I needed to break into the school and read my file after hours. And, I didn't want to wait. I intended on going there tonight.

I CAUTIOUSLY LEFT the trees and skirted around the parking lot. The Academy lay in quiet darkness. I still had no idea how I'd get inside and hoped I wouldn't need to break a window or anything. Creeping closer to the door we used every day, I scanned the area. Quiet night sounds continued as normal. Good.

Covering the last few feet in silence, I grabbed the door's handle and gave a light tug. As I'd expected, it didn't open. Following the building around to the back, I began checking each window.

Near the pool, I got a break. Curls of steam drifted from one of the windows that someone had left open. I only had to pop out the screen to provide a way in.

Quietly, I hoisted myself up and eased through the opening. Warm air enveloped me as I carefully stood on my feet and looked around the dark space. Water lapped at the edges of the pool, making a soothing background sound.

I'd only taken two steps when a louder splash echoed in the cavernous space. Halting, I shifted my gaze to the water and saw, to my horror, a shape floating in the center of the main pool. I waited for whoever it was to say something, but as I watched, the body sank to the bottom.

Please don't be another dead person, I thought, squinting in an effort to see more clearly.

The shape stayed at the bottom for almost a minute before slowly rising again. Another louder splash echoed as it surfaced, then it started to sink again. I exhaled in relief. Not dead.

Taking care to stick to the deep shadows, I moved slowly to the door and exited the pool to the main hall. From there, I hurried toward the atrium. A tiny, blinking green light above the doors caught my attention. I stopped at the edge of the hall and briefly wondered if it was a motion detector before dismissing the idea. A blinking light would give away the detector's presence.

I hurried through the space and down the hall toward Adira's office. The door was closed but not locked. Shutting it softly behind me, I used my penlight to look at the drawer in her desk. It had a tumbler lock on it. Just one tumbler showing the letter J. I left it on J and tested the drawer. It opened with ease, and I stared at a space crammed full of maroon folders for all the students with the last name beginning with J.

I closed the drawer and frowned at the tumbler. It couldn't really be controlling the contents, could it? I turned it to S and opened the drawer again. The contents appeared the same, only this time with all the folders for students with the last name beginning with S. I fingered through the files, looking for Smith. When I found it, I quickly marked the spot and withdrew the folder.

There wasn't much inside. As Adira stated, I found my printed assessments, my transcripts from prior schools, and a single additional piece of paper.

SMITH, *Megan*

Fury

Notes:

Week 1 - Beginning emergence of powers, which she believes to be anger issues.

Week 2 - No knowledge of true self or true form.

Week 3 - No apparent interest in humans, yet. Complete apathy when exposed to their deaths.

Week 4 -

THAT WAS IT? The sum of my existence? The underlined note, "Current fourth generation," was written in the margin near the word, "fury." What the hell did that mean? What was a fury?

I replaced the contents of the folder and tucked it back into its spot in the files.

The whole breaking and entering thing hadn't gotten me much information. I closed the drawer and slipped out of the office. While my mind tried to solve how I would learn about the different creatures that existed, including furies, my feet started the trek back to the main lobby.

The reflection of red and blue lights on the hallway wall stopped me in my tracks. That stupid blinking light had to have been a motion sensor. I wanted to swear.

I focused on the small burgeoning thread of anger inside of me. Trammer. If I kept walking, I'd run into him. The large, raging part of me wanted that. He needed to be hurt. I shook my head and backed away. Was that really who I wanted to be? Was that a fury? All anger and fight? No thanks. What Oanen had said to me at the festival made more sense now. I had a choice, and I refused to choose that.

I retraced my steps to the back stairs. Just as I started up, a beam of light swept the hall behind me.

"Stop!" Trammer yelled.

I ran, taking the steps two at a time. His huffing breaths fell further behind as I passed the second landing. I raced to the third, wondering where I could hide when I saw a slim set of stairs leading up. The roof. Arms pumping, I sprinted for the door. It opened without a sound and closed just as silently.

Gravel crunched under my feet as I moved away from the door. How the hell was I going to get down from here? I leaned over the nearest side, and my stomach dipped at the sight of the very distant ground. Jumping was out.

I straightened just as a shadow passed over me. Oanen

landed several feet away in a spray of gravel. Before the dust settled, he morphed into his very naked human self. My cheeks heated. I really needed to leave. Now.

"I've been looking for you for hours," he said, stalking toward me.

Don't look down. Don't look down.

"And you found me," I said in a rush. I hurried past him toward the student parking lot side of the building and looked over the edge. No gutters.

"And today's word of the day is 'screwed' spelled m-e-g-a-n," I mumbled to myself.

A hand circled my upper arm. I looked up and met Oanen's frustrated gaze.

"What did you do?" he asked.

"I broke into the Academy and read my file in Adira's office."

He glanced at the red and blue light show still going on toward the front of the building then released me.

"I'll help you, but we need to talk afterward."

The very naked Oanen disappeared, replaced by a familiar, large griffin. He dipped his wing, an obvious invitation to climb aboard.

The whole talking thing sounded a bit ominous. Especially when that meant Oanen would need to ditch his feathers. Yet, I didn't see that I had any other option unless I wanted to chance getting caught and potentially attacking Trammer.

"Fine. But you better not let me fall." I scrambled onto his wide back and settled a leg just behind each wing.

His hard muscles bunched between my thighs, and he leapt into the air. My stomach jolted, and I leaned forward, pressing myself against the space between his wings and gripping his neck to stay on. Wind buffeted my face as nothing but night sky and stars filled my view. He leveled out, and I felt each breath expand and contract the massive torso between my legs.

Exhilaration like I'd never felt before filled me. I lifted my head, not wanting to miss a thing. Wind buffeted and cooled my heated cheeks and stung my eyes. I didn't close them, though. I looked around in awe as Oanen soared away from the roof, passing over the parking lot and skimming the tops of the trees. Everything looked dark and peaceful.

With only the soft thwrump of his wings to mark his passing, Oanen moved silently through the night. As soon as he cleared town, he rose higher, and miles passed quickly below us.

In no time, I spotted my house ahead. He started his descent, heading right for it. I squinted at the roof. It looked like something was stuck by the chimney. He flew closer. It looked like a chair. He flew closer, still. I started to panic that he'd crash into the house, but he pulled back at the last moment and landed on the roof with his back feet first.

The feathers under my hands disappeared, and I found myself clinging to Oanen's bare back. He gripped my hands before I could let go and turned in my arms so he was facing me. With little space between us, I stared up at him. His eyes glinted in the weak light.

"Are you going to hit me again, Megan?"

"No. I know this isn't a dream."

His lips twitched, and his hold loosened on my wrists. Instead of stepping away, he reached up with his left hand

and brushed his fingertips along my hairline from temple to jaw. The touch made my heart race. I moved my foot to step back, but he grabbed my arms quickly.

"There's no retreating here. You'll fall." He lifted me, pivoted, and deposited me on the chair wedged against the chimney. The view of his waistline, which was now eye level, made me squeak and scrunch my eyes shut.

"Breaking in was foolish," he said. "What happens when they bring Raiden in to check for scents?"

"Then, I own what I did and tell them they're all assholes for trying to keep stuff from me. You really need pants."

He chuckled, and I listened to the rustle of fabric. When I peeked through one eye, he was just zipping. I opened my eyes and looked up at him.

"Why do you have pants up here? For that matter, why is there a chair?"

"I got tired of standing."

"You've been standing on my roof? Why?"

He sighed and looked out over the trees. I followed his gaze and discovered he had a healthy view of the area surrounding my house.

"I started spending the nights up here after the first body was found. I didn't want you to go through that again, and I wanted to know who did it."

I thought back to all the weird noises I'd heard. Even during the rain. Too many emotions hit me at once. The sweet ache from his willingness to sit up here and lose sleep, in any weather, just for me. The fear over what that indicated. The annoyance that he'd done it all without me knowing. The trepidation for the conversation that still needed to happen.

He moved to the peak of the roof beside me and squatted down on his heels. His expression wasn't so closed off this time. His deep blue gaze held mine, and I could see his interest in me. Megan. The swearing, people puncher.

"Oanen..." My tone held warning, but my stomach twisted when his gaze dipped to my lips. That glance began to erode my resistance.

"Megan..."

He leaned toward me. Everything inside of me went cold then warm.

"I'm a fury," I blurted. "I have anger issues. Well, not issues. Superpowers. They have something to do with what I am."

He stopped his forward progress. I kept talking, panicked.

"That's what the file said anyway. What is a fury? Am I part of the human-eating food chain, too? Honestly, they don't look the least bit tasty. I'd rather hit most of them."

He pulled back and studied me.

"Furies don't eat humans. But, they punish the wicked."

"So, being a fury isn't going to clear my name," I said, disappointed in his answer but relieved we seemed to be respecting personal bubbles again.

"It might help, though," he said.

For a split second, I thought he meant getting back into my personal bubble, and my insides went crazy happy at the idea. His next words set me back on the correct topic.

"Furies can sense the wicked, and I imagine anyone who would kill Camil would need to be pretty wicked."

"You're saying I might be able to sense the killer? How?"

Oanen shrugged lightly.

"I think you'd need to use your superpowers. Why else would Adira keep asking why you thought you were angry with someone?"

Stunned, I sat on my roof in the dark for another moment before the problem with our current location sank in.

"How are we getting down from here?"

He scooped me up in his arms and jumped. I nearly screamed but managed to bury my face against his bare chest instead. The rumble of his laugh and the impact of our touchdown had me lifting my head.

"Not funny," I said.

"No. Cute, though," he said, setting me on my feet.

I swallowed hard and met his gaze as I waged an internal battle. Invite him in or let him go back to the roof?

CHAPTER NINETEEN

THE HINT OF HUMOR IN HIS GAZE ONLY GREW THE LONGER I looked up at him. Oanen had to know what he was doing to me, how conflicted he made me feel.

No, it was how I felt that conflicted me. Why was it so difficult to be near him, yet twice as hard to walk away?

"Have you eaten dinner yet?" I asked.

"No."

"Would you like to? With me? In the house?"

I wanted to smack myself in the head. What was wrong with me?

He smiled widely.

"I'd really like to have dinner with you, Megan."

"Okay." I stepped around him, needing to escape quickly. He didn't allow much distance, though. I heard him following closely behind as I strode to the house.

In the kitchen, I focused on pulling the makings for sandwiches out of the fridge. Like the last time, he sat at the table and watched me move around.

"Something's changed," he said.

"What do you mean?" I asked, not looking up from the plates I'd put on the counter.

"You seem nervous now. Why?"

"Because life is complicated. Because I have no one to talk to about any of it."

"You can talk to me."

His simple words made my heart pound so loudly in my ears that I struggled to think straight. I knew this was the moment to tell him that we wouldn't work. That I was too unpredictable to ever be anyone's girlfriend.

"It's just...I just..."

It felt like I'd swallowed my tongue for a choked moment. Now that the time for the talk was at hand, I wanted to run. With every ounce of willpower I had, I stood my ground and struggled with the words that would make him understand.

"I don't know you, Oanen, and I definitely don't know myself. I feel like I don't know anything. You told me to focus on what I do know, and I'm trying. But anything more than that is—"

"Too much right now. I get it."

I released a slow breath, grateful.

"Good." I turned and brought the sandwiches I'd made to the table. "As long as we're clear, you can stay in the spare room or on the couch tonight. Your pacing on the roof has been keeping me up."

He considered me as I sat then nodded and bit into his sandwich, consuming a quarter of it in one mouthful. I ate my dinner in silence, still unsure if I was making the right choices. Not just with Oanen, but my life.

I was a fury. Now what? Use my anger like a water diviner and seek out the murderer?

"Since I plan on keeping an eye on things," Oanen said, interrupting my thoughts, "I'll clean up down here."

I realized I was playing with the bread crumbs on my plate and took it to the sink.

"Thanks."

"No problem. And, Megan?"

I stopped at the kitchen door and looked back.

"Thanks for letting me stay. Next time, I hope you let me in."

I nodded and, uncertain of his meaning, fled upstairs.

SINGING WOKE ME. Female singing.

I sat up in bed and turned my head toward the door, not believing my ears. Unless Oanen had a third form, there shouldn't have been a sweet female voice singing a current pop hit from within my kitchen.

Easing from bed, I moved to the door. Was that the shower running? I crept down the stairs and caught Eliana busting a dance move in front of my stove.

"Good morning," I said from the kitchen doorway.

She jumped a little but turned with a smile.

"Morning! I'm making you breakfast while Oanen showers. He asked me to bring him a change of clothes for school." Her open smile changed to a knowing smirk. "So... sleepovers, hey?"

"Shut it. He's been standing on my roof like some gargoyle protector."

"Oh come on. He's nothing like a gargoyle. They scare the daylights out of me at night when they take their true forms."

"Wait, gargoyles are real, too?"

She sighed and shook her head at me. "Haven't you figured it out yet? Just about all of the myths are real. Some creatures are misrepresented or exaggerated, but most exist."

The bathroom door opened, and I automatically glanced that direction. My lungs seized, and my brain crashed at the sight of Oanen with a towel wrapped low around his waist. He saw me, and his lips twitched in an almost smile. My heart joined the list of my other malfunctioning organs.

He looked devastating straight out of the shower. Wet strands of his lighter hair hung in short waves around his head. Early morning sunlight reflected off of each damp ridge he possessed. And, the way he moved when he stalked toward me had nothing on the clean, damp smell of him.

"Morning, Megan. Hope you don't mind that I used the shower."

"Oh, she doesn't mind at all," Eliana said, her voice sounding oddly distant.

I glanced over my shoulder at the kitchen and found it empty.

"Put your clothes on already!" she called from outside.

Oanen chuckled, the sound sending a shiver to my belly.

"I'll be back," he said. He grabbed the clothes from the kitchen chair then went upstairs.

Numbly, I walked to the kitchen door. Eliana stood by

her car, her arms crossed and a frown on her face as she looked at me.

"You should take a shower, too," she said. "A cold one."

Instead of listening to her, I went outside and sat on the step. The cool air raised gooseflesh on my exposed arms and legs.

"How do you do it?" I asked.

"Do what?"

"Fight your instincts."

"I don't fight them. I fear them."

She rubbed her arms then walked past me to go inside.

"Breakfast is almost ready," she said.

I nodded but stayed on the step. Instead of dwelling on my non-relationship with Oanen, I turned my thoughts to the instincts I possessed as a fury.

If I could sense the wicked through my anger, as Oanen suggested, I might be able to find the killer. But, so many people made me angry on a daily basis. How would I ever know which was the right one? I couldn't go around trying to beat the truth out of all of them, could I? I shook my head. No. No matter how satisfying it might feel, I didn't want to do that. To become that. Like Eliana, I feared where it might lead. I knew what rejected and alone felt like. I had friends now and didn't want to risk losing them.

After a quick shower of my own, I joined Oanen and Eliana for breakfast then rode with Eliana to school. All the while, my mind remained fixated on the residents of Uttira rather than the students of Girderon Academy. Jesse's death had proven the killer wasn't an unmarked member of Uttira, so I doubted I'd find the killer within the halls of the

Academy. However, my time there wouldn't go to waste. I planned to test my fury power of identifying the wicked.

I stuck with Eliana as much as I could throughout the day. Instead of running to Adira every time someone ticked me off, I asked Eliana questions about the person. I paid attention to what she knew, which wasn't much, and the level of anger I felt. Aubrey still reigned as the top contender for who I'd like to punch in the face when it came to the students. And that made me all the more determined to figure out why. Not an easy task while at the Academy and under Oanen's watchful eye.

By the end of the day, I had a plan.

I waited until we were in the car to involve Eliana.

"Are you up for hanging out tonight?" I asked.

Oanen took flight from the roof and circled above our car as Eliana backed out from her spot.

"Sure. Dinner, too?" she asked. She merged with the flow of cars leaving the Academy grounds.

"Maybe. If there's time."

She glanced at me. "What do you mean?"

"Remember that siren in the hall after our first session?" I asked.

"Yep. Marla."

"And that guy at lunch?"

"Devian."

"Yeah, those two. I want to follow them around tonight and see if I can figure out why they annoy me so much."

Eliana made a face that was a cross between a frown and an "oh-oh".

"Oh, come on. Please?" I begged.

"Yeah, I'll do it. I just hope tonight doesn't result in another dead body. Especially one of ours."

"We'll be fine. We're the perfect team. I kick ass, and you stop me from going too crazy."

"If you had said, 'What could go wrong?' at the end of that little speech, I would have made you walk home. Remember, sirens don't just lure humans with their songs. And, I don't even know what Devian is. We're messing with the unknown."

And that didn't worry me. Not even a little.

Eliana took a right out of the Academy drive.

"So who are we bugging first?" I asked.

"That's Marla's car ahead. I have no idea where she lives. So, we'll need to follow her."

Marla headed out of town going north. After about fifteen minutes, she pulled into a nicer subdivision nestled on the shore of an enormous lake.

"Wow. How far does the barrier go?"

"Around the whole lake. Uttira is larger than it seems because it's sprawled out."

Eliana turned into the subdivision well behind Marla, and we watched the girl's compact yellow car pull into a driveway near the shore. Eliana pulled over and parked on the street.

"You know we're going to get caught, right?"

"That's why you're going to stay in the car, and I'm going on my own. If I'm not back in five minutes, leave without me."

Eliana sighed, which I took as her agreement, and I quickly left the car. Hopefully, my stroll down the sidewalk toward Marla's house looked casual to any observers. The way I pushed through the yard's towering shrub barrier probably didn't, though.

On the other side of the cedars, the soft lilting sound of a sweet voice drew me around to the side of the house. I couldn't make out the words until I was a few feet from the third window. Something about a naughty school girl undressing.

Like some pervy voyeur, I peeked through her window to see what she might be up to. What I saw confused me. She wasn't undressing but sitting on the edge of her bed, filing her nails while singing. She glanced up at the computer on her desk and smirked slightly at the split images of four older men. All of them had their sweaty, flushed faces way too close to their cameras. The sight of their heavy breathing and the expressions on their faces gave away what they were up to.

"Gross," I said under my breath.

I focused on Marla. She looked almost bored as she sang about taking off her underwear, which was damp from all her longing while at school. My anger warred with my need to gag. An alarm went off, and she quickly stood and wrapped herself in a robe.

"You know what this means," she said, ending the song. "My parents will be home soon. If you want to watch me again tomorrow, deposit the money in my account."

She turned off the cameras and went to sit at her computer to bring up a different screen. A list of deposits ranging from fifty dollars to three hundred filled the window. She smiled as two new deposits came in, then stood and removed the robe over her clothes. Using a remote, she reset an alarm on her desk, turned on her camera, and started her song again. This time it was a bit dirtier. Instead of singing about undressing, she sang about undressing and touching herself.

What the men thought they were watching was a lie, an illusion cast by her siren's song. She was cheating them. Definitely something I'd define as wicked. Yet, these were all older men who shouldn't have been watching her in the first place. I didn't really feel too badly for them.

I ducked away from the window and retraced my steps back to the car.

"That was seven minutes," Eliana said as soon as I opened the door.

"Good thing you didn't leave. Now, we need to find Devian."

She rolled her eyes at me and turned around, heading out of the subdivision.

"How are we supposed to do that? I don't know where he lives."

"Who would?"

"Oanen, but I don't think we should ask him. He's probably already freaking out and looking for us because we aren't at your house."

I chose to ignore all Oanen conversation for the moment.

"What's plan B? There's always a plan B."

"We go to the Roost and see who's there who might know. Anyone born and raised here is a likely candidate." She started the car and turned around. "Getting that person to tell us what we want to know will be a problem, though. If you haven't noticed, people in Uttira like to keep to themselves."

The Roost was livelier than I'd thought it would be for a

Monday afternoon. Music thumped inside like always, and bodies filled the dance floor.

I immediately saw who we needed. Fenris danced in the middle of his swarm of females.

"Stay here," I said to Eliana.

Without hesitation, I strode into the crowd. Aubrey saw me first and stiffened. Fenris noticed and turned. As soon as he saw me, he smiled warmly.

"Hey, Megan."

"Hey, Fenris. Can I talk to you for a minute?"

"Sure."

Aubrey immediately grabbed his arm in a cloyingly possessive way.

"Alone, Aubrey," I said. "You can keep your jealousy in check for five minutes, can't you?" My anger begged for her to lunge at me.

Her face flushed scarlet, and I waited, anticipating her next move.

"Keep dancing," Fenris said, patting her hand. "I'll be right back."

Fenris extracted himself, and we moved off to the side without incident. I tried not to look disappointed.

"What's up?" he asked.

"I'm wondering if you know anything about Devian, a kid from school. Where does he go when sessions let out? Where does he live?"

Fenris thought about it for a moment then looked at the people on the dance floor.

"His girlfriend's out there. Give me a minute, and I can probably find out for you."

"Thank you."

He disappeared into the crowd of dancers, and Eliana joined me.

"Did he know?"

"No. He's going to ask Devian's girlfriend."

"Nice."

Aubrey chose that moment to stride toward us. I grinned widely and fisted my hands. Before I could take a step forward, Eliana pushed me back into the nearby couch and sat on my lap, wrapping her arms around me.

All the anger I felt left in an instant.

"Oh, don't you two look cute," Aubrey said with a sneer. "I've warned you, Megan. You keep messing with what's mine, and I'm going to start messing with what's yours."

"Oanen would kick your butt," Eliana said, her words loud in my ear since she was hugging me so close.

"Not Oanen, you dumb box. You."

Her head popped up from my shoulder.

"You think I'm Megan's?"

Eliana's peel of laughter turned several heads before she smothered her giggles in my hair. I couldn't help but grin, too. Aubrey's face grew redder.

"Aubrey, what are you doing over here?" Fenris said, re-emerging from the dancers.

"Talking to Megan."

"I see. Well, while you were talking to Megan, Nala and Brin left with Jenna."

"What?" Aubrey turned on her heel and marched out the door.

Eliana released her tight hold on me and climbed off my

lap. A wisp of anger poked at me, but faded as Aubrey moved further from the Roost.

Fenris offered his hand, a polite but unnecessary gesture that I accepted. His warm fingers wrapped around mine, and he gave a tug, helping me to my feet. Instead of releasing me when I stood, he pulled me into his arms and hugged me close.

Eliana wiggled her eyebrows at me over his shoulder while he inhaled deeply then whispered Devian's address in my ear. Just as quickly as he'd hugged me, he released me and walked away.

"I'm starting to think you're at least half succubus," she teased.

"Shut up. Let's go."

We left the Roost and made our way to the address Fenris had obtained for us. Eliana gave me knowing looks the entire ride to the non-descript white house that sat in a rural area just outside of town.

She slowed down to pull over until we saw the front door open. She quickly resumed speed and passed by but not before I caught sight of Devian French kissing a girl on his front step. Since Fenris had obtained the address from Devian's girlfriend, I was pretty sure I'd just witnessed him cheating on her. I'd definitely classify that as wicked.

"Should I turn around and go back?" Eliana asked.

"No. I think I have my answers now."

"What answers? To what questions?"

"The answer to how a fury finds the wicked."

"Fury?" She glanced at me. "That's what you are?"

"Yeah. You mean Oanen didn't tell you this morning?"

"No. He just called and told me to bring some clean clothes for him to your house. How did you find out?"

"I broke into Adira's office."

"No way."

"Yeah. Oanen found me before Trammer did. And by the way, mermaids are creepy as hell when they sleep."

"I don't even know where to start. What did following Marla and Devian answer? How did Oanen find you? Were you ever going to tell me? Does this mean you have to hate me now?"

Her eyes started to water with the last question.

"Whoa, what? Why would I hate you?"

"Furies punish the wicked. I can't think of any creature more wicked than a succubus."

"Seriously, if you weren't driving and I wasn't afraid of crashing, I'd power hug you right now. I don't know much about being a fury, but I do know that I won't let what I am change how I feel about my best friend. Ever."

She sniffled lightly. "Stop. You're making me even more emotional; I get hungrier when I'm emotional."

"Okay. Subject change. We were following Marla and Devian as a test. Oanen theorized that I can sense the wicked through my temper. Those two mildly upset me today."

Eliana snorted.

"If I hadn't held your hand, you would have tried to hit Devian."

"Well, that's because he's cheating on his girlfriend. I don't like cheaters."

"Why don't you get mad at Fenris, then?"

"He's very open with his interest, and he's not committed to Aubrey, despite what she believes."

"So every time you're angry at someone there's a wicked reason?"

"Based on tonight, that seems to be the case. I'm not done testing it yet."

"What do you mean? What more do you still need to do?"

"I need to follow my temper to Camil's killer."

CHAPTER TWENTY

Oanen stood on the front porch of my house when we pulled into the driveway. His gaze locked onto me. Arms crossed and looking more stoic than usual, he stepped off the porch and followed the car.

"You are in so much trouble," Eliana said.

"Me? Why just me?"

She just shook her head as she parked behind the house.

When I opened the door, he was there, crowding my space.

"What did you do?" he asked softly.

"Do? Why do you think I did something?"

"Because you're an hour late. Because I circled town looking for you, and you weren't there. That means you went somewhere else. For a girl who likes staying away from people, it seems odd that you'd suddenly want to roam around Uttira. Unless it wasn't idle roaming. Unless you had a specific goal. Like looking for a killer."

"Ha!" I said with a triumphant grin. "I was not looking for the killer."

He continued to stare down at me, and I rolled my eyes.

"I had to test what you said to see if it was true. Does my anger indicate a wicked person? I believe it does. I also believe the level of anger hints at the level of wickedness."

"I repeat…what did you do?"

"I followed a siren home and watched her scam some rather nasty older men out of their money. I also saw a guy cheating on his girlfriend. That's it."

He exhaled slowly.

"Megan, when I suggested using your abilities to find the killer, I didn't mean alone."

I frowned. "I wasn't. I had Eliana."

He leaned forward, placing each hand on the roof of the car and caging me in. My chest grew tight and a flutter started in my belly. Vaguely, I heard the kitchen door slam shut as I stared up into his deep blue eyes.

"With me, Megan. You go with me."

His gaze held mine until I nodded. Then, it dipped to my lips. My heart beat painfully in my chest, and I forgot to keep breathing.

He closed his eyes and sighed.

"What do you want to do next?" he asked.

My brain hiccupped on that question. What did I want? I wanted him to do something about that longing look, didn't I? No. I didn't. It was too dangerous. Just standing like this was too dangerous. It felt like a fire was starting inside my stomach. That couldn't be good for either of us. He was already too far under my skin.

"Do you have any idea who the murderer might be?"

That froze the flames that had been licking at my insides.

"What?"

He leaned away from me and released his hold on the car.

"What did you plan to do once you verified that you could use your powers like I said?"

I tried not to blush that I'd misunderstood his first question so thoroughly. He'd been asking what I'd wanted to do next to find the killer.

"I thought I'd spend more time in town around the adults."

"And when you got angry at one?"

"Eliana has my back with her ninja hugging skills."

"You need to take this seriously."

"I am."

"You're talking about adults. People who've had years to hone their skills, not the fledglings in the Academy. Do you know what to do if you piss off a Gorgon? A Sphinx? How about a Minator?"

"Yeah, I hit them."

His hands suddenly cupped my head.

"You are killing me."

I jerked my head from his gentle grasp.

"Don't even joke about that." I pushed past him and stomped into the house.

Eliana, who sat at the table while looking out the window with an unfocused gaze, jumped at the sound of the door. She looked at me then over my shoulder. I didn't miss the hint of black in her eyes.

"You okay?" I asked.

"Yep." Her smile didn't reach her eyes. "I'm not feeling

up for company, though, so I think I'll head home." She stood and escaped the kitchen before I could blink.

"I'll see you in the morning," she called from outside.

She'd left me alone with Oanen. Again.

I looked away from the door to where he leaned against the counter. He watched me with that same careful study he had since the moment I'd punched him in the face weeks ago.

"I have some things I need to do." He straightened away from the counter. "Do you promise to wait for me before going to town?"

"I don't plan on going tonight."

"Whenever you plan to go, do you promise to wait?"

"Yeah. Sure."

He didn't look like he believed me and took a step in my direction.

"I promise. Geez."

He gave me a long look then moved toward the door.

"Am I camping on the roof again, or is your spare room still available?"

Part of me seriously considered saying he could camp. But, despite my irrational temper, I wasn't that mean.

"The spare room is yours until the killer's found."

"Thank you."

He walked out the door, and I focused on pulling out dinner from the fridge rather than watching him strip for take-off. It didn't matter where I looked, though. My imagination gave me all the imagery I needed to match each wisp of sound before his wings beat loudly in the air.

Once he was gone, I brought his folded clothes inside

and set to work preparing all the ingredients for tacos. The activity kept my hands busy but not my mind.

Adira wanted me at the Academy, attending sessions, which meant not being in town when most of the adults were out and about. If I couldn't be in town when the adults were, how could I ever hope to find the killer? A thought brought my head up. I stared out the window and grinned at my genius.

Maybe I didn't need to wander. Two deaths. Both human. Maybe I just needed to stay around the humans.

ELIANA AND OANEN had different plans the next morning.

"What do you mean we're not going? I thought skipping school meant Trammer would come knocking on my door."

"We're not skipping," Eliana said. "We called in and said we couldn't attend today and possibly not tomorrow."

"And Adira was fine with 'hey, I don't feel like coming in today'?"

"We let her know that we're going to town to help you work on your anger," Oanen said. "She only asked that you email her a report with the names of the people who upset you along with a reason why you think they upset you."

An Academy sanctioned leave of absence? I could live with that.

"By the way, thanks for setting dinner aside for me last night," Oanen said. "I didn't think I was going to be gone that long."

"No problem," I said, quickly standing and taking my plate to the sink. I didn't miss Eliana's knowing smirk.

She had made us breakfast again. Only this time when I'd come downstairs, Oanen had already been showered and dressed. It didn't matter. Having him here in any form distracted me in a really weird way. Like I kept wanting to look at him and just stare. As soon as we found the killer, I'd need to tell him he had to stop stalking my roof and sleeping in my guest room. I'd never be able to focus enough to figure out what being a fury meant with him around.

"So where are we going to start?" I asked.

"To keep what we're doing a secret, I thought we could start with the shops and look for a new top since your old one has Taser holes in it," Eliana said.

"You want to actually shop?"

She nodded, grinning widely. I shrugged.

"Fine."

Twenty minutes later, I stood in a dressing room trying on a top that Eliana had picked out for me.

"It's too tight," I said, attempting to wiggle it into place.

"It's supposed to be tight," she said from the other side of the door.

"I don't like tight. I like breathing."

Another shirt appeared over the edge of the door. This one had a modest heart-shaped neckline with a hint of shimmer to the loose material. I wiggled out of the strangler and gave the new option a try. The darker color looked good on me.

Smiling, I opened the door. Oanen sat in the chair opposite the changing room. His relaxed, leaning position didn't change when I stepped out, but the look in his eyes did. Appreciation replaced bored disinterest.

"Megan," Eliana said from beside him, drawing my attention, "that looks amazing on you. It falls over your curves instead of hugging them." A blush colored her cheeks as she spoke.

"Talking about my curves embarrasses you?" I asked.

"That's the first time I've ever heard her use the word," Oanen said.

Eliana narrowed her eyes at him.

"You keep it up, and you're waiting outside each shop."

"Each shop?" I said. "There's no point. Look around. There's no one here. Where do all the mark bearers go every day?"

"A lot of them have day jobs outside of Uttira."

I groaned. "Why didn't you tell me that?" Before the festival, the market district had been teeming with people at this hour. When I'd planned to spend more time in town, it was because I'd thought it would be full of people again.

"How do these businesses stay open?"

"They make their money off the unmarked, like us."

Frustrated, I returned to the dressing room to change out of the shirt. If the adults weren't in town, then there was no point for us to stay, either.

I stepped out again and stopped at the sight of Eliana's large, pleading eyes.

"Please don't say we have to go home. I've never been able to shop like this. Adira will count this as progress."

I snorted. "Progress? You're not the one trying on the hootchy shirts."

"Picking them out counts. It's a baby step."

Sighing, I rolled my eyes and nodded. She clapped and took the shirt from my hands.

"We're getting this, right?"

"Sure."

We walked toward the register where the woman sat reading a novel. She looked up at us and smiled.

"Find what you needed?"

"Yes, thank you," Eliana said, sliding the shirt onto the counter.

The woman started to ring up the purchase. Everything was fine until I handed her a fifty, and she opened the cash drawer.

Anger slammed into me. I reached out for Eliana's hand. Instead of connecting with her small, cool fingers, strong warm ones clasped mine. The shock of holding Oanen's hand distracted me from my anger.

"Here's your change," the woman said, holding out a few bills.

When I didn't reach for them, Eliana did.

"Thank you," she said.

"Enjoy the shirt."

Oanen led me toward the door. I stared at our joined hands, my insides flaring hotter and hotter by the second. At the last minute, I recalled the anger and looked back in time to see the woman slip my fifty from the drawer.

As soon as we reached the sidewalk, I eased my hand from Oanen's. Heat had spread from my stomach to my face.

"Are you okay?" Eliana asked.

"Yeah. She stole money from the cash drawer as we were leaving. I didn't feel anything toward her until I handed over the fifty. As soon as I did, it's like I knew she would do something wicked the moment she thought of it."

"Wow. That's pretty nifty," Eliana said.

I grinned at her. "Nifty?"

"What? It is. We're still shopping some more, right?"

I sighed and ignored the fact Oanen was still watching me closely.

"Lead the way."

I ROLLED over in my bed, pretending to sleep. Pretending that I couldn't hear Eliana singing in the kitchen or Oanen moving around in the shower.

The routine of the last few days was getting under my skin. No, it wasn't the routine. It was Oanen. I didn't know what to do about him. No, that wasn't it, either. I knew what I needed to do, and I hated it. Pushing him away now was better than having him wash his hands of me later. It was safer for both of us if I walked away now. Wasn't it? My insides churned at the thought.

The internal conflict was tearing me apart, and since I didn't know how to resolve it, I planned to hide from it. Besides, there was no reason to get out of bed today.

After that first day's success, we'd gone to town every day that week with Adira's blessing. Sure, I'd identified a few people involved with petty crimes. And I now better understood how the degree of my anger corresponded with the level of the person's wickedness. But, during all that time, I hadn't come close to feeling the level of anger I would have thought could be associated with murder.

Downstairs, the singing stopped, and the kitchen door opened and closed. My eyes widened. Eliana wasn't leaving me alone again, was she?

A minute later, Eliana's voice, just outside my bedroom door, made me jump.

"Get out of bed already. He's gone."

I rolled over and looked at her.

"For how long?"

"Until tonight. I thought we could keep binge watching our shows."

Relieved, I got out of bed. We talked, snacked, watched our shows, and relaxed until after dinner when Eliana's phone beeped with a new message.

She made a face as she read it.

"What's up?"

"Oanen's parents are worried that I'm not socializing enough for a young succubus. They want me to go to the Roost tonight."

I made the same face she'd made a moment ago. I didn't want to spend the evening alone. Not when Oanen had an open invitation to stay over.

"Do you have to?" I asked.

"If I don't, they'll just bring up their concerns to Adira, who will push harder for me to do stuff I really don't want to do. The Quill's mean well. They really do worry that I'm not...eating right." Her face paled with the words, and I could see the dread in her eyes.

"Want me to go with you?" I offered.

"Would you? I know you're tired of town."

"Of course I'll go. Tired or not, it's more fun hanging out with you at the Roost than watching TV alone." I stood and grinned at her. "Besides, I wanna be there when you wear that dress I picked out for you."

Her previously celebratory smile started to fade.

"Come on. Don't be a chicken. You wear your dress, and I'll wear mine."

She laughed and clapped. Of course she would. My dress was far worse than hers.

CHAPTER TWENTY-ONE

"STOP TUGGING," I SAID, SLAPPING ELIANA'S HAND AWAY from her neckline.

"I feel sick," she said, staring at the Roost's red double doors.

"No, you don't. You feel nervous. There's a difference."

"Let's go back to your place."

"No way. I want to see the boys fall all over themselves when they see you in this."

"This" was a tube dress topped with capped sleeves. And, it was a far cry from the typical, prim mid-calf sundresses Eliana usually wore. We both knew the dress would cause every head inside to turn. The material clung to every curve that Eliana owned. And that fact was freaking Eliana out.

I met her nervous gaze. Her makeup looked flawless and natural. The quiver in her glossy lips didn't convey any sense of "I am succubus, hear me roar" but rather damsel in distress. I thought the latter would prove more potent in this crowd.

"You're going to knock the socks off of everyone in there. There's going to be fighting and mayhem because of you. If I'm lucky, I'll get to throw in a few punches in defense of your honor."

She snorted, my words erasing the look of fear in her eyes, as I'd hoped.

"You can't fight tonight. That dress wouldn't survive."

The dress I wore, a black tube that barely reached below the curve of my butt cheeks and the top of my boobs, didn't need to survive more than one night, anyway. I never planned to wear the dumb thing again.

"We'll see," I said, reaching for the door.

We walked into the Roost together, the beat of the music rattling my rib cage. No sultry singers swayed on the stage tonight. Everyone was crammed onto the dance floor.

As I expected, it didn't take long for people to start noticing us. Not that we dressed so seductively compared to the rest of the crowd. I was pretty sure the girl wearing the dress with the opaque panel over her boobs won the seductive, yet tacky, dress contest.

Eliana leaned in to talk so I could hear her.

"I see Ashlyn at the back table. Let's go talk to her."

I nodded and let her lead the way. It wasn't like we were at the Roost to actually socialize. It was about appearances. Eliana needed to look like she was socializing and trying to become more like a typical succubus.

Before we made it to Ashlyn's table, Fenris stepped out from the mob on the floor.

"Ladies," he said, holding his arms out wide. "What a spectacular sight. Come dance."

"Thank you, but we wanted to talk to Ashlyn before she has to go," Eliana said.

"Tell me you'll dance with us afterward, then."

Aubrey chose that moment to step from the crowd. The annoyance that had simmered in the back of my mind flared into full anger. I'd witnessed Aubrey's meanness and certainly thought her level of bullying and bitchery qualified as wicked. But wicked enough for this much anger? No. There was more to Aubrey's story, and I really wanted to know what...after I punched her teeth in.

I stepped toward Fenris, who was unaware of Aubrey closing in behind him.

His arms wrapped around me. Aubrey's eyes widened. Deciding this a better punishment, I wrapped my arms around Fenris in return and ran my fingers through the hair on the back of his head. Chest to chest, I looked up into his amused gaze.

"Get rid of your dead weight, and we'll dance with you all night long," I said.

"Bitch!" Aubrey screeched.

I laughed, and Fenris made a sound that fell somewhere between a groan and a sigh.

"Troublemaker," he said softly before releasing me.

He turned to Aubrey, his hands up in a placating manner. She didn't even spare him a glance. She flew at me, knocking him to the side.

I grinned widely and widened my stance, ready for her. Her curled fingers, now tipped with vicious claws, swiped through the air at my face. I leaned back, avoiding the strike, and swung hard, connecting with Aubrey's left cheek. She snarled and snapped her teeth at me. Dancing out of the way, I waited for my next opening then planted my fist in her ribs. Instead of my anger being alleviated, it burned brighter.

"Come on, Aubrey, tell me your sins," I said softly. "Tell me what wicked things you have planned."

She growled and tried coming at me again. This time Fenris wrapped his arms around her and pulled her off her feet. Slim arms encircled me. I sighed and didn't try to struggle like Aubrey did. I didn't want to hurt Eliana or lose the meager coverage of my dress.

A shrill whistle pierced the air. I turned my head and looked at Trammer, who was glaring at all of us.

"Break it up or take your animalistic hides outside where you belong."

"Come on," Eliana said in my ear, tugging me toward the rear of the building.

While Trammer gave Aubrey's still struggling form a final disgusted glare, Eliana and I took a seat at the table near Ashlyn. The moment Eliana released my hand a flood of anger robbed me of breath. I froze in the act of sitting and looked up at Trammer, who moved toward us. No, not us, but Ashlyn. I tensed, liking that he would never see me coming.

Eliana gripped me with more strength than I thought she possessed and dragged me down beside her. We'd barely settled into our seats when Oanen strode through the crowd, straight toward us. My stomach dipped at the sight of him even as the sound of Trammer's voice needled at my insides. Eliana kept her arm wrapped around my bare shoulders, muting the shit storm of rage that wanted to break its way in.

"Five minutes alone and you managed to fight," Oanen said, looking down at me.

I shrugged like it was no big deal, which it wasn't. The move drew his gaze to my bare shoulders. The look in his eyes changed, and I recalled the time that I'd thought that look was a detached study of me. I couldn't have been more wrong.

He held out his hand, and my pulse jumped.

"Come."

I glanced at Trammer, who was waiting for his niece to gather her things, then shook my head at Oanen.

"I can't leave Eliana right now."

He cocked his head at me, and his hand slowly returned to his side. He stood there in silence as Trammer and Ashlyn moved toward the front door. As soon as it closed, he offered his hand again.

Eliana released me and gave me a shove.

"Go. I'll be fine alone for a bit. Good practice," she said.

I hesitated a moment then lifted my hand to Oanen's. The first touch of his warm fingers against mine made me shiver. He saw it but didn't comment as he helped me stand. Holding my hand in his, he turned and led the way toward the dancers. I really didn't want to dance.

He didn't stop in their midst but pushed his way toward the stairs to the second floor. The whole way up the stairs, I could barely concentrate on each step because his thumb kept moving over my knuckles. If he didn't quit it, I'd trip soon.

Passing the bar, he moved to a door at the far end. Cool night air brushed my face as soon as he pushed it open. We stepped out on a metal landing then went up the stairs that led to the roof. Gravel crunched under my heels, and I looked over at the neon sign for the Roost.

Oanen stopped walking and turned toward me.

"I was getting dressed right here. Even with the loud music and a layer of tar and gravel, I could hear your voice when you told Fenris to get rid of Aubrey." He swallowed and looked down at my hand, which he still held.

"Do you care for him?" he asked quietly.

"Fenris?"

"Yes."

With my insides going wild, I studied Oanen's tense face.

"Fenris is just a friend. Friends are all I can do."

He looked up, his intense gaze pinning me.

"Why? You've learned a lot this past week. You're no longer in the dark about who you are."

"Exactly. And that's why friends are all I can do. Because of what I am. What I've learned this last week has only made things clearer for me. Getting close to anyone is dangerous. Except for maybe Eliana."

"You're afraid of hurting someone."

"I'm afraid of hurting someone I like." More importantly, I was afraid of someone I liked hurting me.

"Maybe the person you like just needs to understand the rules and not do anything wrong."

His words made my chest ache worse. His thumb brushed over my knuckles again, and I realized he was only doing it to my right hand. The one I'd used to hit Aubrey. The soothing gesture swayed me further. Dangerous territory.

I turned my head away and looked at the building's

sign, trying to gain some mental distance from my distracting physical reaction to Oanen.

"Would you be willing to fly me to Trammer's house?" I asked.

"Now?"

I took a long, slow breath and let go of my regret.

"Yeah. I think now would be best. Since the moment I arrived in Uttira, that man has pissed me off for no explainable reason. I need to find out why."

"Okay." Oanen released my hand and turned toward a low set of lockers just behind the sign. He opened one and took off his shirt, throwing it inside.

I took a moment to stare shamelessly at his muscled torso. Was I being stupid for saying no to that? Probably. But it was safer this way.

Turning my back to him, I listened to the soft rustle of clothing as he stripped for flight. At the soft scratch of his claws on the gravel, I faced him once more. He dipped his shoulder to me, an elegant gesture that drew me closer. At the last minute, I kicked off my heels.

"Eyes forward. My dress is way too short for this."

He made a quiet noise then turned his head toward the sign. I lifted my leg over his broad back and settled in behind his wings, his downy feathers caressing my thighs.

"All set," I said.

He turned his head and bumped my leg with his beak before beating his powerful wings. Within seconds, we were in the air, circling over the buildings.

It didn't take Oanen long to find Trammer's house. He set down not far from the driveway. I quickly climbed off and stepped back, but Oanen didn't return to his human form. Tucking his wings, he walked beside me as I crept up the driveway.

Like at the siren's house, I peeked through windows until I found the pair. Ashlyn sat in the living room, reading a book. Trammer moved around in the kitchen, preparing an obviously late dinner.

"What are you hungry for, Hun?" he asked, his muffled voice barely reaching me through the window.

"I'm not really hungry," she said absently and without looking up.

"Ashlyn, you need to eat."

"I did eat. I had fish sticks today."

He stopped moving around in the kitchen and ran a hand through his greying hair.

"That's not enough. You need to eat dinner, too."

"I know Uncle Tram. I will."

He came into the living room and sat across from her.

"I'm worried about you," he said gently.

She closed her book and looked up at him.

"Why? I'm fine."

He shook his head.

"I want you to stay away from Megan and Eliana. They're trouble."

She gave him a doubtful look.

"I like Eliana. She's nice."

"How can you say that after what those monsters did to your father?" Trammer asked, not unkindly.

"I thought that was an accident," I whispered to Oanen.

He bumped me lightly with his head, likely a warning to be quiet.

"You need to let go of your anger," Ashlyn said from

inside. "I did. It was an accident. Human or other, we all make mistakes."

Again, Ashlyn struck me as a truly nice person. Like Eliana.

Trammer stood, his face flushed. He didn't yell at her, though. He patted her shoulder and went back to the kitchen. She watched him go with a sad look in her eyes then picked up her book once more.

I didn't understand how someone, who obviously cared so much for another person, could be making me so angry. Seeing that they were settling in for the night, I backed away from the window and turned toward Oanen.

He dipped his shoulder, an invitation to take flight again. I barely paid attention to the houses passing beneath us. My mind dwelled on the puzzle of Trammer until Oanen landed on the Roost's roof.

I quickly slid off Oanen's back, and feathers abruptly vanished as he shifted to his human form. I squeaked, and turned around again, his soft chuckle teasing me.

"What were you hoping to see back there?" he asked.

"I'm not sure. Something wicked? There has to be a reason Trammer makes me so angry," I said as I picked up my shoes. "I mean, sure he's carrying a grudge for anything non-human because of Ashlyn's father's death, but that doesn't scream wicked killer. If anything, it screams just the opposite because the people dying are human."

The muted thump of the music didn't cover up the sound of Oanen dressing again.

"I don't know, either," he said. "His dislike for us is why he made a good candidate for human liaison. He's less likely to be corrupted by any of us."

"How long ago did Ashlyn's father die?"

"About a year."

The music suddenly grew louder as the main entrance to the Roost opened below. A long, catcall-whistle pierced the air.

"You are looking fine tonight," a male voice said.

"Of course I am." Heels clicked on the sidewalk. "I'm surprised you haven't been run out of here already. You must be sneakier than most."

Oanen frowned and moved toward the edge of the building. I followed, and we stared down at a man dressed in jeans and a leather jacket who spoke to a girl wearing skintight black pants, hooker heels, and a revealing top. My temper flared looking at both of them.

As we watched, the man reached into his pocket and produced a small baggie.

"Since you're looking so fine tonight, how about I give you a free sample?" he asked.

"I have a better idea." She started singing about how he wanted to give her all his money then go slam a car door on his pecker. Oanen stepped back from the ledge as the guy began to hand over his money.

"I need to go tell my parents there's another drug dealer here. There's something about Uttira that seems to attract them."

A car door slammed, and Oanen flinched at the sound of the man's hoarse yell.

"Have Eliana take you home," he said a moment before he shifted, ripping his clothes right off.

Unable to help myself, I looked over the side of the

building once more. The sobbing man clung to the side of the car, his pants loose around his waist.

The siren had done Uttira a favor, but I still wanted to punish her for stealing from the guy. How messed up was that?

CHAPTER TWENTY-TWO

THE MUSIC PULSED LOUDLY AND THE LIGHTS FLASHED annoyingly when I went back inside the Roost.

Moving to the second-floor railing, I looked down at the dancers. They were all having a great time, completely ignorant of the man screaming outside. Or maybe they had great hearing, like Oanen, but didn't care. Probably the latter. And that made life seem just a little too messed up, even for a seventeen-year-old fury. Granted, my life had never been "normal," but I longed to know what "normal" felt like now more than I ever had in the past.

My gaze locked on Fenris and his group of girls, who danced in the middle of the crowded floor. He looked bored and completely miserable. Maybe normal, or at least our version of normal, wasn't that great anyway. His would improve, though, if he would just walk away from his groupies.

Shaking off my reverie, I made my way down the stairs and skirted around the dancers. A few people nodded to me, but I didn't slow. I wanted to get outside and check for that siren.

Eliana waited for me at the back table right where I'd left her and stood as soon as she saw me.

"About time," she said. "What happened?

"We'll talk about it outside."

She slipped her hand into mine, and we both moved toward the door.

Fenris called my name, and I stopped to look back at him. He motioned for us to come join them. His gaze pleaded with me. I shook my head and nodded toward the front door. He gave a playful frown but waved us off. Behind him, Aubrey gave us her usual evil glare.

Ignoring her, I tugged Eliana out the door. The man who had tried giving drugs to the siren still leaned against the car, his face pressed to the roof as quiet sobs shook his shoulders. Eliana gave him a puzzled look.

I released her hand, letting my emotions flood me again, and motioned for her to stay there. The knowledge of the man's damage to himself didn't reduce the incredible amount of anger I felt for him. However, it did allow a very human amount of pity.

I walked toward the man, my bare feet not making a sound on the pavement.

"Do you want me to open the door for you?"

The sound of my voice made him jump, which made him groan and gasp while frantically nodding his head. I reached between him and the car and pulled on the handle. He cried out as he fell to the sidewalk, clutching at his groin.

Having freed him, I no longer felt pity, only disgust. I turned and walked back to Eliana.

"What the hell was that about?" she asked, still staring at the man.

"That was a drug deal gone wrong. A siren took his money and made him slam his dick in the car door."

Eliana winced.

"Yeah, that's what I thought. The guy's an asshole, but the punishment seemed a bit cruel. Ready?"

"Shouldn't we tell someone about him?"

"Oanen flew to tell his parents. I'm sure someone's on their way, and that guy's not going anywhere."

She tore her pitying gaze from him and nodded at me. But, before we made it more than a step, a shimmering hole appeared before us. Adira stepped through and gave us both a warm smile.

"I'm very proud of you, Eliana. I think you dressed beautifully tonight. Any luck?" she asked.

"Luck?" Eliana said. Then a flush covered her cheeks. "Not really. I wasn't trying for that. Baby steps, right? I have a very succubus style dress on."

Adira reached out and gave Eliana's arm a gentle squeeze.

"You've done very well. Progress is good; just make sure to keep moving forward."

"What are you going to do to him?" I asked, tilting my head toward the man behind us.

She looked down at the man, and her expression hardened.

"He is going to have his memory wiped and be

removed from Uttira. There are other human towns he can terrorize instead of ours."

"Do you need help with him?" I asked.

"No, you two are free to continue your evening. I will see you on Monday, Megan. We can talk about your report regarding your week-long break in town."

I nodded, hiding my disappointment. At the end of each day this week, I'd fulfilled her request and had sent an email with names and conjectured reasons about why those people might have ticked me off. Each email had ended with a request to do the same thing the next day. Adira hadn't answered today's email, and I'd already guessed she wanted me back in class before she'd just confirmed it.

Adira stepped past us, and Eliana and I quickly moved to her car. I got in with a sigh of relief.

"Well?" Eliana said as she started the car. "What happened? Why were you gone so long?"

"Adira's been telling me to evaluate why someone is making me angry, right? There are two people in this town who have made me angry since day one. The first is Aubrey. She's a bitch, and she's underage. So, she is obviously not the killer. The other person is Trammer.

"Oanen flew me to Trammer's house so I could try to get a sense of why I might be so angry with him, like Adira keeps suggesting I do. Only, we get there, and Trammer's super sweet to Ashlyn and making dinner and all concerned about her. Doesn't seem like someone who's wicked, does it?"

"Not really," she agrees.

"And not only is he super sweet to his niece, he's got a grudge against anyone not human, which according to

Oanen makes Trammer a perfect liaison. Now, if the bodies that keep showing up were creatures like us, I could totally see Trammer as a suspect. But, they're human. Trammer has no reason to kill humans."

"Well, maybe Jesse but not Camil," Eliana said.

"What do you mean?"

"Jessie was a human trafficker, right? Human. But, he didn't know we weren't human."

"So you think Trammer would want to kill Jesse because of human trafficking?"

The light in the car dimmed as we left town.

"If you were a human adult trying to protect a human niece, wouldn't you?"

I frowned.

"You're right. Jesse's death makes more sense than Camil's. But, why kill Jesse if his mind was wiped, and Trammer had orders to remove him? Removing him from Uttira would have removed the threat from his niece."

"True."

Yeah. True, but something about Trammer still pissed me off. And, until I knew what, could I afford to make any assumptions of innocence when my anger was telling me otherwise?

I took my phone out and sent Oanen a text.

I think we need to follow Trammer when he takes the guy out of town.

I'll be at your place in 10.

"What are you thinking about?" Eliana asked.

"I'm not sure. I just think there's a reason I'm angry at Trammer, and I shouldn't give up on finding out why. I've asked Oanen to help me follow Trammer when he leaves town with the guy from tonight."

She slowed and pulled into my driveway.

"If Oanen's going to come to get you in a little while, I might as well go home." She parked by the back door. "Call me when you're done, though, okay?"

"I will."

I ran inside and up the stairs. Riding a griffin in a dress once had been enough for me. Stripping from my dress, I kicked it aside and quickly put on jeans and a dark, long-sleeved shirt, which I layered with a hoodie for warmth.

Jogging back downstairs, I pulled my hair into a ponytail and drank down a glass of water. When Oanen landed in my backyard, I was outside and ready.

"I hope you know where to go," I said, climbing on his back.

He launched himself into the air, his wings beating hard to gain altitude. Once we soared well above my house, he took off south toward the barrier.

"Just don't run into the thing," I shouted.

A booming cry answered me.

He circled over a section of road twice then started to descend. Just before we dipped below the trees, I caught a glimpse of approaching headlights. Oanen set down near the tree line beside the road. I quickly hopped off his back and ducked behind a tree. Oanen shifted to his skin and moved behind me.

"We should have brought you clothes," I said softly, not taking my eyes off the road.

"I don't feel the temperature unless it's really cold."

"I wasn't worried about you. I was worried about me."

He chuckled, and I blushed.

Trammer's police car sped past and kept going down the road through the barrier.

"I wish we could follow him through that," I said.

"Me, too."

The faint smell of burnt hair reminded me not to think too hard about leaving Uttira. With Oanen standing behind me, I didn't feel the least bit cold. I did, however, feel very nervous. Why hadn't I thought to grab the pants he'd left at my house?

"You looked nice tonight," Oanen said.

My fading blush re-ignited.

"Thank you."

"I wish I would have been there when you arrived. I would have liked to dance."

Heat flared in my middle.

"We need to focus," I said.

"I am focused."

"On watching for Trammer," I clarified.

"I don't think he'll be back anytime soon. The nearest town is a twenty-five minute drive from here. There and back? That's close to an hour. So we have time to pick up our conversation from the roof."

"Huh?"

"The conversation where you were trying to tell me you don't date."

My throat burned, and sweat beaded my forehead as my pulse jumped into hyper speed.

"Are you serious right now?" I asked.

The bark of the tree bit into my palms as I pressed harder against it.

Oanen's hand settled on my shoulders.

"I have excellent hearing, Megan. You need to calm down. We're talking. You're not angry, which means I'm not doing anything wrong."

The approach of headlights from the south saved me from saying anything. With increasing anger, I watched the maroon car speed through the barrier and blinked at the driver.

"Wasn't that—"

"Yeah. Trammer. Hop on." The fallen leaves rustled behind me. When I turned, Oanen dipped his feathered shoulder for me to climb onto his back.

I gripped him tightly as he took off in a rush. Why had Trammer switched cars?

Oanen coasted on the currents, following the car from high above. Trammer signaled on the last left before my house and followed the meandering backroad to its end, not more than two miles from my back door. There he pulled over and killed the engine.

"We need to get closer," I said softly.

Oanen started to descend. Landing quietly on the top of one of the towering pines, he gave us the perfect vantage point to watch Trammer. The man climbed out of his car and looked around as he walked to the trunk. The sight of him tormented me with the need to cause him pain. The intensity of my need to hurt him had increased since the last time I saw him. Why?

I had the answer when he opened his trunk. A long, lumpy form wrapped in black garbage bags lay within the dark interior. Trammer bent forward and tugged the plastic encased body from the trunk, letting it drop right to the ground. He squatted down and cut away the black material. The moonlight cast a pale glow on the drug dealer's lifeless face.

"But why?" I said quietly.

Oanen turned his head and nipped at my jeans with his beak. Yeah, I'd be quiet. For now.

We watched Trammer stuff the plastic back into the trunk then turn toward a nearby tree. He pulled a knife from the bark and squatted by the body once more.

Pressing my face into Oanen's feathers, I didn't watch what he did next. I stayed like that until the car started again, and Trammer drove away.

Oanen's unexpected launch into the air startled a squeak from me. He beat his wings hard, gaining altitude enough that I could see Trammer's headlights. Oanen silently tailed him. At the end of the road, Trammer signaled right, retracing his route.

"Wait," I said when Oanen started to do the same.

"There's no point in following him. We need to go back to that clearing."

None of what we saw was making any sense. Why would Trammer kill a human for trying to deal drugs to a siren? He didn't like any of the creatures in Uttira. And why take the man out of Uttira only to bring him back in? Why not just kill the guy and leave him in a ditch outside the barrier?

Oanen landed not far from the body. I slid off his back and tried to understand Trammer's motive for gutting the guy. Blood and innards spilled out onto the grass. The scent of death tainted the air.

"Why are we here, Megan? We need to report this to the Council."

"This doesn't make sense," I said. I turned and looked at the tree where the knife was once again embedded. "Why have a knife here, waiting? How could Trammer have premeditated this when no one knew we'd report this guy?"

"Trammer and the Council always know when a human enters the barrier."

"They do?"

Oanen nodded.

"Most humans avoid Uttira. Well, the decent ones do. The Council keeps an eye on them all, though, to make sure that any human who happens to find their way into Uttira doesn't discover anything they're not supposed to."

I recalled the way Trammer had conveniently appeared at my front door the day the cable and TV delivery men had shown up.

"Okay. So the Council and Trammer knew about him. That would mean Trammer could have come out here and put a knife in the tree in anticipation of having to remove the guy. But why would Trammer kill him for trying to sell drugs to a siren? Trammer couldn't care less about any of us."

Oanen shrugged. "This guy had been delivering drugs to Camil every week for months. He'd never done more than stop at her house and leave again, though. Since the Council was aware of the deliveries and the man caused no trouble, Trammer's orders were to leave him alone."

"It's just not adding up for me. How many times has Trammer had to remove this level of scum from Uttira?"

"At least a dozen."

"But no deaths until I showed up, right?" I paced around the body, studying it. "Why kill this guy tonight then? Why slice him open like this but not remove anything like Camil in the alley?"

I stopped pacing.

"The other bodies were eaten. Trammer wouldn't eat them." I looked down again at the way he'd cut the man open and let his insides spill out. The scent of blood filled my nose.

"This is bait," I said with shocked realization.

Oanen immediately shifted and dipped his shoulder.

"We need to know who or what Trammer's baiting," I said. "We need to watch."

He nipped at my jeans until I gave in and climbed on. Instead of taking me home, like I'd thought, he flew us back up to the tree.

"Good," I said, running a hand down the feathers of his neck. "I want answers."

We sat in the tree for the next several hours in silence. When my eyes started to stay closed between blinks, he nipped at my pants again.

"Yeah, yeah," I mumbled, holding tighter. "I won't fall off."

He tipped forward, falling out of the tree and catching an updraft with his wings. My heart thudded in my chest from the scare.

"You could have warned me," I said.

Laying my head against his back, I held on as he flew the short distance to my house and enjoyed the warmth radiating from his feathers. Even with my eyes closed, I could feel it the moment he started descending. He reared back slightly as he landed, and he began to shift beneath me. Startled, I grappled for a new hold on bare shoulders as I slid off his back. He twisted and pulled me up into his arms. I blinked up at him.

"You're not going to throw me on my bed again, are you?"

His lips tilted up at the corners.

"No. Not this time."

He set me on my feet but didn't release me. His thumbs moved over my shirt on my biceps.

"I'd like to stay again, tonight."

Warning bells went off in my head, but given what was going on just a few miles from my house, I wasn't stupid enough to say no.

"Yeah, that's fine. I wouldn't want to be alone if Trammer showed up, anyway. I don't know that I'd be able to stop myself from going after him."

Oanen shook his head slightly and nodded toward the house.

I turned and led the way inside. While I opened the fridge to use the door as a shield to keep my gaze from wandering, he grabbed his clothes from the chair in the kitchen and ducked into the bathroom. I glanced at the clock. Just after midnight. Despite seeing a dead body, I considered making us a snack since I already had the fridge open.

Pounding on the front door interrupted my thoughts. I moved to answer it. Oanen stepped out of the bathroom and blocked my path.

"I'll get it," he said.

He turned away from me, and my gaze swept over the jeans riding low on his hips and the t-shirt hugging his back.

I made a little face of longing before shaking myself from my mental cloud. Maybe I needed to tell him to hit the roof.

He pulled open the door, and my temper flared at the sight of Aubrey.

"He's not here," Oanen said before she could speak. "And I've been with Megan since she left the club, so there's no need for threats, either."

She snarled and turned away, marching down the porch steps as he closed the door.

"That girl needs a leash," I said as tires squealed on the road.

"Or maybe Fenris does," he said, frowning. "How many times has Fenris been missing just before a body is found?"

CHAPTER TWENTY-THREE

"YOU THINK FENRIS HAS BEEN CHEWING ON THE BODIES? NO way," I said firmly.

"Why not?"

"Because he's not that kind of werewolf. He's nice to everyone. He likes hugging, not biting." Way too much hugging, I thought.

Oanen quietly studied me for a long minute.

"Is your opinion based on how you feel about him?" he asked quietly.

"Yes, it is. He doesn't make me angry. Besides Eliana, he's one of the easiest people for me to be around."

Oanen stepped around me and walked to the kitchen. I wasn't stupid. I knew why.

"You know what? It's after midnight on one of the longest days of my life. You don't get to have hurt feelings because you're reading something into words that have no deeper meaning than the surface."

He stopped walking and looked back at me.

"What are you saying?"

"That we already talked about this, and I don't want to rehash it. If you didn't believe me the first time, saying it all again won't change your mind. So, the only feelings I want to discuss right now are how tired and hungry I am."

"I wasn't walking away because of what you said. I believe you and trust your instincts. Fenris isn't the one eating human flesh. But, with him missing, the females will be running around the woods looking for him. That means I need to go back and watch the body."

Females? There was only one who kept knocking on my damn door. A door not far from the dump site.

"You want to go alone?" I asked, unsure.

"I wouldn't mind company. Still want to snack?"

"No. I want to catch Aubrey red-handed," I said.

"It might not be Aubrey."

"What other reason is there for my anger every time she's around?"

"I'm not sure."

He motioned for me to follow him into the kitchen then held the back door for me.

"I'll leave my clothes in here, again."

I took the hint and stepped outside. Alone in the backyard, I watched the stars and listened for the door to open. He didn't take long. Not wanting to turn too soon, I stayed as I was until something nipped at my finger, startling me.

I turned and found Oanen already shifted. His feathers glinted in the moonlight, as did his beautiful golden eyes.

"Ready?" I asked.

He dipped his shoulder, and I climbed on his back. In no

time, we once again soared the skies, flying toward the clearing. When we reached it, nothing looked different. Below us lay the remains of the drug dealer.

He circled, lazily spiraling downward. As he glided, a pale shape slunk from the trees. The familiar rage that I associated with Aubrey flared up inside me.

"I knew it," I said softly. "That's Aubrey."

Yet part of me wondered why I needed to feel so much anger toward her. The man was already dead. She hadn't caused it. Not that I agreed with eating humans, but was it fair to want to beat her bloody for instincts she probably couldn't control? I thought of Eliana's struggle to contain what she didn't like about herself. She fought her instincts constantly.

Any pity I had for Aubrey disappeared as she dove for the man's open middle. I gagged as she dipped her head inside and started devouring his soft bits. She wasn't attempting to control anything. She was gorging herself.

"Oh, that's so gross."

Oanen screeched loudly and tipped forward, descending rapidly. I clung tightly to his feathers and watched Aubrey's head jerk up at the sound of his cry.

She snarled but didn't run or back away. Instead, she hunched over the drug dealer like she was guarding a treat.

Oanen landed with a hard thump that clacked my teeth together and almost jarred me from my seat. A nearby snarl had me looking up in time to see Aubrey launch herself at us. My heart thudded with adrenaline, and I embraced the rage that filled me. Before I could slide off to face her, Oanen reared back, almost unseating me again.

I gripped his feathers as he swiped at her with his front

talons. She hopped back but didn't give up. Darting forward again, she went for his throat. Oanen moved to dodge her and used his talons once more. The vicious tips caught her hindquarters, ripping a swath of red into her fluffy white coat. She yelped and rolled away.

Oanen dipped his shoulder, indicating I could finally get off. The wrong shoulder, though. I didn't want to hide by the trees. Ignoring the direction he wanted me to go, I tried to dismount toward Aubrey. However, Oanen tilted his shoulders so I slid off the opposite side.

Aubrey had regained her feet by the time I landed on mine. But instead of facing me, she twisted around to look at her wound. She gave it a tentative lick and whined before turning on Oanen with another snarl. Bloody saliva dripped from her stiff, angry mouth.

I took a step to the side, ready to go around Oanen, but he half-opened his wings, blocking me. Aubrey's gaze finally darted my way. Oanen's feathers ruffled, making him look bigger and scarier. The deep, threatening cry he emitted at her made me shiver.

Aubrey didn't try attacking again. With a stagger, her fur receded until she stood before us naked, bleeding, and filthy.

"Did you leave this here?" she demanded, glaring at me.

Oanen shifted quickly and lurched forward, grabbing Aubrey by the throat.

"Is this the first time you've fed on a human?" Rage filled his words.

Stunned, I did nothing as Aubrey pulled ineffectively at his hands and made a strangled sound in answer. He lifted her off her feet in response and gave her a little shake.

"Is this the first time?" he yelled at her.

Her eyes darted to me before a choked yes came out of her.

"I don't believe you." He dropped her.

Aubrey landed on the ground in a heap, favoring her wounded leg. Moonlight glinted off her pale hair and exposed breasts as she looked up at Oanen. A tiny part of my mind hated that they were seeing each other naked.

"Report to Raiden and tell him everything. He'll know if you lie. Go!" he yelled when she didn't immediately move.

She hopped to her feet and limped off into the trees. I stayed where I was, letting my anger fade slowly with her retreat.

Once I knew she was gone, I looked at Oanen's back. Wisps of steam rose from his skin, and his shoulders moved with each angry breath as he continued to watch the trees where she'd disappeared. I wasn't sure what to do. I hadn't expected such a violent reaction out of him. He'd always been so controlled.

"Are you okay?" I asked when he continued to face away from me.

"No."

That single word sent a bolt of panic through me, and I rushed around him.

"Did she hurt you?" My gaze swept over him from head to toe, more worried about a potential injury than modesty. However, seeing the unmarred perfection of everything Oanen erased my concern. It erased everything but yum-yum thoughts.

"Megan," he said with impatience, and I realized it wasn't the first time he'd had to say my name.

I tore my gaze from his abs and met his eyes.

"Yeah?"

"Are you okay?"

"Yeah. Sure. Fine. Why?"

"You look flushed."

"Nope." My gaze remained laser-focused on his. "Just confused. You were pretty aggressive with Aubrey."

"Shouldn't I have been?"

"I don't know. I mean, my anger says yes, but my brain is questioning why I'm so angry with her. She didn't kill this guy. We know that. Yeah, she ate him, but I think Trammer put the guy here to bait her or someone like her. I don't know much about werewolves, but I do know that if you leave out food around a dog, it's going to be eaten. We all have instincts we're fighting to control. I suck at controlling mine. Is it fair for me to condemn Aubrey when she can't control hers?"

"This is more than just punching someone in the face. This is about eating humans. We can feed on their energy, on their blood, even on their life force, but we cannot feed on their flesh. Seeing her, I snapped. What she did not only goes against my nature, but it's against our laws, too. We can no longer delay reporting this."

Without another word, he shifted back to his griffin form. I smoothed my hand over his neck feathers and climbed on. I hoped he didn't think I'd been justifying Aubrey's actions. I hadn't. I was empathizing with them.

The flight to Oanen's house took longer than I anticipated. My fingers were numb by the time he landed on the roof of the stone mansion. Dismounting, I paid more attention to the glass greenhouse that took up half the space than bare Oanen.

"Dad built this so Mom could watch me learn to fly."

"Your Mom doesn't fly?"

"There's no such thing as a female griffin," he said with an amused smile.

"Hey. How am I supposed to know?"

"Come on." He clasped my cold hand, and I enjoyed the warm contact as he led me inside the greenhouse. He stopped at the shelves near the back of it and quickly dressed before opening the door that led down a set of stairs.

I shivered slightly at the sudden change in temperature and rubbed my arms. At the bottom of the steps, Oanen tapped the digital display mounted on the wall.

"Mother. Father. Please meet me in the study," he said, his voice echoing from different locations around the house. He tapped the screen again and started walking.

"Your house has a freaking intercom?"

"Yes. Yelling for me wasn't cutting it. Mom wanted it installed. Dad made it happen."

He led the way down the hall, another set of stairs, turned right, and opened a set of heavy double doors to a very manly, grand room that only vaguely looked study-ish because of a mahogany desk in the back corner near the balcony doors.

"This place is ridiculous," I said quietly, looking around.

"Yep. It is. Family homes usually are around here. Are you still hungry? I can get you something."

"No. I'm fine." I wandered to one of the overstuffed leather chairs and took a seat.

When I glanced at the door, I found Oanen's parents there, dressed as if it weren't close to two in the morning but mid-afternoon. Neither one said anything as they studied me. Crap. I stood again. How much had they heard?

"Hello," I said, unsure.

"Megan. Oanen. What's going on?" his mom asked.

"Quite a bit. You might want to contact Adira as we explain." His father pulled his phone from his pocket and sent off a quick text as Oanen recounted what we'd witnessed in the last few hours.

"Where is Aubrey now?" Mr. Quill asked.

"I sent her to report to Raiden."

Oanen's mom walked further into the room. She kissed Oanen on the cheek then turned to me.

"Megan, please sit. Can I get you anything while we wait for Adira?"

"No, thank you." I sat, feeling more than a little nervous. Oanen moved next to me, sitting on the arm of my chair. Surprisingly, the move made me feel better instead of more freaked out.

Oanen's father slowly joined us, his attention on the text message he was typing into his phone. When he looked up, he let out a heavy exhale.

"Adira is bringing Raiden."

"Raiden?" I asked. "Why not Trammer?" The guy was running around killing people, and we'd witnessed it. What more proof did they need?

Oanen's mom reached out and put her hand on mine. A soothing calm filled me. Not quite like what Eliana did but close.

"All will be well. We will address Trammer's crimes. However, he is not the greatest threat at the moment."

"How is he not? Just because humans are his victims and not us?" I only barely managed to keep the resentment from my tone.

Eliana shuffled into the room, rubbing her eyes. "Trammer's killing people?"

"And Aubrey's eating them," Oanen added.

His mom didn't look away from me.

"There is a reason consuming flesh is against our laws. It changes the nature of the creature. Makes them more violent. Makes them crave more at any cost. Even at the risk of exposing our world to the humans. For most of us, ingesting flesh holds no appeal. No temptation.

"That is not true for some, though. We need to ensure Aubrey is the only one to have succumbed and is dealt with appropriately, so her actions do not tempt others to do the same."

I understood what Mrs. Quill was politely saying. They needed to get to Aubrey so she didn't spread her brand of crazy. It might be a little late for that, given how long ago the first body was found, but I kept that bit of criticism to myself.

Oanen's mom's eyes sparkled with amusement almost as if she knew what I'd just thought. I gently eased my hand out from hers, and she smiled.

Eliana came over and sat on the other arm of my chair. Oanen's mom reached out and ran a soothing hand down Eliana's bare arm.

"You should sleep, dear one," Mrs. Quill said.

They might not be mother and daughter by blood, but I

could see the true affection Mrs. Quill had for her ward.

"I'm okay. I want to know what happens."

A shiny portal opened near the door, drawing our attention. Adira and Raiden stepped through. The older man's hard, silver gaze swept the room and landed on me.

"Are you sure it was Aubrey?" Raiden asked without preamble.

"Yes," I said before Oanen could. "I recognized her white fur when she was a wolf and saw her as a human, as well."

Raiden's shoulder seemed to sag just a bit.

"We need to know if this was her first time," Mr. Quill said. "Or if there are others responsible for the prior incidents."

"Agreed," Raiden said.

"How was she missed when you questioned the pack?" Mrs. Quill asked without censure.

"I didn't question the young without the mark since the human was killed outside Uttira. Now that we know what Trammer was doing, I will question them all."

"Good. Perhaps you should issue a ban on solo runs while this is unresolved. If any others have had a taste of flesh, we don't want them hunting for more of it," Mr. Quill said.

Raiden gave a curt nod, and Oanen's father looked at Adira.

"Given the number of deaths, I feel it's unwise to wait until morning to question Trammer."

"I agree," Adira said.

"Agreed," Raiden added. "I believe my presence isn't as necessary here as it is with the pack now. With your agreement, I will return and start seeking answers from my own while you direct the interview with the liaison."

Mr. Quill nodded to him, and Raiden stepped back through the portal.

"I will return shortly," Adira said then disappeared.

CHAPTER TWENTY-FOUR

THE SILENCE IN THE STUDY GREW TO DEAFENING PROPORTIONS in my mind. What was the council going to do with Trammer? No one seemed overly upset that he'd been killing his own kind. Why not? And, why was no one talking? Was it because of my presence or because their son was sitting right next to me with his thumb giving my back a discreet and occasional caress? I hoped they weren't noticing that. I hoped they were instead speculating about why Trammer had killed those humans. They had to be at least a little curious, right? I sure the hell was.

When the shimmer finally returned, Oanen's stroke paused and I exhaled in relief.

Trammer stepped through first, dressed in full uniform. The shirt was a bit wrinkled, and his hair wasn't as neat as usual. The sight of him made my blood boil, and only Oanen's restraining hand on my shoulder kept me in my seat.

Trammer's gaze swept over us all before settling on Oanen's father.

"Mr. Quill," he said. "What seems to be the problem?"

"Oanen and Megan witnessed what you did to Mr. Ryan tonight."

Trammer's whole demeanor changed. He didn't look worried; he looked pissed.

"Mr. Ryan? That shitbag gets a fancy 'Mr.' for selling drugs in your town while plain 'ol Trammer is burning bodies to clean up your messes? Your standards are screwed up. You treat me like I'm inferior, but I'm not a parasite that only exists to feed off of others."

His gaze went straight to Eliana. She made a small, hurt noise; and I glared at Trammer while reaching for her hand. Her fingers shook in mine.

"Do you admit to killing Mr. Ryan?" Mr. Quill asked.

"Unbelievable," Trammer said. "Yeah, I killed him."

"Why? He's your own kind."

Finally, I thought.

Trammer laughed angrily.

"Neither of those men I killed was my kind any more than I'm your kind, you ignorant prick."

"Those men? What about Camil?" I asked.

His accusatory gaze pinned me.

"Do you seriously still think I killed that girl? I had no reason to."

He gave me a dismissive glare before facing Mr. Quill.

"Camil died from an overdose. The very man who you wanted to let go is responsible for her death."

"Is that why you killed him?" Mr. Quill asked.

Trammer snorted angrily.

"You remove what you consider trash to keep Uttira safe, but you're looking at it all wrong. Those men feed on humans just like you do. Do you even know what happens when you return them to their depraved lives? You claim to exist to protect humanity. But by letting the scum live, you're condemning hundreds of innocents to death. You're not protectors of anything but your self-interests."

"Fine," I said. "You killed those men to keep others safe and had nothing to do with Camil's death. But why bring the bodies back here? Why put Camil in the dumpster?"

He barked out a laugh again.

"I brought the first guy back to prove you're all just animals waiting to kill us humans. I don't know who found the body, but they sure had a feast despite your no flesh law. Camil, I didn't touch. I saw her after you did, and I only realized what happened when Mr. Ryan got a glance at her file in my car on the way here. I don't know who cut her open and fed on her, but I hear, once a wolf gets a taste of human flesh, they can't stop craving it. Bringing Mr. Ryan back inside the barrier and leaving him in the clearing was to prove that. We all know I'm not the monster here. Or, at least, not the worst monster."

He was talking about all of them. Us, actually. But, in my mind, I only saw Aubrey's face the night I'd discovered Camil's body. Aubrey had tried to get me to leave Ashlyn's table, and I'd sent her on a wild goose chase looking for Fenris. She would have had the time and opportunity to discover Camil's body before I did. Aubrey also would have already had her first taste of flesh and the motive to try to set me up for the kill. All of that just because of jealousy?

My head was starting to hurt. When I tried to see past the fury-anger, I wasn't sure what to think. Aubrey lost to her jealousy and instincts. But, what about Trammer? Yes, Trammer had killed people but only ones who were hurting other people. He wasn't just some vigilante; he wore the town badge.

"Given your statement, we no longer believe you hold the best interest for all humans in your position. As such, we find you no longer suitable as human liaison."

Trammer snorted.

"We sentence you to a memory wipe and removal."

So they were going to make him forget about Uttira and just send him back out in the real world?

"Wait," I said. "What about Ashlyn?"

"Was she involved with your actions?" Mr. Quill asked.

"Of course not!" Trammer said angrily.

"That wasn't what I meant," I said. "What happens to her when his memory is wiped?"

"She continues with her responsibilities."

"She doesn't get a choice to go with him? He's her uncle. From what I understand, she has no parents. No one else."

"Haven't you been listening?" Trammer said. "They only pretend to care about humans. But they don't."

"That is untrue, Trammer. The council will continue to provide for her like it has always done," Adira said.

"So she has no choice?" I asked.

"If she would want to leave, her memory would need to be wiped as well," Adira explained. "Since she has been here for three years, that would be a traumatic experience."

"But shouldn't it be her decision? And if she does choose to stay, shouldn't you get her so she can talk to her uncle and at least say goodbye?"

Some of Trammer's anger faded from his expression.

"Megan, maybe living in the real world helped you become more human. Don't let them kill that part of you."

With speed I couldn't have anticipated, he grabbed his gun from his holster and put it to his temple.

"Keep an eye on her," he said.

The sudden explosion of noise and brain matter made me jump. Trammer crumpled to the ground. I stared at the heap as Eliana leaned into me and started to cry. Absently petting her hair, I looked at the adults. They shared a look, but none of them seemed overly upset that yet another human had met his end in their town.

Keep an eye on her.

He'd said it while looking at me. I knew he meant Ashlyn. How could he leave her like that? So much like my mom had left me.

"Children," Mrs. Quill said. "I think it's time for you to sleep. We will talk more in the morning."

I couldn't believe they were telling us to go to bed with Trammer still twitching on the floor.

"What about Aubrey?" I asked.

"We will let Raiden know Trammer's confession, and she will be dealt with accordingly. Now go. Help Eliana to bed."

Eliana shook against me. Maybe leaving was for the best. I pulled Eliana to her feet and looked at Mr. Quill.

"I think Aubrey sent me a text from Camil's phone to get me into the alley that night. Have Raiden ask her about that." In my heart, I knew my mom hadn't come back, but I needed it confirmed.

Mr. Quill nodded, and with Eliana's face buried in my shoulder, I led her past Trammer's fallen body.

"Let me take her," Oanen said.

He scooped Eliana up in his arms and headed out the door. I followed slowly, pausing in the doorway to look back. I couldn't stop thinking about Trammer's last words.

"What about Ashlyn?" I asked.

"I will tell her in the morning," Adira said. "She will be given a choice, as you suggested."

"Let us know what she decides. I'd like to say goodbye if she chooses to leave."

Adira nodded, and I left to catch up with Oanen.

They weren't more than a few steps from the door.

"Oanen, put me down," Eliana said. "I just didn't want to see him."

Oanen set Eliana on her feet. She looked at me with sad eyes.

"At least everyone will believe you, now, that you're not the killer."

"I couldn't care less about that. Well, maybe not being the center of everyone's attention will be nice. But, I'm more worried about Ashlyn now."

"What he said in there wasn't true. They do care," Oanen said. "But we don't understand humans the way the two of you do. Like he did. That's why a liaison is necessary." He gave a troubled exhale. "Why would he kill himself like that?"

"I don't know," I said. "Maybe shame. He was angry and defiant until I brought up Ashlyn. Maybe he didn't want her to know what he'd done. Whether justified or not, he was killing people in secret. That's not something rational humans do."

"And now Ashlyn's all alone," Eliana said.

"No. She'll have us if she wants. We'll keep an eye on her."

Eliana rubbed her brow.

"I'm never going to unsee that. I'm tired, but I know I won't be able to sleep."

"Want to come to my house? Maybe a change of scenery will help?"

"I don't think so. Let's watch a movie in our living room," she said, looking at Oanen.

"You guys have your own living room?"

She smiled slightly and grabbed my hand.

"Come see."

She led me to a spacious room on the third floor. It wasn't just a living room. It had a kitchenette with a full-sized fridge, a pool table, two large TVs at the back of the room attached to every gaming console known to man, and a TV toward the front surrounded by a full sofa and two loveseats.

"Holy crap. Why have we been hanging out at my house?"

I sat on the sofa while Eliana browsed the paid movie selection. Oanen brought me a bottle of water and a bag of snacks before sitting next to me. Eliana sat on the other side of me.

The movie started to play. I munched on my chips and stared at the screen, not really seeing it. I was tired. So was Eliana, because she fell asleep on my shoulder within minutes. Oanen sat beside me, seemingly unbothered by the need for sleep.

As soon as I finished my last chip, he took the wrapper and empty bottle from me. I leaned back and closed my eyes as I listened to him throw away my trash. I was glad I wasn't alone because behind my closed eyes all I saw was red.

I FELT HOT. Way too hot. I wasn't sweaty, though. All the heat was inside me, building in size and making me uncomfortable. It had nothing to do with my temper and everything to do with using Oanen as the best body pillow ever.

His hand rested on the middle of my back as if holding me in place against his muscled chest. My cheek lay on his shirt, right over his heart. The steady beat skipped when I lifted my hand to brush some hair from my face. Knowing that he was awake made the heat worse. As did the sensation of his other hand smoothing over my hair.

I lifted my head and looked for Eliana but didn't see her. Oanen and I lay on the long couch together. Alone.

"How did this happen?" I asked, finally meeting Oanen's gaze.

"Mom would say Freya answered my prayers. Dad would say Hera."

His prayers? Heat spread to my cheeks.

"What would you say?" I asked.

"That I only care how you answer them. You know what your anger's for now, and you know I'm not afraid of it. Stop hiding from life and start living it."

His steady gaze held mine.

"Say yes to me," he said softly.

He was asking me to let him in. I knew I should get up.

That I should make up some excuse for why this wouldn't work and just walk away. But I couldn't.

"And if I hurt you?"

"Then I'll have probably deserved it."

"What exactly would I be saying yes to? Dating? Being your girlfriend?"

"Sure. We can start with that."

The heat whirled inside me, creating an uncomfortable ache.

"I'll think about it," I said before scrambling off of him.

"Perfect timing," his mother said, walking into the room. "I was just about to wake you two. Eliana offered to make breakfast while we talk."

Oanen stood and walked beside me as we passed through the halls. Although I should have been wondering what Mrs. Quill wanted to talk about, my mind wouldn't let go of the conversation Oanen and I had been having. Was I truly going to date him? Was I ready to risk decking him again and see his eyes fill with hate or disgust? My insides went hot and cold just thinking about it. So I tried not to.

Adira and Oanen's father were already in the study, waiting for our arrival.

"Good morning, Megan. Did you sleep well?" Adira asked as Mrs. Quill joined Mr. Quill on the sofa.

"Well enough. How's Ashlyn?"

Oanen led me to a chair and perched on the arm after I took the seat. His nearness made it a little hard to focus on Adira's answer.

"She is upset over the events that took place and her uncle's death but chose to remain in Uttira. She is considering possible guardianship but will remain in the home she knows for now. I did let her know you are concerned about her."

"Thank you. And what about Aubrey?"

I needed to know the Council had done something about her. She might not have killed any people yet, but her level of wicked probably meant she wasn't far from it.

"Aubrey was the one to text you from Camil's phone. She'd gotten your number from Fenris' phone. Because Aubrey does not have the mark and did not kill her victims, the council didn't sentence her to death. However, the pack did sentence her for reconditioning. She has been removed from Uttira and will not return until the pack deems her cured."

"Is that enough?" I asked. Not that I wanted her put down, but I sure as hell didn't want her back in Uttira being a pain in my ass, either.

"The pack believes so. The first incident was an accident. She was jealous and angry with you because of Fenris' interest and sought to drag the body to your house so you would be accused of his death. However, she couldn't resist the taste of human flesh after the first mile."

"Ew. I'm so not going to eat breakfast now."

"I apologize."

"Okay, so Ashlyn's good, and Aubrey's still bad but dealt with. What's next?"

"Next, we talk about this past week away from the Academy. You missed several sessions, but your online notes don't reflect a negative change."

"No offense, but all the sessions I'm in are pointless. I already know how to order a pizza and not kill the delivery guy. Blending with the human world isn't going to be a problem for me. This world is. I don't know anything about the creatures that exist or what they might be capable of. If I'm in this world, shouldn't I know more about it?"

"I agree." She looked at the Quills. "I'd like Megan to be given access to the Academy Library."

"Granted," Mrs. Quill said.

"What's in the Academy Library?"

"The most extensive collection of written information on our creation and history. While the other students attend sessions, you may read whatever you choose in the library."

"Your access comes at a price, Megan," Mr. Quill said. "We want you to fill in as temporary human liaison until we can acquire a new one. The information you gain from the library will help you understand who you will be dealing with in your new role."

"You want me to liaison? Why? I thought that was a human's job?"

"It is, and it will be. However, after last night, you've proven that you also have the humans' best interests in mind. You have the qualifications to fill in for the short term."

"And, you will continue to report any flares in your temper to me," Adira said.

All three adults watched me, waiting for some kind of response.

"Sure," I said.

The Quills stood. "We hope you'll join us for breakfast, Adira."

"Thank you. I will."

They left the room, but Adira didn't move from her spot. Her gaze flicked between Oanen and me.

"Have you finally agreed to his protection?" she asked me.

"Protection?" I echoed, confused.

"Humans call it dating, Adira," Oanen said.

"Ah. That's good. None of us are meant to be solitary. Not even furies." She started for the door then paused and looked back. "Oh, and don't break into my office again. I will not forgive it a second time."

My mouth dropped open as she left.

"I told you she'd find out," Oanen said.

I closed my mouth and gave him a sour look.

"This relationship won't work if you say 'I told you so,' every time I'm wrong."

"Do you plan on being wrong often?" he asked with the corners of his mouth twitching.

"No."

"Then let me have my moment."

He tugged my hand, pulling me closer and threading his fingers through mine. My heart started to pound hard at the simple contact.

"You won't regret saying yes," he said.

"I didn't say yes; I said I'd think about it."

He smiled slightly.

"I'm optimistic."

I snorted. "That's not the word I'd use to describe you."

"What word would you use?"

"Persistent."

He laughed.

"Come on. Let's feed you and find out what your liaison duties are for the day."

"They're going to give me duties already? I thought it would just be harassing delinquents."

He grew slightly serious.

"Now that you know what you are, they're going to want to use you to fill the role you were meant to fill."

"What do you mean?"

"You're meant to find and punish the wicked. They're going to want you on the Council."

"What they want and what they get probably won't be the same. I haven't even graduated yet."

"We'll see."

Thanks for reading Fury Frayed, book 1 in the Of Fates and Furies series. The series continues with Fury Focused.
Now available!

AUTHOR'S NOTE

Fury Frayed is Megan's introduction to the world of Mantirum!

Don't worry, she still has a ton to learn and will be back in Fury Focused.

Ready for a little trivia?

Mantirum is a blend of Norse and Greek mythology. The mythos between the two is often very similar with several of the gods having the same characteristics/ability but different names (and sometimes even different genders or backstories like Hel and Hades).

Megan's full name is Megan Grace Smith. All the women in Megan's family tree have "peace" oriented names, which you will learn more about in book 3.

Oanen's full name is Oanen Alister Quill. Typically, griffin's will have names pertaining to flight, like Oanen's father, Lander. However, Oanen's mother wanted something different for her son. Something to reflect the protector he would one day become.

As part of the research for this book, I rode the Avatar Flight of Passage ride at Disney World. Loved it! Flying a griffin in real life would be heart-stoppingly epic, and I would probably yell and hoot the whole time.

If you've enjoyed Fury Frayed, be sure to check out Fury Focused, book 2 in the Of Fates and Furies series. But don't forget to show your support (or not) for this book first! Leaving a review is one of the best ways to support an author. Your review might just be the one that persuades more readers to pick up a book you've loved (or hated). And, reviews increase a book's visibility on retailer sites. Please consider leaving a review to help keep my books visible!

Don't forget to sign up for my newsletter at melissahaag.com/subscribe to find out when a new book in this world releases. (You can also follow me on Amazon or BookBub for new release alerts.)

If you're a Judgement of the Six fan, keep reading for an extra little thank you.

Happy reading!

Melissa

MORE BOOKS BY MELISSA HAAG

**Judgement of the Six Series
(and Companion Books) in order:**
Hope(less)
*Clay's Hope**
(Mis)fortune
*Emmitt's Treasure**
(Un)wise
*Luke's Dream**
(Un)bidden
*Thomas' Treasure**
(Dis)content
*Carlos' Peace**
*(Sur)real***

optional companion book
**written in dual point of view*

Of Fates and Furies Series
Fury Frayed
Fury Focused
Fury Freed

By Kiss and Claw Series

The Howl
more titles coming soon

Other Titles

Touch

Moved

Warwolf

Nephilim

BONUS SCENE

Bonus scene for fans of the Judgement of the Six series
DO NOT READ if you have not yet finished the series!
Spoilers ahead
(You've been warned!)

Clay...

I could feel Gabby's anxiety and sent a reassuring wave of love her way. She'd warned me not to "do that head talk thing" today, but I was tempted to do it anyway. Feeling my Mate's stress made my own kick up a few notches.

In an attempt to distract myself, I focused on the TV that was turned on with the volume low. Since Winifred revealed the existence of werewolves to the world, our group had been monitoring current events. With Gabby's insistence to finish school, I kept an even closer eye on things.

The initial turmoil had only grown. People were still showing up dead with fingernails removed. Neighbor continued to suspect neighbor, ignoring all the years of backyard barbeques and playdates that had once been the foundation for friendships.

I wished we didn't live in town, but I couldn't forget Gabby's first conversation with me. Had it really been almost a year since she'd pointed out that she didn't have fur like I did and couldn't just live in the trees? I missed the trees.

The news anchor grew serious and warned viewers that we were about to see some disturbing and graphic images. Since the onset of the revelation of our existence, censorship had slowly gone out the window. If someone died a horrible death, the news not only reported it, they had footage of the aftermath.

The screen switched to a pile of human-shaped red. I figured out what I was looking at before the news anchor spoke.

"The remains of a human male, completely stripped of his skin, were found this morning in the street adjacent to the capital building. There are no leads regarding who or what did this at this time."

The co-anchor added his opinion, something that had also increased in our daily dose of "factual" reporting.

"I think the 'what' seems pretty obvious, though, don't you? Based on the surveillance footage," which the screen started to show, "the victim is less than two minutes ahead of the person who called in his death. No human could do what was done that quickly."

The now deceased man walked off camera. A second man started on the same path after a few moments. Before the second man disappeared from view, he started running.

"According to the witness who called in the death, he heard a scream unlike anything he's heard before. He was carrying a permitted, concealed weapon and thought he could help. When he arrived, the man was already skinned and dead."

The concealed weapon part had me shaking my head. Every human was carrying now, making the world more dangerous not just for werewolves and Urbat but for themselves, too.

The TV suddenly went black.

"That's probably not the best choice of distraction right now," Emmitt said.

He leaned back in his chair and looked at his watch.

"You need to get your head in the game. Michelle should be here in a few minutes."

Luke, the other inhabitant of the room, chuckled.

"If Gabby finds out that was what you were watching right before you exchange vows, you're going to be the skinned man."

I threw the remote at his head. He caught the device before it connected with his skull and grinned at me.

"I don't see why we have to do this," I said. "It's dangerous. We've been Mated for weeks."

"Being Mated doesn't replace their need for the ceremony. Plus, this is just another layer of protection. Her name will change yet again," Emmitt said.

Name changes were something that Michelle and her lawyer had worked on as soon as the Judgement was made. The girls all changed their last names. Winifred, too, since she had most everything registered under her name. We'd had to leave behind the Compound and Emmitt's Montana home and start up elsewhere. For the moment, we lived in the hate-filled cities and blended.

"I thought the Judgement was supposed to fix the world," I said. "Instead, it's falling apart."

"Not falling apart, shifting alliances. It'll take time," Emmitt said.

From what we'd been seeing, it would take more than our lifetime for humans to accept werewolves among them.

"And don't say anything in front of the girls about thinking this ceremony is a waste of time unless you want to be sleeping on the sofa for the next month," Emmitt said, returning to the topic at hand.

"Is that what happened to you?" Luke asked.

"No. I'm smarter than you two."

Luke snorted. I ignored them both.

I didn't mind the ceremony. I minded the danger. When Emmitt and Michelle had their small wedding the week after we'd said goodbye to his parents and our fallen friends, the world had been calmer. The government had still been following Blake's paper trail, keeping them distracted. Once they'd figured out that he'd died in Arizona, though, the government's attention had shifted. Suddenly, all the news showed was the images taken of us while we were at the station in New York.

Michelle and Winifred assured us that changed names and giving up the lives we'd known would help hide us. Would help keep our Mates safe. Yet, the hunt hadn't settled down. Gabby's face was still shown daily. Grainy, but to me, easily recognizable. What if someone today identified her despite her current phony last name?

"I can smell your worry," Emmitt said. "It'll be fine.

Winifred's here, and Grey's nearby. Nothing will happen today. It'll be perfect for the girls."

I glanced at Luke, who didn't seem nearly as concerned as I was.

The door to our room opened, and Michelle walked in. The faint, rapid beat of her child's heart became my sole focus. I stared at the slight swell of her stomach in fascination.

"Is he behaving in there, Clay?" Michelle asked with a knowing smile.

I could feel my face flush at being caught again. In the days leading up to this, Gabby, Bethi, and Michelle had spent a lot of time together. And, every time Michelle had entered a room, I'd stopped to listen. I couldn't wait until Gabby carried our child.

"Given who this cub's uncle is, we can only hope this one will be well-behaved," Emmitt said, setting a hand on her stomach and kissing her.

"What are Jim and Olivia up to?" Luke asked.

"They're at Rachel's parents' place. They spent the night there just to be extra safe."

I thought of Rachel and felt a pang of regret. Gabby had really wanted her to be here for our wedding.

In the days following the Judgement, Gabby had managed to talk to Rachel and explain everything. Rachel hadn't believed Gabby right away, but when I'd shifted to the dog Rachel had known and loved, she'd changed her mind. After delivering a harsh scolding about deception, she'd hugged me and told me she liked me better as Clay-the-man because I made Gabby so happy. Rachel's easy approval of me and my kind proved that humans were capable of acceptance. Most just chose not to.

The reunion between the pair had been short-lived, though. Because of Rachel's association with Gabby, it hadn't taken long for government officials to track her down and start asking questions. As much as she'd wanted to be here on Gabby's special day, like me, she'd been worried about Gabby's safety. Their compromise was to live stream the ceremony. Rachel, Jim, and Olivia wouldn't be the only ones watching. Several members of the pack, including Paul and Henry, would be watching too.

"Well, are you two ready?" Michelle asked, glancing at me then Luke.

"I was born ready, Luv," Luke said, standing and straightening his suit jacket.

I hated when he poured on the accent.

A rush of love brushed my mind, and I smiled slightly. Gabby was the one who'd suggested a dual wedding, stating it felt right. The girls had bonded after everything they'd gone through. Luke and I? Not as much. But, he was growing on me.

I stood and nodded to Michelle.

"Ready."

She led the way out of the room and down the vacant hall to the officiant's room. This wasn't a cheap, Vegas in-and-out marriage. Michelle had gone all out.

The ceremony would take place in a tastefully decorated room, surrounded by friends. More importantly, we had the place to ourselves.

Luke and I stood at the front of the room near the officiant while Michelle moved off to one side and picked up a tablet to aim our way. Emmitt stepped to our left, taking his place as a witness to our marriages.

Luke and I both turned to watch the door. Winifred, the second witness, entered first. The scent of her sorrow filled my nose. She smiled at us as she made her way to the front, but the smile didn't quite reach her eyes. It hadn't since that day in Arizona, the day all of our lives had changed forever.

Music started, pulling me from my somber thoughts.

My gaze shifted back to the door in anticipation, and my chest squeezed at the sight of Gabby. My Mate. My wife. My everything. She wore a white dress that came to her knees and a white flower in her hair. I'd never seen anything prettier than my wife in that moment.

She smiled softly as she walked toward me. I itched to go to her and hold her close. Instead, I stood my ground and waited until she stopped in front of me. I didn't touch her. I didn't want to mess up the perfection. But, I said the words that were burning my mind.

"You are my yesterday, my today, and my tomorrow. I can't remember a single day before I met you, and I can't imagine a future without you at my side."

"Aw." Gabby's eyes watered, and she stood on her toes to kiss me softly.

Her lips against mine made the ache in my chest worse. But, she retreated quickly. If she hadn't, I would have likely messed something up by pulling her into my arms.

With the palm of her hand on my cheek, she held my gaze.

"You are the best thing in my life, Clayton Michael Lawe. Thank you for stepping out from behind that door."

"Why don't you say sweet things like that to me?" Bethi asked Luke from beside us, interrupting our moment.

Gabby released me with a laugh and looked at the pair. Like Gabby, Bethi wore a modest white dress and had a flower in her hair.

"Probably because he knows you," Gabby said. "Knee length dresses in case we need to run, no heels, and no veils because they're too easy to grab." Gabby changed her tone to mimic Bethi's voice. "Gabby, you should really add a garter. It's a great place to conceal a knife."

"A girl's gotta be ready," Bethi said with a scolding look at Gabby.

"Bethony, please," a voice said. "It's your wedding. Let yourself be a bride."

Michelle held the tablet aimed at us, a live video feed.

"That's your mom, Bethi," she said.

Bethi rolled her eyes.

"I know my mom's voice."

The officiant cleared his throat. "Would you like to begin?"

Luke wrapped Bethi in his arms and stared down at his Mate.

"What do you say, Luv? Will you be my bride?"

Gabby laced her fingers through mine, and the four of us stood together...like we had in the past and like we would in the future.

The officiant was quick and got us to the exchange of vows. Luke and Bethi went first.

"You've given me the world," Luke said, holding Bethi's hands. "All I can offer you is my heart in return. I will use every day of my life to show you how much I love you."

Bethi's mom started crying.

"I'll take your heart," Bethi said with a small smile. "And your shoulder to lean on when things get hard."

"What are you going to give me?" he asked.

"My amazing wit and candor."

Jim's laugh came over the tablet's microphone. Bethi grinned widely then grew serious.

"And, I promise to love you not just in this life but in every life I live. You are the one dream I will embrace. Forever."

The officiant turned to us. Gabby sniffled a little and looked up at me. I gently squeezed her hand and opened myself to her so she would feel everything I felt for her.

"Gabrielle May Winters, you've given up so much because of me, and I never meant for you to give up anything. If you'll have me, I'll do everything I can to give you the life you deserve."

She nodded, sniffled louder, and released my hand to pull a tissue from the neckline of her dress. She dabbed her eyes then met my gaze.

"You are the most patient, kind, and fully bearded man I know. The past is behind us. And, the future is ours. I love you, Clay."

We exchanged rings. The tremble in Gabby's fingers and the nervousness teasing my mind were driving me insane. I just wanted to get to the part where I could hold her.

"I pronounce you man and wife and man and wife," the officiant finally said.

I wrapped Gabby in my arms and kissed her like it was our first and last moment together.

Gabby...

His absolute love filled my mind, followed closely by his desire for me. I still wanted to kick myself for waiting so long to complete our bond.

Letting his need control the kiss, it took until Emmitt cleared his throat for me to recall where we were and what we were doing.

I pulled away with one last caress and breathlessly smiled up at my husband before turning to take the tablet from Michelle.

I smiled at all the familiar faces of my surrogate family, including Henry's new, human Mate. Rachel's face filled one of the windows at the bottom. Even when she cried, she looked perfectly beautiful.

"Thank you all so much for sharing our day," I said. "I'm sorry you couldn't be here in person."

"Tell Bethi and Luke, I'll see them in a bit," Bethi's mom said. She logged off as did the others until it was just Rachel with Jim, Olivia, and Peter talking quietly in the background.

"It's your turn next, Rachel."

"It might be a while."

"Why?"

"Because I want you to be there when I say I do. The world is changing. They won't care about finding you forever. Eventually, they'll go away, and then we can start planning."

Her words made my eyes water anew.

"You are the best friend I've ever had," I said, "and because of that, I can't let you wait. Not when what you and Peter have is so perfect. Like you said, the world is changing, and you don't know what tomorrow might bring. Don't postpone a moment of your happiness. You don't want to look back and live with regrets."

She cried a little harder then nodded. Peter walked up behind her and set a hand on her shoulder in silent comfort.

"We'll do a small ceremony like you," he said. "And, when the world is ready, we'll do a big wedding and invite every werewolf we know."

"That'll cost a fortune," Luke said, turning away from his quiet conversation with Emmit. "Werewolves eat four times what humans do."

"I just need your signatures," the officiant said, "then you can have the room to yourselves."

"I better go," I said to Rachel.

"Call me when you can," she said. "I'll answer any unknown number."

I smiled, promised I would, and disconnected the feed.

The officiant waited patiently while we signed. I almost wrote Winters instead of my new, fake name but caught myself in time.

"Thank you for doing this for us, Will," Winifred said to the officiant. "Stay safe. If you need anything, don't hesitate to reach out. We've already lost too many of us already to silence."

"You have my word, Winifred. I'll reach out occasionally just to let you know we're all right here."

"Thank you."

She faced me and hugged me hard.

"Sam would be so proud of you."

"I know. He'll never be gone or far from my mind. He

was the best father I could have asked for." And, I wished he would have been here to give me away and so I could have told him what he meant to me.

Clay's mind nudged mine, the warmth of his love a reminder that I wasn't alone. That I had a real family now, too.

"I'll check in with you two tomorrow," Winifred said. "Go enjoy your quiet time while I visit with Bethi's mom."

I released Winifred and took Clay's hand.

We left the building separately from the others, just like we'd arrived. Clay held the car door open for me and gave me a quick kiss before closing it and jogging to his side.

Wherever we lived, he never seemed bothered by traffic and drove with ease to our current home. This time, however, I could feel his distraction, and my stomach lurched. I'd insisted on following the time-honored tradition of spending the night before the wedding apart and had him stay with Luke last night while Winifred stayed with me. She and I had talked late into the night and had gotten the house ready for our return.

Did he know what I'd done? What I had planned?

"I can smell and feel your worry, Gabby," he said. "Talk to me."

"Nope. Not this time. It's a surprise."

He glanced my way.

"I'm serious, Clay. I'm not telling you. Out of my head." I'd gotten better at closing myself off from him. It wasn't easy and made me feel lonely, but I was determined to keep him from figuring the surprise out until we got home.

He chuckled, the low sound making my insides melt. I watched the route with increasing impatience. When he finally pulled into the driveway, I beat him to opening my door. With all the potential watchful eyes on us, it was easier to do lately. It was too dangerous for werewolves to use their super speed.

"Impatient, Mrs. Lawe?" he asked, coming around to my side.

"Very."

A slow grin parted his lips, and I felt the heat of his thoughts in my head.

"I did not realize how much you thought about *that* until after we were Mated," I said softly.

"Not *that*. Just you." He scooped me up into his arms, which made me squeak. Then, I sighed contentedly and set my head against his shoulder.

"Feel free to carry me over the threshold, Mr. Lawe."

He strode to the front door, and I struggled to suppress a flutter of nervous anticipation as I reached out to let us in. The door swung wide, revealing my surprise, but Clay didn't see what I'd done. He was too busy looking down at me hungrily while crossing the threshold.

His lips touched mine, and his shameless thoughts threatened to distract us both. The sound of the door closing pulled me back to reality.

"Wait," I said, pulling away. "Set me down."

He did, right in front of him. I stared up at him and raised my eyebrows, waiting for him to notice what was in the room behind me.

His gaze finally shifted to the crib I'd set up in the living room with Winifred's help. She'd even stocked it full of diapers for us.

For several long seconds, he said nothing. But I felt what

he was feeling. Confusion. Then, disbelief. Then, a storm of everything.

He dropped to his knees before me and pressed his ear to my middle.

"How did I miss this?" he said. "It's so perfect. And fast." He looked up at me, his eyes full of so much love, I wasn't sure how much longer I'd be able to keep back my tears.

"You're happy then?"

"Happy? You've given me everything, Gabby. The family I've always wanted but never thought I could have."

He stood and wrapped me in his arms again, pressing his lips to my forehead.

"I love you so much it hurts," he said gruffly. "I'm not letting you out of my sight for the rest of my life. Our cubs either."

I smiled and hugged him back.

"I'm okay with that."

"Have you thought of names?" he asked.

I laughed. "I've only known a few days."

"I'd like to suggest two. If it's a girl, Samantha. If it's a boy, Sam."

The tears I'd been fighting to hold back let loose.

"I'd like that very much."

He set his hand on my stomach.

"The world is changing so much. I hope this cub's future is full of joy and love."

"With you as its father, it will be. But, we can ask him in fifteen or so years."

Clay chuckled, and his lips met mine.

This scene was added to thank the fans of the *Judgement of the Six* series for jumping into a new world with me (Fury Frayed). My hope is to release an *After Judgement* novella eventually. This scene and the *After Judgement* novella will be the bridge that links the *Judgement Series* to another series (yet unnamed) that I hope to write, someday, in the same world.

If you haven't read the Judgement of the Six series yet, start with Hope(less).

CPSIA information can be obtained
at www.ICGtesting.com
Printed in the USA
LVHW041221011020
667641LV00004B/349

9 781943 051717